Colin Falconer is the author of more than thirty books of fiction and non-fiction, which have been published in Australia, UK and the USA and translated into sixteen languages. A former journalist, he was born in London and now lives in Western Australia. Colin Falconer writes contemporary fiction as Mark D'Arbanville.

PEARLS

COLIN FALCONER

BANTAM

SYDNEY AUCKLAND TORONTO NEW YORK LONDON

PEARLS
A BANTAM BOOK

First published in Australia and New Zealand in 2006
by Bantam

National Library of Australia
Cataloguing-in-Publication Entry

Falconer, Colin, 1953-.
    Pearls.

    ISBN 978 1 86325 512 7.
    ISBN 1 86325 512 5.

    1. Pearls – Fiction. I. Title.

A823.3

Transworld Publishers,
a division of Random House Australia Pty Ltd
20 Alfred Street, Milsons Point, NSW 2061
http://www.randomhouse.com.au

Random House New Zealand Limited
18 Poland Road, Glenfield, Auckland

Transworld Publishers,
a division of The Random House Group Ltd
61–63 Uxbridge Road, Ealing, London W5 5SA

Random House Inc
1745 Broadway, New York, New York 10036

Text designed by Nada Backovic Designs and typeset in 12.5/16 pt Granjon by
Midland Typesetters, Australia
Printed and bound by Griffin Press, Netley, South Australia

10 9 8 7 6 5 4 3 2 1

For Rones. The pearl I reached for.

'I cannot die unless it is my day to die.'
— saying common among
the Japanese pearl divers of Broome

1

Lacepede Islands, off Point Lagrange
Broome, Western Australia. November 1913

Tanaka hung motionless on the lifeline, the monstrous canvas arms of his diving suit limp at his side, streaming seawater. Wes, his tender, unscrewed the face plate of the helmet, and shook his head when he saw the watery blood streaming from the diver's mouth and ears. He unscrewed the helmet from the corselet, and Tanaka was hauled up. He lay on the deck inside the monstrous suit, like some ancient pelagic fish brought from the deeps. His only movements were the irregular, spastic twitching of his fingers.

Cam McKenzie frowned, his hands on his hips. He

looked at the big West Indian bosun for his verdict. 'Well?'

'Dead, skip.'

'How the hell did it happen? Didn't you stage him, like I told you?'

Wes stared at the deck. 'Mebbe his luck run out, skip.'

'There's no such thing as luck,' Cam said. There was only one thing to do to save the man, and he dreaded it. But he would not stand by and watch any man die. 'Put his helmet back on!'

'You send him back down, skip?'

'Just do it, Wes.'

There was a buzz of protest from the crew, who were mainly Koepangers and Malays.

'He be dead, skip,' Wes repeated.

'His fingers are still moving. Do it!'

'Mebbe more better lettin' a man die when it's his day,' Wes mumbled. The reproach in the big West Indian's eyes was plain. But he nodded to the crew and, grumbling, they hauled Tanaka's body back over the side of the *China Cloud*. Wes picked up the helmet and screwed it back in place on the corselet.

'Now you can help me into the spare diving dress,' Cam said.

'You is better lettin' a man die,' Wes repeated, but he did as his skipper said and lowered Tanaka into the water. The men went back to work on the hand pumps as Wes fed out the hose and the line over the port gunwale.

✦ ✦ ✦

Cam did not see the sun go down. He hung suspended six fathoms below the hull of the *China Cloud*. The water slowly lost its luminescence and the silent alien world of the sea closed around him.

Fear settled like cold lead in his gut. Even when the sea was clear and green, huge sickle-mouthed monsters would sometimes appear silently and unannounced, only to disappear again just as rapidly into the underworld mist. Now, in the deepening green, he felt like bait on the end of a line.

From above he heard the clack-clack of the compressor engine, sniffed at the familiar smell of the galley smoke that was carried down his air pipe. The weed-encrusted hull of the *China Cloud* bobbed on the mercury skin of the sea.

The sea darkened to a grim mist. The sun fell. He was alone.

He was alone and he was afraid.

✦　✦　✦

After an hour Tanaka regained consciousness; Cam saw his eyes flicker open through the face glass, widening in panic and confusion.

Cam had tied the diver's hands with rope, knowing a man's instinctive reaction on coming around would be to close his air valve and ascend to the surface. Instead, as soon as Tanaka was conscious, Cameron signalled on his lifeline for Wes to bring them up to staging depth, and as they hung there in the water he regulated Tanaka's air valve himself.

Tanaka finally stopped struggling, accepting his helplessness. All light faded now from the green water. Occasionally a luminous shape would dart through the blackness, quick and terrible. Cam fought back his own panic, the instinct to signal *Come up!* A man shows

3

weakness, shows fear, he is dead in the world. His father had taught him that.

Wes had his instructions. Another five hours they would wait, helpless and blind.

They hung on the end of the line.

2

The deck of the *China Cloud* was bathed in silver; it was a full moon, almost blue, a 'pearler's moon' they called it, so bright after the dark sea it was like coming out of a mine into full sunlight. Cameron blinked as Wes unscrewed the face glass.

'Hokkay, skip?'

'I'm okay. How's Mister Tanaka?'

'Alive, skip. You put voodoo on him?'

'No voodoo, Wes. Just Navy science. Now get this damned helmet off me. And tell Curry-Curry to get my dinner!'

Wes helped him out of the diving suit and Curry-Curry, the Malay cook-boy, put a mug of steaming coffee in his hand. Cam stared at the churning black sea and shivered. Not Tanaka's day to die after all; he wondered if he would know his own when it came.

Christ. His hands were shaking. He didn't want anyone to see.

He went down the scuttle. Tanaka lay on his bunk, his eyes fixed on the planking over his head.

'How are you feeling, Mister Tanaka? Much pain?'

'Bit. Not much.'

'You're lucky to be alive!' Cam took a bottle of square-face gin from a trunk in the corner. He splashed some into the coffee in his enamel cup. He offered it to Tanaka.

The Japanese shook his head, his face expressionless.

'You might at least thank me.'

'Not my day to die, boss.'

Cam leaned on the bunk, his face close to Tanaka's. 'It was your day to die, Mister Tanaka. For good or ill, I took your destiny in my own hands. But this time you've tried the patience of your Shinto gods a little far.'

Tanaka turned away. 'I dive for you again tomorrow, boss.'

'There's no more diving for you, not on this boat. If you want to kill yourself, it will be on another man's lugger.' Cam felt suddenly bone weary as the tension of the last few hours emptied out of him. 'We're sailing for Broome. You're alive thanks to the good graces of the Royal Navy and Cameron McKenzie. I just pray you'll walk again.'

He lifted himself onto his own bunk. He lay back and closed his eyes.

As he waited for sleep he heard Tanaka whisper: 'One day I pay you back, boss.'

Cam did not answer. He was exhausted to his bones but every time he shut his eyes the green phantoms of the deep swarmed from the darkness to torment him. He despised his own fear, could smell the taint of it in his own sweat, and it disgusted him. A year he had lived this way, during his Royal Navy days, battling this yellow streak in himself, and he had never won, he had never lost. His will and his fear were equally matched; one would never stop coming on, the other would never take a step back.

He would never let anyone know how it terrified him, the stink of wet canvas, the panicked feeling of suffocation as they screwed the helmet into place. His imagination painted for him in vivid colour the possibility of a slow and agonising death at the bottom of the sea, cold and alone.

'You fucking cry like a baby,' he heard his father say long ago as he took off his leather belt and wrapped a loop around his knuckles. 'You and your brothers. When will you learn to be a man?'

Cam was breathing fast. His nose wrinkled at the stench of rotting shellfish. He heard a cockroach scuttle across the deck. Sleep would not come.

✦   ✦   ✦

Tanaka was stretchered off the *China Cloud*. A good diver could not be replaced in the middle of the season. He would have to dive out the year himself.

Few Europeans dived their own boats; the Japanese were far better divers than the whites or even the Malays. They did not suffer so badly from 'squeeze', or from ear bleeds, and they could stay down longer and deeper without getting the diver's sickness.

But he had no choice. He tried not to think of what lay ahead, getting up each dawn to climb shivering into the wet canvas suit and heavy lead boots, steeling himself against the dread of suffocation every time the helmet was lifted onto his head and the face plate screwed in place.

You can do it, Cam, you've done it before.

He had spent an entire year with the Royal Navy in the freezing lochs of Scotland. He remembered the first time he discovered his claustrophobia, the overwhelming panic as the black water bubbled around his copper helmet and the silent cold blackness of the water swallowed him. He had conquered it then; he would conquer it now.

As soon as Tanaka was on his way to the Japanese hospital he ordered full sail and the *China Cloud* headed back out to sea. His pearl – the perfect, beautiful, wondrous pearl that would sell for a prince's ransom and change his life – was out there waiting for him, somewhere. He felt it in his bones. And he was right. It waited, patient and perfect and inevitable, like fate, like destiny, the flawless beauty around which the wheel of his soul would turn.

It is said there are two things that can alter the course of a man's destiny; one is luck, and the other is courage. Without courage, a man cannot make anything of his luck. But without luck, a man might run scared all his life and it will make no difference to his fortune. But in that one moment when he senses the turning of the tide and the smell of change in the wind, if he has the balls for it, he might just change his life forever.

3

Like all oyster shells this one was not easy to see in the
green gloom of ten fathoms. A russet tree of sea fern
grew on the shell, making it almost indistinguishable from
the mass of coral that surrounded it. Cam did not see it and
would have passed it, but another creature of the sea was
more diligent, and was stalking it with exaggerated care.

The sentinel fish that lived in the oyster's mouth had not
as yet detected the danger. The octopus was small, its tentacles barely a foot long. A chameleon of the sea, it altered the
colour of its body as it crept towards its quarry, changing
from dun-yellow to green to orange as it swam from sand to
weed to coral. The unblinking eyes were fixed on the oyster,
waiting its opportunity.

As the oyster breathed it opened its shell a fraction to filter the sea for food through the fleshy curtain of its lips. At that moment the octopus darted forward, plunged its long arms inside the shell, and tried to prise it apart.

The oyster instinctively attempted to clench tight the lips of its shell, but its attacker was prepared. The octopus clamped its remaining tentacles on the coral, while those inside the oyster's mouth strained to wrench apart its victim's abductor muscles and render it helpless.

The life and death struggle made the sea fern tremble and threw up tiny puffs of sand on the reef; and it was this that finally attracted Cam's attention. By the time he had lumbered across, the octopus had succeeded in opening the shell and was contemplating a succulent and hard-earned meal.

Suddenly its prize was snatched away. Outraged, it squirted a cloud of ink at the terrible bubble-headed monster that had stolen its dinner and darted away.

Cam placed the shell in the bag around his neck and moved on. It was just another shell, part of that day's dread labour. He had no sense of premonition. But then it was not the shell that changed his life's course. Luck is just what happens to us; life is what we do with it.

✦　✦　✦

It was late afternoon and the sun hung low and fat and copper on the horizon. The rigging was festooned with shellfish hung out to dry, like washing. The crew would get thirty shillings a bag for it, landed in Singapore.

The Koepangers were forward, leaning on the rigging,

chattering and laughing among themselves. Cam worked on the catch, the empty shells thudding onto the deck as he finished with each one. He was wearing only a Malay sarong at his waist. Unlike most of the Europeans in this part of the world his skin was not pale; it had tanned over the months to the colour of fresh-cut jarrah. His chest and arms were finely muscled, and he was tall, almost six feet three inches. He had dark hair and fine, even features, though after three weeks at sea these were hidden behind the dark pelt of his beard.

'A bonnie-looking boy,' his mother had said before he went away to sea.

He picked up another oyster, working the thin blade of the knife through the muscle. The shell fell apart, and he felt with his fingers under the slimy meat for a pearl or 'blister' on the shell that might indicate a 'baroque' or 'barrack', the malformed nacre that was sold by the carat to the buyers back in Broome. He worked steadily, mechanically; opening shell was monotonous work. Only one shell in a thousand provided a pearl, and few of those were of any great value.

Cam looked up. 'Curry-Curry! What's for dinner tonight?'

The cook-boy's head bobbed out of the galley, perfect white teeth framed against a nut-brown face. 'Curry-curry, *tuan*,' he said.

Cam grinned at Wes. It was an old joke. Their cook-boy had not earned his nickname for nothing.

The next shell was already open, prised apart by the octopus. He ran his finger inside the slimy meat, feeling for a hard stone, expecting to find nothing. But this time

11

he felt something under his fingers, and he stopped breathing for a moment, his heart hammering almost painfully against his ribs.

Sweat formed little blisters on his forehead. He could not believe the size of it. He drew out a large pearl, rolling it between finger and thumb. 'Good God Almighty,' he murmured. It was huge.

He looked up. Wes was staring, open-mouthed. He rolled his eyes in his head and made the sign to ward off the evil eye. The rest of the crew had stopped what they were doing and were staring too, hushed in awe.

It was the most beautiful thing he had ever seen in his whole life. It shimmered like the moon. Good God Almighty. First season out, he had what some men search a lifetime for and never find; he was holding his dreams right there in his hand.

✦ ✦ ✦

Cam was below in his cabin with Wes. Curry-Curry had brought them their dinner but Cam was too excited to eat. He had placed the pearl into a small leather pouch looped on a thong around his neck, and every few minutes he would put his hand to his throat to touch it, make sure he was not dreaming.

'Dat pearl worth a fortune, skip,' Wes said as he scooped another heaped spoonful of rice into his mouth. 'What you do with all dat money?'

'This is my future, Wes. I'll buy more luggers, build my destiny on pearls.' He clapped a hand on his shoulder. 'Stay with me, Wes. You'll not go poor. Not now.'

Paddy Mick, the Koepang bosun, scampered down the scuttle. 'Storm she come,' he said to Cam. 'More better you look him.'

Cam put down his plate and followed Paddy Mick up to the deck. The wind was from the southeast and a mist of rain had begun to fall. He checked the barometer. It always fell in the afternoon but by now it should have recovered.

Wes shook his head. 'Willy-willy season come soon now, skip. Must be close to lay-up.'

'Aye, looks like it. We'd better head for shelter.'

The *China Cloud* set sail for the pearlers' camp at Barred Creek.

4

Cam stood on the prow in a white shirt and canvas trousers. Above him, the stars were extinguished by low darting clouds. A quickening breeze, salt on his skin and his breath still tight in his chest. Twenty-five years old and the world at his feet. He had never felt elation like this. Nothing could stop him now. He would not be poor again; he had made a promise to himself and he would keep it. He had done it by force of will alone. He wished his father were here to see it.

'Weigh anchor!'

The riding lights of four other luggers bobbed in the darkness, other pearlers seeking shelter from the uncertain weather. Cam heard the twang of a guitar from the deck of one of the boats.

He turned to Wes. 'Tell Curry-Curry to get the men's dinner. We'll ride anchor here tonight and take another look at the weather in the morning.'

'Aye, skip.'

Cam put a hand to the pearl under his shirt. It was still tempting to make the run home for Broome with his prize – but there might be a few more weeks in the season yet. Time enough to find more.

He heard the click of rowlocks. A whaleboat emerged from the darkness into the arc of light thrown by the kerosene lanterns on the port side.

'Ahoy there, *China Cloud*!'

Cam leaned over the port rail. 'Ahoy!'

'My mastah belong *Koepang*,' a voice shouted in pidgin. 'Say you come longa me for chow, orright?'

It was a common courtesy on the pearling grounds, sharing a poor dinner in another white skipper's cabin, a chance to talk with another European after weeks, perhaps months, with only native crew for company. And also, in this case, a welcome opportunity to eat something different from Curry-Curry's infernal stews. And he had been too excited to eat dinner earlier.

'Aye,' Cam shouted back, 'I'll be there!'

◆　◆　◆

The sparse silver strands of hair were combed tight across the man's head, taut as guitar strings. There was several day's growth of white stubble on his chin and his breath reeked of gin. He thrust out an enormous hand and clapped Cam on the shoulder with the other. 'Welcome aboard the *Koepang*! The name's Patrick Flynn, late of Donegal, Ireland, bless her rolling green hills, and more lately of Broome, and pleased to see another white face after six weeks at sea! And who do I have the pleasure of addressing?'

'My name's McKenzie, sir, Cameron McKenzie.'

'A Scot! Well praise the good Lord for that then, there I was thinking I'd have to try and be pleasant to another damned Englishman. You look like a drinking man to me. Would you care for a little gin?'

A charlatan, Cam thought. Too hail-fellow-well-met for his liking, a little too forced. But he went along with it. 'As long as it's not too little.'

Flynn slapped him hard between the shoulderblades. 'Not on the *Koepang* it won't be! Come down to the state-room and we'll oil your throat!'

The stateroom was a cramped and squalid cabin reeking of shellfish and bilge, like Cam's. But there was a tablecloth on the dinner table and even silver service. A passing attempt to be civilised.

There were two carved mahogany chairs – Cameron usually ate perched on the edge of his bunk or squatting on the deck – and when Flynn clapped his hands a Malay steward appeared, in white ducks.

Cam accepted a brimming pot of gin from him.

Flynn raised his own glass in a toast: 'To your health and prosperity,' he said, and the gin gurgled down his throat. He held out his glass for another.

Cam, who prided himself that he could drink any man under the table, did the same.

'Where are you from, Mister McKenzie? I've been in Broome nearly ten years and I can't say I've ever seen your face.'

'I arrived at the beginning of the season. I was lucky to get a crew.'

'Who's your diver?'

'A Jap named Tanaka.'

'Tanaka? Over the hill, my boy, take it from me.'

'Aye, and nearly crippled too. He's back in Broome these last two weeks. He got the paralysis.'

'So who does your diving now?'

'You're looking at him,' Cam said quietly.

'You?' Flynn raised an eyebrow and there was new respect in his eyes. 'Not many white men dive their own boat.'

'This one does. I have some knowledge of it.'

'In what way now?'

'When I was in the Royal Navy, the Admiralty's Deep Water Diving Commission wanted volunteers for their trials. They thought they had a way of beating the diver's sickness.'

'The Japs reckon their paper charms and some cajeput oil does the job well enough.'

'Which is why so many of them end up in the grave-yard.' Cam leaned forward, elbows on his knees. 'You see, down there in the deeps, a man's body is under pressure from the water above, and nitrogen is more readily absorbed into the blood, and it bubbles into the joints and the brain when he comes back to the air. In the Navy we learned that to overcome it, you wait at a certain depth below the surface, where the pressure is not so great, until all the nitrogen in the blood is breathed out again.'

Flynn shook his head. 'They tried all that once a few years back. Sent some Royal Navy divers out here with their fancy

17

ideas. One of them died and the other went back a cripple.'

'The Japs sabotaged the trials. I heard about it. They didn't want whites taking over the diving. They want to keep it for themselves.'

'So what went wrong with your man Tanaka then?'

'I don't know. Perhaps the tide rose faster than we thought. Or perhaps he had just pushed his body too far. He's been diving now for thirteen years and most of these Japs don't last more than five, even the best of them.'

'Well, a man who does his own diving must work up an appetite. The *Koepang* has one of the best cooks this side of Ceylon, my boy, even if I do say so myself.'

'What are we having?' Cam said, eagerly.

Flynn gulped another gin. 'Curry,' he said.

◆   ◆   ◆

Flynn settled back in his chair and belched. There were yellow-brown stains on the front of his shirt. He ate with the same gusto that he drank his gin.

The Malay steward attempted to clear away the plates, but Flynn shooed him off. 'Never mind that, man! Get me another drink!'

'A fine dinner,' Cam said. Holy Mother of God, it had been even worse than one of Curry-Curry's concoctions! He made a mental note to go easier on the boy.

Flynn took a tin of Egyptian hand-rolled cheroots from the pocket of his shirt and offered one to Cam. He blew smoke in a dense cloud towards the ceiling and drummed impatiently on the table with the fingers of his left hand while he waited for his drink to arrive. He listened to the creak of cordage and timbers as the *Koepang* shifted with the tide, heard the sighing *wah, wah!* of the Malay crew as they gathered around their story-teller.

'What brought you all the way here, to this godforsaken part of the world?' Flynn asked.

'I heard it was the place a brave man could make his fortune. A few hundred pounds, they said, and you could lease a lugger and crew. I'd saved the money His Majesty's Navy paid me for risking my neck in that gloomy Scottish loch. It nearly cost me my life so I wasn't about to piss it up against a wall.'

'Good for you, my boy. Was it all worth it?'

Cam felt the weight of the pearl in the pouch at his neck. If he only knew! 'All right so far.'

Flynn leaned eagerly across the table. 'Did you find any pearls?'

'Some small ones.' This was partly true. Until today they had all been small.

'Let me show you something,' Flynn said. He pushed his plate to one side, reached into his pocket and pulled out a tobacco tin. He took off the lid and tipped the contents onto the table. There were a dozen pearls, mostly small ones; but there was one much larger than the others, a perfect round with a shimmering lustre, faintly pink against the white tablecloth.

'Look at that!' Flynn said.

Cam leaned forward. He could smell Flynn's breath, an oily mixture of gin and curry.

'Seventy, eighty grains,' Flynn said. 'Worth a thousand pounds at least! A thousand pounds!' Flynn repeated the words like a benediction. 'That's what you call a pearl!'

Cam tried to appear impressed. 'Aye, it's a beauty all right.'

Flynn frowned, sensitive to the caveat in his voice. 'You'll never see another like it!'

'Aye, perhaps.'

'No doubt about it! It's the find of the season!' Offended by Cam's lack of enthusiasm, Flynn scooped the little pile back into the tobacco tin with an imperious gesture. 'The find of the season!' he repeated.

Cam hesitated but could not help himself. He pulled the leather thong over his head and opened the pouch. He let the pearl drop in his palm and stared at it for a moment, marvelling at its texture, its weight, the roseate sheen that lent it an almost other-worldly beauty. In the manner of a magician producing a rabbit from a hat, he grinned and let it fall onto the table.

Flynn's jaw fell open and he stared. When he spoke again his voice was hoarse with admiration: 'Jesus Fucking Christ and all the Blesséd Saints in Heaven. Where did you find that?'

✦   ✦   ✦

The pearl rested again in the leather pouch about Cam's neck, but Flynn could still talk of nothing else. The gin had made him emotional and his eyes were wet. 'I've been on these pearling grounds near ten years and I've never seen the like,' he murmured. He took another gulp of his gin. 'The sea makes a pearl like that just once in every lifetime. And you found it, my boy, you found it! That pearl will grace the neck of an empress or a queen one day, you mark my words. Maybe even the Queen of England herself.'

20

Then he added, quickly: 'And may God bring down hail and punishment on the English and their bloody empire just the same.'

'Well, it's the making of Cameron McKenzie's empire, I know that.'

'And good luck to you too, my boy,' Flynn said, and he raised his glass again. He looked around for his steward. 'Mahomet! Where are you, you black bastard? We need some more gin!'

Cam got to his feet, had to put out a hand to steady himself. 'Where's the gentlemen's bathroom, Flynn?'

Flynn grinned back. 'Right there at the stern, same as on the *China Cloud*. But if you feel the end getting wet stand back a bit, my boy. The sharks bite hard along this part of the coast.'

'It's been that long, I don't think I'd miss it.'

'Good-looking young buck like you, you'd miss it as soon as you stepped on the dock in Broome. And watch out for that pearl. Don't go dropping it over the side!'

'The devil himself couldn't get it away from me,' Cam said, and went up the scuttle. Flynn waited for his footfall on the deck above his head.

'The devil himself?' Flynn murmured. 'We'll see about that. *Mahomet!*'

The Malay steward appeared in the doorway, head bobbing.

'This bastard drinks like a fish. I'm nearly done and he looks fresh as a Donegal daisy. Get some opium and stir it into his gin. And make sure you don't mix up the drinks or I'll flog your arse so hard you'll have to shit through your ears!'

5

Cam opened his eyes. His mouth was dry, and pain lanced his eyeballs. He was lying on his bunk, still in his shirt and ducks. He tried to sit up but the room started to spin around him, and he lay down again. A shock of cold grease erupted on his skin.

Wes came down the companionway. 'You awake at last, skip.'

'Sweet Christ, what happened?'

'You got plenty drunk. Jay-sus! I had to carry you down to yo' bunk. You like a dead man.'

'Flynn and his damned gin,' Cameron groaned. 'Help me up to the deck.' Wes helped him out of his bunk and up the scuttle to the deck. Cam held on to the port gunwale, white knuckled, taking deep breaths of clean salt air.

He squinted against the harsh glare of the sunlight; it was like a thousand needles being pushed into his eyes. The sky was cloudless and blue; the weather had passed during the night. Cameron felt a sudden unease. The *Koepang* and the other luggers were gone.

He checked the sun; it was almost directly overhead.

'Have I been asleep all morning?' he said, and saw the reproach in Wes's eyes.

He leaned forward and retched over the side.

When he had done he closed his eyes, fighting another wave of nausea, skin crawling and damp. He tried to remember what had happened last night, felt a gradual stirring of unease. There was something wrong. He felt for the pouch at his throat.

It was gone. Dear God in heaven! He fought down the welling of panic and rage.

'Where's the *Koepang,* Wes?'

'Long gone, skip,' Wes said. 'She sail wid da tide first light.'

'Why did you not wake me? It's nearly midday!'

Wes took a step back. 'When you drink like dat, skip, more easy to wake a dead man.'

My pearl! My beautiful goddamned pearl! Cam wanted to rip out the main mast and hurl it into the sea. The bastard! That fucking, goddamned, treacherous Irish bastard!

Curry-Curry appeared from the galley, offered Cam a mug of steaming black coffee. Cam knocked it out of his hand and sent it rolling across the deck. Curry-Curry yelped and raced for the scuttle.

'My pearl! He's got my damned pearl!'

Cam hit his fist against the foremast so hard that he smashed two of his knuckles. Blood dripped from his fingers onto the deck. He didn't feel anything. 'MY PEARL!'

No one spoke, or moved. The crew of the *China Cloud* watched Cam with huge, frightened eyes.

When Cam spoke again, his voice was as quiet and deadly as the hiss of a snake. 'Hoist sail, bosun. We're going after them. When I catch that bastard Flynn I'm going to rip out his heart with my bare hands.'

6

When the *China Cloud* limped into Roebuck Bay, the *Koepang* and the rest of Flynn's small fleet were already drawn up onto the beach, preparing for refitting. It had taken longer to get back to Broome than Cam had hoped. For the last four days he had railed and cursed against the vagaries of the sea; five hours out of Barred Creek they had been hit by another wild squall that had torn the mainsail and damaged the rudder, leaving him with no chance of catching Flynn before he reached port. The pearl might already have been sold snide in some back-room bar.

The *China Cloud* weighed anchor and Cam jumped into his whaleboat. He and Wes rowed to the shore. He leapt out while they were still knee-deep in the shallows.

That bastard! Ever since he left Glasgow he had dreamed of that pearl. Cam strode up the hard strand among the detritus of rusting anchor chains, driftwood, packing boxes and shell, he thought about what that one single pearl meant to him; he had overcome his terror of the deeps, climbed shivering and cold into that damned canvas suit each dawn, lain sleepless and aching and exhausted every night in his bunk, searching for that one stone. You're a braggart and a fool, Cameron McKenzie. How did you let your own boastfulness get in the way of everything you ever dreamed of? Why did you ever show that bastard Irishman the pearl?

He found Flynn's foreshore camp, a ramshackle huddle of corrugated iron huts and timber lean-to's. The first man he saw was Mahomet, Flynn's steward, no longer dressed in stiff whites, looking more at ease in a native sarong.

'Where's Flynn?' Cam shouted at him.

Mahomet looked up, startled. As soon as he saw him he started to run but Cam caught him easily and wrestled the little Malay to the sand.

'Where's Flynn, I said?'

'Don't know, boss!'

Cam grabbed him by the throat. 'Tell me, or by God I'll wring it out of you!'

Mahomet screamed and closed his eyes.

'Where?'

Mahomet tried to wriggle away. Cam put his fingers around his throat and squeezed. 'Tell me where he is or by God I'll break your neck like a chicken!'

He meant it. And so Mahomet told him.

❖   ❖   ❖

It was lay-up time in Broome and almost all the luggers and their crews were back in port. These were the roaring days; the price of shell was high, labour was cheap, and the brothels and gambling houses and hotels were packed. Japanese, Chinese, Javanese, Malays and Manilamen, their pockets stuffed with the season's profits, milled around the crowded, Asian-smelling streets of Chinatown.

Cam found the billiard hall in John Chi Lane, a corrugated iron shack with two tables and a rough, timber-hewn bar. It was stifling hot inside, the air thick with tobacco smoke and the fug of gin and sweat. Cam strode in, Wes running to keep up.

Flynn leaned over one of the tables, attempting a snooker against the cushion.

'Flynn!'

Flynn's ball snickered along the baize and dropped in the far pocket. 'Jesus, Mary and Joseph,' he muttered. He surveyed the newcomer with a frown. Then his face brightened and he held out his hand. 'Cameron, my boy! Back in port already!'

Cam ignored the proffered handshake. 'Where's my pearl, Flynn?'

'Pearl, my boy? What are you talking about?'

'You had your shifty-eyed little cabin boy drug me! What was it you put in my drink – opium, was it?'

Flynn stared at Cam open-mouthed. Then he started to laugh. 'What's that you're saying? That I drugged you? Now why would I want to do that?'

'For the pearl!'

'Your pearl?' Flynn was aghast. 'You lost that beautiful pearl?'

'I didn't lose it. You stole it!'

Silence. Cam was aware of the press of hostile faces around them. No friends here. This was Flynn's town. At least big Wes was behind him, watching his back. Cam had no intention of leaving without his pearl.

A bear of a man in a beer-stained shirt barged a path through the crowd. 'Mister Flynn's a respected customer in this establishment,' he said, as if he was the manager of the Ritz. 'I'd advise you to clear out of here.'

'And I'd advise you to keep your nose out of other people's business,' Cam said.

Flynn chuckled again. 'It's all right, Joe,' Flynn said. 'It's just a little misunderstanding. We can sort this out like gentlemen.' He turned to Cam. 'Now look, my boy, I'm sorry about your pearl. I really am. It was a fine stone. But I'm an honest man, as my friends here will all vouch. I swear on my mother's grave – God rest her poor martyred soul – I never took your pearl. Now how about I buy you a drink and we'll talk about this?'

He reached out to put a hand on Cam's shoulder. Cam shoved it away. 'I want my pearl or God help me I'll tear you apart with my bare hands, here and now.'

Flynn shrugged and made as if to turn away; instead he pivoted on his right foot and drove his billiard cue with all his force into Cam's midriff. As Cam doubled over Flynn smashed the cue on his head.

Cam staggered but did not fall. He lurched sideways into the jeering crowd, who pushed him back towards Flynn, hoping to see the Irishman finish him off. Cam used the impetus to drop his shoulder into Flynn's body. He gripped his arms around the Irishman's waist and drove him backwards. They smashed into a billiard table and rolled onto the floor, locked together.

Flynn reached for Cam's face and tried to force his knuckles into his eyes. Cam turned his head away, brought his knee up into Flynn's groin. Flynn screamed in pain and rolled away.

Cam got to his feet, stood over him, fists clenched. 'Get up, you thieving bastard.'

Flynn struggled slowly to his knees, one hand cupping his crotch. 'There's no need for name-calling, my boy. Let's keep it a fair fight.' He hooked his fingers around the edge of the billiard table and pulled himself to his feet, his back to Cam. His fist closed around a billiard ball. He span around and threw it at Cam's head.

Cam ducked; he heard a muffled scream of pain as the ball hit a man standing directly behind him.

Flynn had grabbed another ball and was winding up to throw again. Cam launched himself at him. His fist caught Flynn on the point of the chin and the Irishman fell backwards, his head striking the heavy carved leg of the billiard table. Cam bent down, grabbed Flynn by the hair and pulled him half upright. His fist came from somewhere near his right knee and smashed into Flynn's midriff.

The Irishman gasped and would have collapsed onto his face but Cam held a fistful of long, silver-grey hair, like Flynn was some grotesque marionette with broken strings. 'Where's – my – pearl?' Cameron hissed in his ear.

Flynn's arms flapped in a spastic attempt to push

Cameron away. There was blood in his hair and his mouth gaped open like a beached fish as he tried to get his breath.

Cam frisked his clothes. 'Where is it, Flynn? Tell me, or by God I'll beat it out of you!'

The big man Flynn had called Joe took a step forward. 'Best let him go now, mate.' He was holding the broken billiard cue in his right hand and tapping it on the palm of his left hand. Several Malays and Manilamen were ranged behind him – some of Flynn's crew, no doubt – and Cameron saw the glint of a knife.

For a few moments the only sound was Flynn snuffling and spitting blood.

Cam considered his situation. Even with Wes backing him, they had no chance against this mob, and the Malays were renowned for their abilities with their curved *kris* knives.

Cam released his hold on Flynn. The Irishman fell forwards onto his face.

'The pearl's mine,' Cam said, 'and I swear to you I will have it back – or you'll pay, Mister Flynn. You'll regret the day you ever crossed Cameron McKenzie!'

The crowd parted to let him pass and he walked out into the bright sun.

7

Cam sat in his cabin on the *China Cloud*, a bottle of square-face in his right fist. He took out his tin of cigarettes and lit one.

He stared morose at the ashtray on the table in front of him. The ashtray was, in fact, a pearl shell, and on the shell was a pearl 'blister'. The blister had once been formed by a parasite boring into the shell; in defence the oyster had covered the wound with nacre. Water pressure had caused a bubble to form, which in turn had filled with mud. These so-called 'blister pearls' were sold for a cheap price in Broome, and were used to make hatpins. The blister was the first pearl Cam had ever found and so he had kept it as a souvenir.

He stared at the illusory pearl, thinking of the real one Flynn had stolen from him at Barred Creek.

Wes watched him gloomily. 'Mebbe he tell you true. Mebbe you drop this one pearl, skip. You was powerful drunk.'

'I wasn't drunk,' Cam said softly. 'I've not been that drunk in my whole life, and never will be. I was drugged, I know it!'

Wes knew better than to argue, but he looked doubtful. 'Mebbe.'

'I have to get it back.'

'If he steal yo' pearl,' Wes said, and he lingered on the word 'if', 'if he steal it, mebbe he sell dis one pearl already. A man doan keep snide too long.'

'Perhaps.'

Curry-Curry's face appeared at the scuttle. 'Somebody come, *tuan*.'

Cam heard footfall on the deck overhead. 'Find out who it is, Wes.'

'Aye, skip.'

A few minutes later a pair of spotless white canvas shoes was followed down the scuttle by an impeccably ironed white linen suit, although the cuffs were already stained by the characteristic brick-red dust of the northwest. This vision of sartorial elegance was crowned by a splendid white sola topee.

Cam stared at this apparition. George Niland.

'How are you, Cam?' He removed his topee and held out a hand.

George Niland had a florid, boyish face and sleek, close-groomed fair hair. He smiled a lot – it was why Cam had

32

never completely trusted him – and there was something soft about him. He was a big man, but heavy rather than muscular. Like dough, Cameron thought.

First job Cam had had when he'd sailed from England was crew on one of the Niland crayboats out of Fremantle. Niland's father owned the biggest fleet in Western Australia and George had managed the operation from an office in Cantonment Street. It was George who helped Cam get his skipper's ticket.

'What are you doing way up here?' Cam said.

'Father bought himself a pearling fleet. Lot of money in shell.'

'I've not seen it yet, George.'

'Perhaps you spent too much of the season in port picking fights with other skippers.'

So that was why he was here. Not a social visit then. 'You heard the way that Irish bastard thieved me?'

'Mister Flynn is regarded as an upstanding member of this community.' He fanned himself with his topee. 'You'll have to tread gently there, my boy.'

My boy. Something in his tone rankled. He thinks he's still the boss. 'He has something that belongs to me and I intend to get it back. Still, that's my problem, not yours.'

George took out a handkerchief and mopped at his forehead. 'Not in port five minutes and you've got your knuckles bloody already. Haven't changed much, have you, Cam?'

Cameron was suddenly conscious of his cramped quarters, the spartan bunk in the corner. 'Like a drink?' Cam said.

'Too early in the day for me.' He looked around,

wrinkled his nose. 'How did you find your way to this godforsaken part of the world?'

'Same as you, I suppose. Sunk all I have into the *China Cloud*.'

'You own her?'

'Only leased her for a season. I'll make enough from my shell to try my luck another year. Would own her now and perhaps a few others if it wasn't for Flynn. You sure you'll not have a drink with me?'

George pulled a gold fob watch from his pocket. 'I have a meeting with my bankers. Remember what I said about Flynn.' He hesitated at the scuttle. 'You've heard about the At Home Captain Gregory is having tomorrow afternoon.'

'I have. I'm told all the pearlers in the town will be there.'

'You won't be making a scene, I hope.'

Cam supposed he was used to getting his way with most people. Not this time.

George replaced the sola topee with a flourish and turned to go. Then, as an afterthought, he added: 'Patrick Flynn has a lot of powerful friends in Broome.'

'Are you one of them?'

George smiled and disappeared up the scuttle.

8

Broome's settlements were clustered on either side of a headland known as Buccaneer Rock. On one side of the town the tin shanties of Chinatown huddled between the mile-long jetty and the mangrove swamps. On the other, the pearlers' palm-shaded bungalows sprawled in fragrant gardens on either side of wide shell-grit streets.

The Gregorys' bungalow was surrounded by sweeping verandas wreathed in purple bougainvillea. As Cam walked up the path, he was assaulted by the heady scent of mock orange blossom and frangipani. Trestle tables had been laid out on the verandas and iced champagne and claret-cup was served by white-jacketed Malay stewards. There was the sound of braying laughter from the tennis courts and the croquet lawn.

George came towards Cam, his hand outstretched. He was wearing a Tussore jacket and trousers, white linen shirt and soft collar.

'Cam. Good to see you again.'

'You look very fine, George.'

'You look quite the white master yourself. Things have changed since that time you first walked into my office in Cantonment Street.'

'Just a new suit and a shave. I nearly wore my old Navy uniform but people sometimes mistake me for an admiral.'

George's nose wrinkled in another of his ingratiating smiles. 'Excuse me a moment. I must go and say hello to the Graveneys. He's our banker. Duty calls.'

Cam watched him go, feeling sour and regretting now that he had come. Beggar at the feast, as the saying went. By God, it was like a little bit of England transplanted here among the palms and the red dust.

He allowed a Malay steward to pour him champagne. 'No opium in this, is there?'

'Master?' the man said.

'It doesn't matter.'

Cam looked around. The guests at the garden party were all white Europeans. Even though it was late afternoon it was close to a hundred degrees; the men were sweating in tropical whites, the women in long gowns, with parasols to keep off the sun. The English never really leave England behind.

And then he saw her.

There are those who will tell you that there is no such

thing as love at first sight, that love is a compromise worked out over years, not a knowing and wanting experienced in a first few breathless seconds. Perhaps they have never felt it, or if they have, are frightened of it and where it might lead fainter hearts. Cam had never felt anything quite like it before; she literally took his breath away. Why this was so he could never afterwards explain to himself or anyone else. But then love at first sight bears no relation to common sense. It is a twist of fate, like the saving of a life or the finding of a pearl.

She was standing alone, at the far end of the veranda, watching the croquet game. She was achingly lovely, with her green eyes and strawberry curls and willowy figure, yet not the most classically beautiful woman he had ever seen. There was something else that captivated him and till the day he died he was never able to say quite what it was.

Two women were squeaking with laughter as they shuffled around the lawn with their mallets. She looked thoroughly bored.

As he approached he felt his own heart banging against his ribs. He had never been nervous around women before and he did not know why he should have felt this way now.

'They say the French gave this game to the English,' he said to her. 'It was their revenge for the battle of Waterloo.'

Kate Flynn turned her head and stared at him. 'I beg your pardon?'

'Croquet. Do you not find it an enthralling and intellectually demanding game?'

'It's chess for the gormless. Do I know you?'

He held out his hand. 'My name's Cameron.'

'I don't believe we've met.'

'No, we haven't. I couldn't wait for a formal introduction.'

'It's what a gentleman would do.'

'The gentlemen of this town spend all their time playing
games instead of talking to young ladies who must otherwise stand on the verandas with nothing to entertain them
and nothing in their glasses.'

Kate pursed her lips to disguise a smile. She was charm-
ed by the man's boldness. She studied him, speculating. He
was appallingly handsome. He looked dangerous.

'I don't think I've ever seen you before. Were you
actually invited to this party?'

'I've not been in Broome long, it's true. My ship's the
China Cloud.'

'You're a pearler then.'

'I am, though I've little to show for it so far.'

Kate pushed a curl from her face with a long finger and
Cam felt himself fall under her acute and critical gaze.

'Do I detect an accent?'

'I'm a Scot and proud of it. One of God's tender mercies
that I was born on the civilised side of the border. You too
by the lilt in your voice.'

'I was born here but my family are from County Cork.'

He affected a slight bow. 'Cameron McKenzie. Friends
call me Cam. I am a little bold, I suppose, making my introduction myself. A lot of women pretend they don't like that
in a man, but I suspect they do not hate it as much as they
say. What do you think?'

'I find it vulgar,' she said.

'Can you at least not tell me your name?'

'Not without a proper introduction.'

'You look like a Beatrice.'

Ah, a flash of fire in the eyes. 'I do not look like a Beatrice.'

'Prudence would be my second guess. It implies good breeding with a conservative nature.'

'If I had something in my glass I should pour it over you.'

'Then I should refill it. What might I get you?'

'Kerosene and a match.'

He laughed at that. 'I should be offended but I know you don't mean that, Prudence. Or may I call you Pru?'

She smiled in spite of herself at his teasing. She held up her glass. 'This is fruit punch. My father put it in my hand. I should rather prefer champagne. Do you think you might find me a glass?'

'Of course. We Celts must stick together.'

She was about to hand him her empty glass but stopped when she heard someone shouting her name. The timbers shook as Patrick Flynn bounded up the veranda steps. He was resplendent in his white tropical suit, but the two black eyes and swathe of plaster across his nose detracted from an otherwise dignified appearance.

'Kathleen, get away from that scoundrel!' He rounded on Cam. 'What in God's name are you doing here?'

'Flynn! I see your nose is a little shorter and broader than it used to be.'

'Get away from my daughter!'

Cam stared at him then at Kate, his jaw slack with astonishment. 'Your daughter?'

'Are you leaving or shall I have you thrown out?'

'I did not know that this was your daughter, Flynn.

She certainly does not look like the daughter of a thief and a liar.'

Flynn flushed to his collar line. People were staring.

'Will someone please tell me what is going on?' Kate said.

'Stay out of this!' Flynn barked.

'Do not talk to me in that manner,' Kate hissed at him. 'I may be your daughter, Patrick Flynn, and God help me for it, but I'll not be dismissed like a servant girl!'

George Niland suddenly appeared, an ingratiating smile in place, the peacemaker. 'Ah, Patrick, you've met my old friend Cam then. He skippered a crayboat for me down in Fremantle a couple of years back. Wonderful fellow. He's a pearler too, now.' He put a hand on Flynn's shoulder and whispered: 'For God's sake, keep your voice down. My father's watching. This isn't the hotel.'

Flynn said nothing, his fists opening and closing in impotent rage. Cam glanced at Kate, but could not read the expression on her face. 'It's all right, George. I do not want to spoil the party. I can't play croquet anyway.' He gave a small bow to Kate. 'Miss Flynn. It was a very real pleasure. I hope I have not spoiled the afternoon for you. Goodbye, George.'

He turned on Flynn. 'Till we meet again.'

As he marched away down the shell-grit path, she called to him from the veranda. He turned around. 'The name's Kate,' she said.

◆　◆　◆

Kate sat next to Flynn in the sulky, fanning herself gently with a scented handkerchief. They passed the long jetty. A

40

passenger ship, the *Koolinda*, was docked there, a twinkling fairyland of lights.

Flynn was morose. He had hardly said a word to her since they left the party.

'What's wrong?' Kate asked him.

'I don't want you speaking to that man again. Do you understand me now, girl?'

She hated to be told what she could or could not do, especially by her father. She tried to keep her voice even. 'What's your quarrel with Mister McKenzie?'

'That's men's business,' Flynn said.

Kate pursed her lips in anger. Men's business! He treated her as if she was a child. It was an incalculable arrogance, considering how she had fed him and washed his clothes for him all her life.

'He called you a pearl thief. Why?'

'I'll thank you not to question me in that manner, my girl. You're not too old to put across my knee, mind.'

'I should like to see you try it, Patrick Flynn. You're likely to get your nose broken again.'

'Enough, girl! I'll not have you speak to your father that way!'

There was a strident note in his voice now. Their horse pricked its ears and tossed its head, jolting the sulky. Kate turned away, tight-lipped with anger.

When they reached their bungalow, Flynn jumped off and helped his daughter down from the running board. Then he climbed back on and picked up the reins.

'And where are you off to now?' she asked him.

'To the hotel. I need a drink.' He looked down at her, and his face creased into a frown. 'And don't look at me like that! I'll do whatever I damned well please!'

He jerked the reins and the sulky clattered away up the road. Kate watched him go with a mixture of sadness and frustration. He was drinking himself into an early grave. He was only fifty years old and he looked like a man of seventy. Dear God. Men.

She went into the house and removed her bonnet and her shoes. The house was like a furnace. She went out onto the veranda, breathing in the scent of the oleander and Japanese honeysuckle that clung to the hot, moist air. She slumped into a cane chair and ran her fingers through her hair, feeling the moisture on her forehead, the dampness of her blouse. The surf was breaking on Cable Beach, five miles distant, and its whisper mingled with the faint and alien melodies from Singapore that drifted from the radio transmitting station next door.

She saw a shadow move among the bushes in the garden and felt a thrill of alarm. 'Who's there?'

A cigarette glowed in the darkness. 'I'm sorry, I didn't mean to scare you,' a voice said.

Kate recognised the soft brogue immediately. She smiled to herself. It was him!

'Why, Mister McKenzie,' she purred, crossing her legs. 'What a fright you gave me.'

✦ ✦ ✦

Flynn jumped off the running board, tethered his horse and went through a door which read: 'Niland and Company.' There was a light burning inside.

George Niland had his feet perched on the edge of the

desk, his teeth clenched on a cheroot. He looked up as Flynn entered. 'You said it was important,' he said.

Flynn shut the door behind him. 'Are we alone, my boy?'

'It's Sunday, Patrick, of course we are. For goodness sake, sit down. You're making me nervous.'

But Flynn did not sit. Instead he reached into his pocket and took out an old tobacco tin. He took off the lid and removed a roll of tissue paper. 'I thought you might like to see this,' he said. He unwrapped the paper. 'Now then, my boy, tell me if you've ever seen another like this.'

George sat bolt upright. In the darkened room the pearl seemed to take on a luminescence of its own.

'My God,' he breathed, 'where did you get it?'

'It doesn't matter where it came from, my boy. The question is – what's it worth?'

9

The bane of the pearler's life was the cockroaches. They thrived on the reeking gristle that clung to the pearl shells stored in the holds of the luggers; at night they swarmed from their hiding places to feast on the sailors' toenails and the calluses on their feet as they slept. It was impossible to keep them off the boats; all the pearlers could do was sink their luggers in the creeks at high tide every lay-up season and drown that season's infestation.

The next time Cam saw George Niland he was standing on the foreshore watching the incoming tide wash over the decks of the *China Cloud*. George was passing in his sulky on his way to the Niland and Company offices but reined in his horse when he saw him.

'McKenzie, my boy!'

Cam turned. Niland's smug bonhomie grated on him. He still sees me as one of his crew, Cam thought. 'Hello, George. Off to count your money?'

George ignored the jibe with a smile. 'So you've decided to stay on in Broome.'

'For a while anyway.'

'Have you got yourself a foreshore permit?'

'I do not intend to build a camp just yet. I'll sleep on the *China Cloud* as soon as my wee guests have floated away on the tide.'

George screwed up his face in disgust. 'It's a hard life, Cam.' He smiled again, wrinkling his nose. 'I was hoping I'd see you this morning. I have a proposition for you.'

'What sort of proposition, George?'

'Have you seen the *Elizabeth*?'

Cam looked out at Roebuck Bay, where the Niland company schooner rode at anchor on the glittering blue water. 'She's a fine ship.'

'And we need a new master for her. I suggested to my father that you were the ideal man. The pay's good and the company always looks after its people. What do you say?'

Cameron shook his head. 'Thanks for the offer, George. But I want to be my own man.'

'You know, Cam, everyone comes here thinking they're going to make a fortune out there . . .' He nodded his head in the direction of the pearling grounds beyond Gantheaume Point. 'But you're more likely to lose everything. You have to be a good businessman to survive here, not an adventurer.'

'If I lose everything I'll not be too much worse off than

I was before.' Cam patted the horse's flank. 'Thanks again though.'

'If you change your mind . . .'

'I never change my mind.'

George shrugged. 'Well, be careful, Cam. It's a hard business.'

He jerked the reins and the sulky clattered away down the red dirt road towards Streeter's jetty.

✦   ✦   ✦

George did not go directly to the Niland and Company offices. He stopped first at the office of TJ Ellies. All pearls had tiny blemishes or indentations that spoiled their value; Tom Ellies was a Sinhalese with a special talent for polishing a pearl so that it found its greatest profit. The work meant cleaning the outer skins of a pearl, like peeling the layers of an onion, until it was smooth and perfect. It required exceptional, almost psychic, skill for one mistake could cost hundreds, even thousands, of pounds.

Flynn was already there waiting for him.

'You're late.'

'My apologies,' Niland said easily. He reached into his waistcoat pocket and produced a small velvet-lined box. He gave it to Ellies, who opened it and took out the pearl with the reverence of a pilgrim approaching a holy relic. He put on a green eyeshade, looking every bit like a croupier in a down-at-heel casino, and held the pearl against the glow of the desk lamp.

A gasp. 'A very fine stone,' he breathed. 'A very fine stone indeed.'

'We've called it the Queen of the North,' George said. He leaned in. 'And we'd prefer to keep the news of our find just between ourselves. It's worth a little extra. Do you understand?'

Ellies sighed. He understood. He understood perfectly.

10

The Southern Cross had wheeled through the sky so that it hung almost directly above the tin roof, but it was still stifling hot. Even at night the feathery fronds of the poincianas drooped. There were low murmurs of thunder all around, flashes of sheet lightning on the rim of the ocean. The Wet was close.

Cam sat next to her on the veranda, casually rolled a cigarette and lit it. Hours they had been sitting out here, yet it seemed like a few minutes. They had talked about their childhoods, their families, the dreams they had for the lives they would live after Broome, after the pearling days were done. He had told her he had grown up in a Glasgow tenement near the shipyards, the second oldest of eight brothers and sisters.

'I remember Friday night was the big treat,' he was saying. 'My ma used to buy my dad a piece of haddock, and she'd give us each a cup of the water she cooked it in, and some bread to dip in it. Never owned a pair of shoes until I was twelve. Summer and winter it was all the same.'

The way he talked about it, she thought, it was like it had happened to someone else. Almost a kind of nostalgia in his voice.

'Where are they now?'

'My family? They're still in Glasgow. My brothers work in the shipyards like my da'. Or like he used to, before the drink got him.'

'But not you.'

'Not me. I was always good at figuring, numbers and such, and my ma hoped I'd get a job in the office at the shipyards. That was the height of her ambitions for me. Then one night when I was twelve years old she sent me down the pub to fetch my da' home for his tea. And this Friday night I went in there and there was this sailor, not crew on the coal steamers, a proper skipper, skin like mahogany, and he was standing at the bar, and everyone was listening. He was talking about white beaches and brown-skinned women and pearls as big as bottle stoppers. And I stood there and I listened to him, and I thought: that's what I'm about. I'm going to get out of this dreary city and these drunks and these tenements and find the sun and find my fortune. So me and me da', we were both late home for tea that night.'

He realised she was staring at him and he stopped and drew on his cigarette, suddenly shy of talking so much.

'That brought you here?'

'There were some detours along the way. I joined the Navy as a rating, then I heard of these trials they were doing in Scotland, sending men underwater in diving suits. I volunteered.'

'You've got courage, Cameron McKenzie.'

He laughed, easily. 'A man's nothing without it.'

There was something about him, she thought. She'd never felt safe around a man before; they were either bullies or blustering fools like George Niland, and she was impatient with all of them. But not this man. He was comfortable in his own skin, even if he didn't have much in the bank, and he knew how to treat a woman. She liked the way he looked at her.

She reached out tentatively and traced the line of a scar on his right forearm, among the dark hairs. She loved the touch of him, God forgive her.

'Where did you get that?'

'A knife fight in Manila,' he said, and then he saw her expression and laughed.

'What's funny?'

'Your face. I was just teasing you. There was no knife fight. A ship's cat did it.'

She punched him playfully on the arm. He grinned at her. Suddenly she felt herself melt inside. The effect of those deep blue eyes and that flashing white smile. It was devastating.

'Do you ever hear from your family?' she said, looking away to hide her sudden confusion.

'My ma writes me every month. All the news.'

'You miss them?' Kate asked. Her own father was all she had left now. She wondered what her life would be like

without him, no matter how much she hated him sometimes.

'I miss them. But I can't go back. I have it in my mind to
be a man of means some day. And I shall. I will find my
pearl and I shall have fine suits and a house like this one
and perhaps even a motor car. I shall not have any man look
down on me again.'

'Again?'

'Once you're poor, Kate, you never forget it. It rusts into
your soul.'

The way he said it scared her. She didn't know why.

'And what of you? Do you no have any brothers and
sisters?'

'I had two brothers. They were both older than me.'

'What happened?'

Just give him the facts, she thought. Like you do anyone
who asks. Don't let them see it still hurts you. 'Jack, he was
the eldest. He drowned when I was twelve, off Cable Beach.
Then a couple of years ago, Will died of blood poisoning.'

He touched her hand lightly with his. 'I'm sorry.'

'Life goes on,' she said, just like her father used to say
before he reached for the gin bottle. She took her hand
away.

'What about your ma?'

'She died when I was a baby. I never knew her.'

He held her eyes. Those eyes, she could lose herself in
them. It was as if he could see into her. She felt a fluttering
inside, like a nest of warm puppies in her. Now how did he
do that to her? Even at twenty she already thought herself
battle hardened to men. From a child she had been expected
to look after her brothers and do the keeping of the house.

When they died she did the keeping of her father too. She did not think it would ever be in her nature to feel anything for a man but resentment and worry.

'It's been a hard life for you, Kate.'

Well, she didn't want his pity and she felt herself immediately throwing her feelings back into their box and hiding them away again. She decided it was time to talk of something else. 'You still think my father stole your pearl from you?' she asked him.

He did not answer her straight away. The silence went on, and she thought he had not heard her. But finally he said: 'He's your father, Kate, so I would not expect you to hear a word against him. But yes, he stole my pearl. There's nothing surer.'

'And do you plan to get even with him? Because if you do, then it's best you take yourself off our veranda right now.'

'You're a spirited girl, Kate.'

'I may be a lady but I could fight as well as any boy at school.'

'You'd blow away in an offshore breeze.'

'I'm still my father's daughter.'

She felt his hand touch hers again. His fingers traced the contours of her wrist and the fold of her arm. It sent a shiver right through her.

He leaned forward and she realised with panic that he was about to kiss her. She turned away.

'I'm sorry,' he said.

Why had she done that? She wanted him to.

'So here we are,' he said finally, to cover the aching silence.

She felt embarrassed with her own fumbling reaction

to his attempt at a kiss. She had never kissed a man before, not properly. George didn't count.

'Why are you here, Mister McKenzie?'

'I told you that already, Kate Flynn. You're the most beautiful woman I've ever seen in my whole life and the first time I saw you, you set my heart racing.'

She had never thought a man to say such a thing to her. Did men and women really talk to each other like this?

'Were you about to kiss me just then?'

'I was.'

She lifted her face towards him. 'Then would you mind trying that again? Perhaps you'll have better luck.'

He leaned towards her. As their lips touched she heard cursing from the street and the crunch of boots on the shell-grit path. Flynn was home.

She got to her feet and smoothed down her skirts. 'Go!' she hissed at him. Cam melted into the shadows of the garden.

She touched her fingers to her lips. My God. Flynn and his rotten timing.

✦　✦　✦

The dinner had been a stately affair. The tablecloth and napkins were Irish linen, the napkins rolled in carved ivory rings, the tableware was Wedgwood, the cutlery sterling silver. They were served turtle soup, barramundi with saffron rice, and fresh mangos for dessert. There was champagne in fluted crystal glasses with every course, and afterwards coffee and crème de menthe. Kate could see her father was impressed, even as he marked out his territory on the table with soup and saffron stains.

For their part the Nilands had ignored Flynn's more eccentric behaviour – such as the sound effects that accompanied his enjoyment of the soup course – but she knew from the glances that passed between Henry Niland and his wife, Elizabeth, that they were participating in this meal under sufferance.

Flynn released a thunderous belch but at least had the manners, Kate observed, to hold his soiled napkin over his mouth as he did so. She felt her skin crawl with embarrassment. At times like this she wanted the earth to open up and swallow her.

'That was a damned good feed,' Flynn said, and then, bowing his head in Elizabeth Niland's direction, 'begging your pardon, ma'am.'

George coughed to cover his embarrassment and then turned to Kate. 'I think I'll step out onto the veranda and have a cigarette. Would you care to join me, my dear?'

Kate hated being referred to as 'my dear', but she smiled and said: 'That would be most pleasant,' as she was expected to do, and followed George outside. She saw Henry and Elizabeth stare at each other, aghast at being abandoned to Flynn, who had already launched into a long and convoluted tale about his early days on a trans-Atlantic ketch, the punchline to which Kate knew was not repeatable in the presence of well brought up women.

George led her onto the gaslit veranda. The parting in his hair appeared to have been made with a slide rule; a small ruby gleamed in his tiepin. He was wearing a charcoal grey Savile Row double-breasted suit, a sharp contrast to the Hong Kong tailored clothes worn almost exclusively by his contemporaries.

He seemed nervous. She noticed a tremor in his fingers as he lit a cigarette.

'Did you enjoy your dinner, my dear?'

'Stop calling me "my dear",' she said. 'I hate it.'

He flushed with embarrassment. 'I'm sorry. It's just that . . . well . . . I've grown very fond of you.'

'Then I wish you would find some other way of showing your affection.' As soon as the words were out of her mouth, she regretted them.

'Do you really mean that?'

She took a deep breath. 'Look, George –'

'No, please, let me finish. We've known each other for a long time and . . . you must know how I feel.'

Kate had been expecting this, but she had not expected him to appear so forlorn and fumbling as he made his proposal. She almost felt sorry for him.

'Are you asking me to marry you, George?'

George looked at her with a mixture of relief and surprise. 'Well . . . yes. My father will be retiring soon and I will have sole control of –'

'No.'

'– of Niland and Company here in Broome and . . .' He stared at her. 'What?'

'Thank you, George. You do me a great honour in asking me. But I must refuse.'

'No?'

'I don't love you, George.'

He put his hands on his hips. For a long time the only sound was the hissing of the gas lamp. 'How dare you,' he said finally.

'George?'

'I am the most eligible bachelor in Broome. How dare you refuse me.'

Kate stared at him, astonished. How dare she? Wasn't this what men had said to her all her life? She was supposed to be grateful but not one of them asked her what she really wanted.

'When my father retires I will be the most important man in Broome. I can give you anything you want.'

'Except love.'

'But I do love you!'

'But I don't love you.'

He threw his cigarette into the garden in an uncharacteristic display of petulance. 'You ungrateful little . . .' He turned away, thrusting his fists deep into the pockets of his trousers.

'You could live for a hundred years and not understand the first thing about me. Goodnight, George.'

Kate went back into the dining room where Flynn was regaling Henry and Elizabeth with the story of how he had once eaten a live cockroach for a bet. She was confident the Nilands would both be most relieved to discover they need never have her father's knees under their dinner table again.

Her heart was in utter turmoil but not a hint of it showed on her face or in her demeanour. It came from a lifetime's practice of disguising what she truly felt, her agony of loss when her brothers died, her cringing embarrassment at her father's arrogant boasting and unbridled drinking, her own loneliness at never knowing a mother who could have helped her navigate the overbearing and brutalising world of men.

✦   ✦   ✦

'You … you … you refused him?' Flynn was almost speechless with outrage. The polished jarrah floorboards shook as he stalked the living room of their bungalow. 'But he's the most eligible man in Broome!'

'Yes, that's what he said.'

'Then why did you turn him down, for God's sake? I had to endure hours of Henry Niland droning on about his dreary bookkeeping methods and all for nothing! Why in God's name did you say no?'

'Because I don't love him.'

A vein in Flynn's temple formed into a hard, bulging knot. 'What's that got to do with it? An alliance with the Nilands would have assured both our futures! I would have become a partner in one of the biggest pearling companies in Australia and you would have been the wife of the man who owned it!'

'There's more to life than money and appearances,' Kate said. She turned on her heel and went into her bedroom, slamming the door.

'No there isn't!' Flynn screamed after her. Then he took off his shoe and threw it. 'There bloody well is not!'

11

Her secret life.

He came at night, late at night, and they talked in low whispers in the darkness, the smell of tobacco on his shirt and frangipani in the air, the buzzing of myriad insects, the sticky heat of the Wet. She could talk to him about anything, the way she had never talked to anyone in her life.

Once, sitting there in the companionable silence, she asked him if he ever felt afraid.

'Afraid? A man can't afford to be afraid.'

'Isn't everyone afraid of something?'

'What are you afraid of, lass?'

She noted the way he had turned the question around. But she let it go. 'I'm afraid of being trapped in a marriage with a man I don't love. I'm afraid I will lose everyone in my life that I truly care about.'

He touched her hand in the darkness. It sent a shiver through her.

'Everyone I ever loved has left me. My mother. My brothers. It's like a curse.'

'What about Flynn? Do you not love him?'

'Sometimes,' she said.

He rolled a cigarette one-handed. He had large hands, but his fingers were quick and nimble and belied the size of him.

A match flared for a moment in the darkness, and she smelled the rich aroma of the tobacco smoke as he drew on the cigarette. 'What do you want from life, Kate?'

'I want to be loved. And I don't want to die in this horrible town like my brothers and like my ma.'

It didn't seem so much to ask of life. But she didn't know how she would manage it. How would she get out of Broome? Perhaps if she married someone as wealthy as George he might take her to live down in Perth and settle there. Hardly the pinnacle of her aspirations.

'What about you, Cam?'

'You know what I want.'

'Is there a woman in this picture?'

A breathless silence. He knew what she was asking him. 'Flynn would call the police if he knew I was even talking to you.'

'Well you did break his nose. Not that he hasn't had it broken before. But you could bury the past, if you wanted.'

'Why would I do that?'

'For my sake.'

He didn't answer her.

In truth, she knew she should not be sitting here with him at all. It was disloyal to her father and it would be a stain on her good character if anyone ever found out. He had humiliated Flynn in public and assaulted him. What was she thinking?

But what if he was telling the truth about the pearl? She loved Flynn but it was the kind of thing she imagined he might do. But he was her father, and that should be the end of it.

'I have to go,' he said suddenly, and slipped away into the darkness without even a kiss. She watched him go with as much relief as regret.

◆　◆　◆

Tom Ellies would only work on a pearl after he had examined it in the soft light of early morning. He said that only then were its secrets, its hidden ridges and whorls, clearly visible.

Flynn watched as he turned the stone slowly between his index finger and thumb and gave a soft sigh which could have meant anything. Flynn twitched, like a wild horse. 'What?' he said, leaning towards Ellies. 'What?'

Ellies cautioned him to silence with an impatient movement of his hand. George patted Flynn on the arm. 'Let the man do his job, Patrick.'

Ellies dropped the pearl onto a piece of black velvet. He rolled it with his finger to test its shape. If it rolled evenly it meant it was a perfect round, the best and most valued kind.

Finally Ellies removed the glass from his eye. 'You have the luck,' he announced. 'Perhaps.'

'Perhaps?' Flynn said. His hands were shaking and his breath smelled of the gin he had drunk that morning to fortify himself for the ordeal of the cleaning.

'Perhaps. Sometimes a pearl has a flaw. Sometimes the flaw goes to its heart and there is nothing to be done about it. You cannot destroy the flaw without destroying the pearl also. Like with a man.'

Fucking philosophy now. He could have strangled the bastard. He just wanted to know how much the damn pearl was worth.

Ellies went to work with the simple tool that was his stock in trade: a three-cornered file with one end stuck in a champagne cork. Flynn and Niland watched him, hardly daring to breathe, as the first bright shreds of pearl skin fell to the table.

♦   ♦   ♦

Ellies straightened with a sigh, and rubbed the pearl with a silk handkerchief that he had produced from his pocket.

'Well?' Flynn said.

Ellies laid the stone on the table. 'You have the good luck,' Tom said, 'the very good luck.' He considered a moment. 'Five thousand pounds.'

Flynn sagged in his chair as if he had been shot. George licked his lips, a dog with his eyes on a meat scrap.

'What would I get in Europe?' he asked.

'Perhaps twice this amount. More. Who knows? For such a stone a man might pay anything.'

George picked up the brown leather briefcase at his feet and took out his cheque book. 'Thank you very much, Mister Ellies. I believe you have earned your commission today.'

✦ ✦ ✦

George closed the door of his office and went to the metal safe in the corner. When the Queen of the North was locked away he went to the drinks cabinet and took out a bottle of square-face gin. 'A little early in the day but I think a celebration is called for.'

He put two glasses on his desk and poured a healthy measure of gin into each. 'A toast. To the Queen of the North.'

'The Queen of the North,' Flynn repeated, and drained his glass. He held it out for another measure.

George poured Flynn another gin then took out his cheque book and fountain pen. 'Five thousand pounds less Mister Ellies' commission . . . that's four thousand, seven hundred and fifty pounds.' He tore the cheque from the book and slid it across the desk. 'Not a bad day's work, Patrick old boy. What do you intend to do with your profit? Buy a bigger fleet, I suppose?'

Flynn tucked the cheque into his waistcoat pocket and patted it with affection. He crossed his legs and leaned back in his chair. 'That would look a little obvious now, wouldn't it? I don't want McKenzie breathing down my neck.' His two blackened eyes had started to heal, and the bruises had turned an unattractive chicken-yolk yellow, streaked with plum. His face, George thought with sudden amusement, had the appearance of a salad wilting in the heat.

'What are you grinning at?' Flynn snapped.

'Nothing, old boy. Just smiling over Dame Fortune. She is a fickle mistress.'

'That she is.'

'So, you were saying what you were going to do with the money . . .'

Flynn drummed gently on the arm of his chair with his fingertips. 'I'm getting too old for the sea. Besides, as you told me yourself, the nature of the business is changing. It's not for fortune hunters anymore. The future belongs to hard-headed businessmen like you – and me.'

'Out with it, Patrick. I smell a plot simmering in that scurrilous brain of yours.'

'I want to invest in Niland and Company.'

George folded his hands across his belly. 'Really? Have you spoken to my father about this?'

'Your father? He's not the future of Niland and Company. You are!'

George noted the deliberate, if clumsy, attempt at flattery, but enjoyed it anyway. He raised an eyebrow. 'Do you think so?'

'Does he know about the little piece of business we have just concluded?'

'Of course not.'

Flynn shrugged. 'There you are then, my boy.'

George's smile froze on his face. 'You're not thinking about blackmail, are you?'

Flynn gave a short, barking laugh. 'I'm sure your father will be delighted when he hears how much profit you just made for Niland and Company.' It was a lie, of course, as Flynn well knew. If Henry ever found out his son was dealing in snides he would horsewhip him. 'The point is this. I'm getting too old for the sea. Besides, there's going to be a war in Europe soon. Any fool can see it. The Kaiser is spoiling for a fight. And what will that do to the pearl market?'

'It may interrupt trade for a while.'

'It will decimate it!' Flynn said, smacking his fist onto the desk. 'What I had in mind was a two-way bet. I was thinking of buying myself a pastoral station down south. I've had a little experience with farming, before I came to pearling.'

'Farming, Patrick? Why in God's name do you want to do that?'

'Think about it, my boy! It's as certain as a goldmine. War means uniforms – and uniforms mean wool!'

George raised an eyebrow. Perhaps Flynn was on to something. 'An interesting proposition. Go on.'

'I fancy doing things on a grand scale – a big station, twenty thousand sheep, maybe more. But I'll need partners of course, and that's where Niland and Company comes in. You become my silent partner, and if war comes, we'll both be rich.'

'And if it doesn't?'

'Think of it as a hedge against the shell market.'

Niland was silent for a long time, considering. When he finally spoke, he measured each sentence carefully. 'It might work. I'll talk to my father about it, although I can't be certain how he'll react.' George knew exactly how he would react. With scorn. 'Of course there is a way you could make the offer irresistible, if you wanted.'

'And how would I do that?'

George leaned forward. His nose wrinkled as he smiled. 'What are you going to do with young Kate? You can hardly expect a pretty and spirited girl like your daughter to live on a sheep station in the middle of nowhere, can you?'

Flynn suddenly appeared less confident. 'She's a stubborn girl, George.'

'Surely not so stubborn that she would openly defy her father's wishes?'

Flynn looked worried.

'I'll leave that part of it to you then, shall I?' George said, slipping the cheque book back into his drawer. 'You leave the business end to me.'

Flynn finished his gin and held out his glass for another. George ignored the proffered glass and stood up. 'Better get back to work. There's a lot to be done.' He put the gin back in the drinks cabinet. 'Good day to you, Patrick.'

'Right you are, my boy,' Flynn said. He gave George a blowzy smile and went out.

George watched him leave the office and climb into his sulky. Ah, my little Kathleen. You thought I would give you up so easily. But as they say: all's fair in love and war.

12

Liddy Punyulpilpil muttered darkly to herself as she cleared away the dinner things from the table.

'What's the matter, Liddy?' Kate asked.

'Not right,' Liddy mumbled.

'What's not right?'

Liddy lowered her voice even further, though it was quite unnecessary. There was no one else in the house. Flynn had still not returned home. In all likelihood he was at the hotel, drinking or gambling the season's profits away.

'I see you b'long him,' Liddy said, rolling her eyes. 'I see you b'long that one white boss.'

Kate grabbed her wrist. Liddy was a recent convert of the local Catholic missionary and the young Bandi girl had since dedicated her life to the hunting down of sin of every kind. 'What? What did you see?'

'I see what happen orright. Got eyes.'

'You are not to mention this to anyone, do you hear?'

Liddy shook her head. 'All same sin!'

Kate shook her finger in her face. 'You say longa Flynn and I send you the hot place b'long debil-debil, you hear?'

Liddy was not impressed. She crossed herself and went into the kitchen grumbling dire predictions. Kate heard the dishes crashing into the sink. Kate slapped her hand petulantly on the table and went outside.

The Wet was very close now. Ominous black clouds were gathering on the horizon and lightning flashed across the sky like distant shellfire. There were no stars and the clouds seemed close enough to touch. She waited.

He came every night, an hour after dark. If her father was home – and that was rare enough these days – she would simply stay inside and she would see his cigarette glowing in the garden from her bedroom window. If she did not come out he would smoke his cigarette and leave. But most nights she would wait for him on the darkened veranda and they would sit side by side on the steps and talk long into the breathless night.

She loved talking to him for he brought the world alive for her, from the cold, dark lochs of Scotland to the green and shadowy deeps of the Lacepedes. Listening to him, she could almost feel the scratchy wool of the jumpers they wore under their diving suits, the drag of the lead boots on her feet, hear the hiss of bubbles in the helmet valves.

She loved the way he didn't hector her like her father and like George. He listened to her opinions and he didn't ridicule them or treat her like a decoration or slightly vain house-keeper. He had seen worlds she longed to know about – Glasgow, London, Inverness, Singapore, Hong Kong, Manila.

But what she loved most of all was the way he looked at her when he spoke. He wanted her, she knew that, and she knew he would not always be content just to talk. That knowledge both scared her and enthralled her.

She waited. At last she saw the glow of his cigarette in the darkness. She felt a familiar tightness in her belly, fear and longing together.

He stepped out of the shadows. 'Pa's not here,' she said. 'Come up.'

The veranda boards creaked under his boots. 'Kate.'

She let him kiss her, his lips brushing hers. She felt her breath catch in her throat. She felt the heat of him, wanted to crush him against her, and she felt ashamed. A decent woman shouldn't harbour such thoughts.

'I live for this,' he whispered.

'So do I.'

'Your father's at the hotel?'

'Yes. But we have to be careful. Liddy has seen you.'

'Liddy?'

'Our housekeeper. She thinks you're the devil.'

He grinned. 'I do my best.'

Cam put his hands on her waist. She froze. No man had ever touched her so intimately. 'What must you think of me?' she said.

'You know what I think of you.'

'I'm a whore.'

'For God's sake, you're no whore! Where did that come from?'

'I let you kiss me. I let you touch me. What kind of woman does that?'

'It's a natural thing between a man and a woman.'

Is it? Kate wondered. Is it such a natural thing? She had no idea. She knew that many men, even her father on occasion, had a certain lewd fondness for the barmaids at the Roebuck Hotel but they showed them scant respect in their conversation and no man would ever think of marrying one. It seemed to her you were either a girl who had fun and was treated like dirt for it or a girl who got married.

She didn't even know what it was that men and women did together, although she wanted badly to find out. If her father knew that she thought about it sometimes, he would die of shame.

He held her closer. Her senses were on fire; she could hear the growl of distant thunder, feel the heat of the night, the heat of wanting. He had aroused not only her wanting but her anger and her loneliness with it.

Damn her father and his drinking and his fury and his lies. Damn the God that had taken away her mother and her brothers. Damn the world that had made her a woman and left her here at home to fret and grow bored and frustrated with the stupidity of men!

She felt his hand on her breast and it took her breath away. No one in her whole life had ever touched her there. Longing like a runaway horse. She would go straight to hell for this. Why, suddenly, did it seem like such a reasonable price to pay?

'No, Cam,' she whispered. 'Don't.'

She imagined her mother watching from the shadows of

the veranda. She had to stop this, and now. She had already allowed it to go too far.

◆ ◆ ◆

The storm, known as a cock-eye bob, came with a roar, just after midnight. The wind slammed the shutters and doors all over the house.

Kate got up from her bed and slipped into a black silk kimono. She went to the windows and pulled them shut against the rain and wind. A lightning flash illuminated the room for a moment and she glimpsed Cameron's naked body sprawled on his back on her bed.

Oh my God, what have I done?

If her father ever found out he would kill her. She was supposed to go to her marriage bed a virgin. Now she had surrendered her virtue to a man who hated him and called him his enemy. That alone was mortal sin but to do this in his own house! And if Flynn didn't discover her perfidy, God already knew of it. She was damned for all time. A whore, like any of the cheap bar girls in the town.

And yet she had never felt so utterly alive.

She heard another crash from outside, and at first she thought the wind had blown open the front door. But then she heard her father's muffled curses in the hallway.

Cameron sat up and beckoned to her. She thought her knees would give way. She slumped down beside him on the bed. The doorknob turned and the key rattled in its lock.

No. God no.

'Kathleen! Are you awake, girl? I've something to tell you.'

Flynn's voice was slurred from drink. Kate stared at the door. She was shaking, like a child. Cam's arm went around her and held her to him.

'Kathleen! Are you awake, girl?'

Her mouth was suddenly dry. She couldn't have answered him if she wanted to. Couldn't move.

Another crash as Flynn staggered away and collided with something in the hallway.

She realised she had been holding her breath and she let it out in a long, shuddering sigh. 'It's all right, lass,' Cam whispered. 'It's all right.'

She felt his hand slip inside the fold of her kimono and cup her breast. This was godless. Her father was just down the corridor. Cameron pulled the kimono from her shoulders so that her arms were pinned to her sides and his tongue traced a line down her shoulder to her nipple.

It felt so good. She was going to hell.

She should stop him. But wasn't it a little late to be a good woman? She wanted him to leave right this moment and she wanted him to love her and never let her go.

He pushed her back onto the bed.

The Wet had come and the storm thundered above their heads and rain beat on the tin roof like a barrage of small stones. Everything dry, like the earth, parched and dusty for so long. Outside the succulents opened gently to the moisture, to the healing rhythm of rain. The pounding of the storm rains disguised the whispers and moans and murmurings of pleasure. She ran her fingers through his hair and closed her eyes and ears to the entreaties of the town and of her father. The saints in their heaven gasped and groaned as he filled her again.

✦ ✦ ✦

Flynn eyed his breakfast in the manner of a man examining his own entrails. He pushed away the plate of eggs, uneaten, and yelled to Liddy to bring him some more black coffee, damn her.

Liddy came to the table, her face dark and troubled. 'Drink b'long debil-debil,' she muttered. 'You drink him too mus.'

'I'll thank you not to lecture me in my own house,' Flynn growled. He sipped the coffee and grimaced. Liddy went away, still muttering gloomily to herself.

Flynn looked up at Kate. 'I've got some good news, girl,' he said.

'You're taking the Oath?'

'Don't you start on me.'

Kate could not meet his eyes. She was sure her guilt was written as plainly on her face as a confession in black ink on white vellum. 'What is this good news?'

'How would you like to go down to Perth this lay-up? We can rent a house, near the beach somewhere.' He waited for her eager acceptance, but it did not come. 'It will be cooler there, girl.'

And leave Cam? For three months? No! 'You know I get seasick.'

'But, darlin', you're always complaining about the heat. I thought you'd jump at the chance.'

'Perhaps I'm getting used to it. It was such a rough voyage last time. It took me the whole holiday to get over it.'

Flynn pushed his coffee away, bewildered. His daughter's whimsies were a perpetual mystery to him.

Everyone who could afford it got away from Broome during the Wet season.

Flynn was not too disappointed on his own regard; if she came, she would only harp at him about his drinking. But this was not just a holiday, as he had intimated to her. He planned to stop in Geraldton to look at a pastoral holding.

The real problem was George Niland. He would be travelling to Perth on the same steamer. Flynn had hoped it would be the ideal opportunity for him to press his case for marriage with Kate.

'Well, you'll have to put up with the seasickness, girl,' Flynn said. 'We're going, and that's that.'

'I'm not going anywhere.'

Flynn slammed his fist on the table, spilling his coffee on the tablecloth. 'Must you defy me at every turn?'

'I simply do not want to go. Must you decide everything I do without consulting me?'

'I'm your father!'

Kate stood up. 'That just makes it worse,' she said, and swept from the room.

Flynn watched her go. Damn the girl! What had he done to be afflicted with a daughter of such wilful ways? He threw his napkin across the table. Why in God's name did she not want to go to Perth?

❖   ❖   ❖

Cam stood at the bow of the *China Cloud* and stared across the bay towards the foreshore. The beach was strewn with rusted cable and anchor chains. The rotting bones of old ships were slowly sinking into the mud like the carcasses of prehistoric beasts. Aboriginal children played among the flotsam and their shrieks of laughter carried across the water.

A dinghy pushed away from the beach and began to row out. He knew the occupants of the boat, even from this distance. One was Wes; the other was his old Japanese diver, Tanaka.

A few minutes later they reached the lugger and clambered aboard.

'You have news?' Cam said.

Wes looked at the Japanese. Tanaka hesitated.

'Well?' Cam repeated.

'It's for true, boss,' Tanaka said. 'My brother have son who dive for Flynn on the *Koepang*. He see pearl, hear Mahomet say he take that one from you. He sell it snide.'

'To who?'

'He not know, boss,' Tanaka said.

Cam turned away. 'That was not just my pearl, that was my future. I may never find another like it!'

Wes looked worried. 'What you plannin' to do, skip?'

'I intend to get even with Mister Flynn, Wes. I'll not let him get away with this.'

'Mebbe you go kill him, skip, dey hang you for sure.'

'I'll not kill him. That would be too kind. There are other ways to cut out a man's heart. Fortune will find it.'

13

The *Koolinda* sat at the end of the long jetty. Beyond the great ship, the still waters of Roebuck Bay shone like a sheet of rolled steel.

Four stocky Aborigines wearing nothing but ripped trousers padded along the broad wooden planks of the jetty with the Nilands' luggage on their shoulders. As they passed George wrinkled his nose at the heavy must of sweat and dirt that accompanied them.

He watched as Flynn and his daughter walked along the jetty towards him. One of the nuns from the convent followed a pace or two behind.

'Good morning, Mister Flynn, Miss Flynn.' He bowed in Kate's direction. 'I was distressed to learn that we shall not have the pleasure of your company on the voyage. It will be a very dull journey without you.'

'I'm sure you'll find something to entertain you. My father, perhaps.'

'With all due respect to your father, it's not quite the same thing.'

Privately Flynn blamed George for his failure to secure an alliance with Niland and Company. If he was half a man he would stop pussy-footing around and make the girl see sense. He was too much the gentleman by half.

'Shall we get on board?' Flynn said. 'It's damned hot out here.' He turned to Kate. 'Be a good girl while I'm away.'

'I don't have much choice, do I now?' She nodded towards the nun, who was standing at a respectable distance with an expression of infuriating piety.

'I'll thank you not to talk like that,' Flynn snapped. He had made arrangements for Kate to lodge at the convent while he was away.

It's a man's town, he had told her when he finally accepted that she would not accompany him to Perth: 'I'll not have you stay at the house on your own, girl. Not without me there to look out for you.'

She kissed him gently on the cheek. 'Have a pleasant trip, Papa. Take care of yourself and don't drink too much.'

He was abashed by the sudden and real affection in her eyes. For all her contrary ways, Patrick Flynn did not know what he would do without his daughter. 'Goodbye, darlin',' he said, and put his arms around her and embraced her. Such a pretty young thing. If only she would do as she was told, she would be perfect.

A few minutes later George Niland and Patrick Flynn

stood side by side on the deck of the *Koolinda* and watched Kate waving to them from the jetty.

'A fine girl,' Flynn murmured.

'Yes,' George said. 'Yes, she is.' And she's going to be mine one day, he promised himself. I'll bring her haughty spirit to heel, see if I don't.

He watched her walk to the end of the jetty and climb into the sulky with the nun. He felt a moment's unease when he saw a familiar figure approach and speak with her briefly before the sulky drew away and headed back towards the town.

'Is that McKenzie?' George said.

'What's he doing out here?'

'I think he has designs on Kate.'

Flynn gaped at him. 'That bastard! Over my dead body!'

'Watch out for him, Flynn. A shark can take you just as easily close to the shore as it can ten miles out in the deeps.'

'What's that supposed to mean?'

'I've known him for some time. Hired him to work for me in Fremantle, on one of our fishing boats. Good skipper and his crews loved him. But not a man to forgive. I'll never forget losing one of my skippers the day before a sailing. He crossed McKenzie in a card game and McKenzie righted the matter with his fists. Poor man ended up in the hospital. McKenzie never forgets a slight.'

'He doesn't scare me.'

'Well he should.'

'He's not coming within a mile of my daughter. That's the end of it.'

George shrugged his misgivings aside. Flynn had given

him his word. The girl was as good as his. He would just have to be patient, that's all.

✦ ✦ ✦

Cam looked up at her in the sulky and grinned. 'So he's sent you to the nunnery.'

'For my own protection.'

'Of course.'

Sister Josephine was glaring at him as if he was the devil himself. She urged the sulky driver to ride on, but Cam held the traces.

Kate leaned towards him and whispered: 'There'll be no more rendezvous at the bungalow for a while.'

'Never mind, lass. Love will find a way.' He grinned at her, then gave the pony a slap and watched the sulky clatter off through the red mud along Dampier Terrace.

14

March 1914

John Chi Lane smelled of fish and urine and mildew and oilcoth. Old Asian women dressed in short black pyjamas squatted on the doorsteps; Manilamen in khaki trousers lounged in the doorways; bare-chested coffee-skinned Malays in scarlet sarongs rubbed shoulders with stocky little Japanese in snow-white singlets; chickens fussed and pecked under the verandas and a galah, fluttering and squawking in its cage on one of the balconies, heckled passers-by with a salty selection of Anglo-Saxon abuse.

Cam made his way along the narrow, crowded street to Sam Wong's boarding house. He found Tanaka sitting on the wooden steps outside eating a breakfast of watery noodles.

Tanaka put his bowl on the step and jumped up. 'McKenzie-san,' he said, bowing.

'Mister Tanaka.'

'You look for diver, boss?'

'Aye, I do. But not you, Mister Tanaka. You've used up all your luck. If you take my advice you'll not step on a pearl lugger again.'

'Yes, boss. I not dive for anyone else, not dive again. Tanaka finish.'

'Glad you've seen the sense of it.' Cam shook his head in genuine regret. It was hard to find experienced divers and he would be sorry to lose the little Japanese. 'What will you do now?'

'Still have dive money. Maybe I open store, or maybe fan-tan parlour. Maybe I still make money from pearl – but I do it here in Chinatown where I not die so quick!'

Cam watched a surly group of Malays pass, their *kris* knives glinting in their sarongs. 'You can die just as quick in the town as you can under the sea.'

'Only if it is my day to die.'

Cam shrugged. 'Well, I'll be sorry to lose you, Mister Tanaka, but I'm glad you've taken my advice.' He held out his hand. 'Good luck.'

'Thank you, McKenzie-san,' Tanaka said, and bowed again. 'I not forget I owe you my life. Perhaps one day I pay you back.'

'Perhaps,' Cam said carelessly. He didn't think the day would ever dawn when he might need a Jap to save him.

He headed down the lane towards John Chi's boarding

house. There was always a ready supply of new divers there, eager for their chance. They took appalling risks, especially the Japanese, and many ended up crippled with the diver's disease, and returned home to live on the streets as beggars. Others left the luggers feet first.

Cam remembered the advertisement he had seen in the program of a travelling vaudeville show a month ago:

PUBLIC NOTICE TO DIVERS

Why live when you can die and be buried for £7.10s. No waiting, no delay. First come, first served. 10% reduction for a quantity.

THE HURRY MOTOR UNDERTAKING COMPANY PORT DARWIN

He wondered if he would know himself when he had tested the Fates too far. He pushed the thought from his mind. Cameron McKenzie would know when it was his day to die. Of that he was certain.

✦　✦　✦

It was the end of the Wet. The *China Cloud* had been refitted and had taken on fresh stores and water, enough for six weeks at sea and the start of a new season. This would be his second full season; he had promised himself that this year he would find his pearl, and his future. There would be money and respect and position; and there would be no more Flynns.

Two Koepangers from his crew were waiting for him on the beach, by the rowboat. They took him out to the *China Cloud*, where Wes was on deck to meet him.

'We got a visitor, skip,' he whispered.

'Who is it?'

Wes rolled his eyes in the direction of the cabin. 'It's a lady, skip.'

'A lady?'

He went down the scuttle. The lady was sitting on the edge of his bunk, head down, her long mane of hair falling across her face. She looked as out of place in the stinking below-decks as a piece of Dresden china in a coal ship's galley.

'Kate?'

She looked up.

Dear God. Her face was pale as chalk, her eyes red-rimmed and swollen from crying. He knew straight away what it was; there was only one reason she would come here in this state. But he asked the question anyway.

'What's wrong, lass?'

She tried to speak but choked on the words.

'What is it? What are you doing here?'

She made an effort to gather herself.

'Did anyone see you come?'

'I don't care . . . about that anymore.'

He sat down on the bunk beside her and held her shoulders. 'Tell me, lass. What is it?'

'I'm going to . . . have a baby.'

For a long time neither of them spoke.

Finally: 'You're sure?'

'What kind of question is that?' she shouted at him. 'Of course I'm sure!'

He felt suddenly as stiff and clumsy as if he was wearing the diving suit. All lead boots and struggling for air.

She searched his face for some clue to what he was thinking. 'What are we going to do?'

A baby. 'When's your father back from Perth?'

'Tomorrow. On the *Koolinda*!'

She broke down. She sagged against him and sobbed. He felt numb.

'It's all right,' he said, over and over. 'Everything is going to be all right.'

'How?' she wailed.

He stroked her hair, soothed her, as he made his calculations of what to do next.

He loved her, yes. But love can make a man forget himself, can make him weak. He had come here to make his fortune, so that he would never live on haddock water again. This woman threatened all of that. Love, what did he want with love?

He had seen men marry for love, they were still back in Glasgow trying to feed a nest of bairns. They were trapped before their lives had even begun, and they would stay in the slums the rest of their lives as he might have done, if he had not the courage and the spirit to fight his way out. Yet he was honour bound, for it was his baby.

Had her father felt the same pricking of conscience when he stole his pearl?

No.

When a man falls in love he loses all control over his life

and destiny. It was a sickness he had seen in others and had always promised himself he would be immune. He heard his father's voice, could still feel the kiss of that belt. Don't be weak. Be a man.

◆　◆　◆

Patrick Flynn was drunk. He surveyed the bar of the Governor Broome through a fug of self pity and sour regret. On the trip down to Perth he had passed the time by playing poker with George Niland and had lost heavily. It had only made him more determined to recoup his losses some other way; in the attempt, he had lost another £200 in one session at a two-up school in Fremantle. He lost another hundred to a whore he found by the docks; when he woke in the morning both the girl and his wallet were gone.

To compound his miseries, he had found an excellent sheep station for sale in the Murchison, north of Geraldton, but Niland had refused to commit himself to the rest of the money.

'You keep your end of the bargain, old boy,' he had told him, 'and I'll keep mine.'

Kathleen! Now how in the name of all that was holy could he persuade the damned girl that what was good for him was good for her too? If she did not want to marry the son of the richest, most powerful man in all of Broome, who would she marry?

'Christ, if the Prince of Wales himself walked in and asked for her hand, she'd want for time to think about it,' he muttered to himself, and dropped some more coins in the barmaid's jar to get her attention.

He ordered another gin.

Flynn looked up as Cameron McKenzie walked into the bar. Jesus Christ and all the blessed saints. More trouble.

'Well! Patrick Flynn.'

Flynn straightened. 'What can I do for you now, Mister McKenzie?'

'I see your nose has mended. Not too well, I'd say. It's about as crooked as you are.'

Flynn looked around. Everyone in the bar was watching. And where's a policeman when you want one?

'State your business, sir,' Flynn said, 'and then I'd be obliged if you'd leave me in peace.'

Cam leaned forward. His eyes were out of focus and Flynn smelled the sour taint of drink on his breath. 'Has Kate told you the happy news?'

'What are you talking about?'

'You're to be a grandfather. Why, I almost feel part of the family already.'

Flynn felt an icy chill in his gut. Holy Mary, Mother of God, surely not? He tried to speak but his mouth was suddenly dry. It was as if someone had swung a sledge-hammer into his chest.

'*My* baby,' Cam went on. 'You have my pearl, and now ye have my blood as well. It seems too much bounty for any one man, doesn't it? Do you not feel lucky, Mister Flynn?'

'You *bastard*!'

'Aye, maybe. But what does that make you? Fate has turned around and dealt your cards back to you.'

He turned away.

Flynn stared after him. The thought of that man dirtying his daughter made him feel physically sick. What

85

was he going to do now? Niland would not have her. No one would. He had ruined her. They would have to leave Broome. They would never be able to hold up their heads in the streets again.

'McKenzie!'

Flynn came barrelling out of the door of the hotel and threw himself at Cam. They rolled over and over in the dirt, Flynn clawing and spitting like a feral cat. But drink had made him clumsy and slow and Cam pushed him away easily and rolled back onto his feet. As Flynn charged again Cam caught him on the point of his chin with his fist and Flynn hit the ground as if poleaxed.

Cam stood over him, his breath sawing in his chest. 'Damn you, Flynn. Damn you for stealing my future!'

Blood seeped from Flynn's mouth. He tried to get up but his limbs would not respond. *Kathleen, what have you done?*

What have you done?

*　　✦　　✦　　✦*

The blue and red flag with its huge white stars fluttered in the breeze at the Residency masthead as the first fleets raced each other for the honour of being first past Entrance Point. The gulls followed the luggers, screeching and swooping for any scraps that might be for the taking.

Cameron climbed into his rowboat. The *China Cloud* rode at anchor in the blue calm of Roebuck Bay.

A sulky pulled up on the road above the foreshore and a woman climbed gracefully out and waited by the running board. He recognised the familiar strawberry curls under the bonnet. Had he hoped to be at sea before she found him? Some hangovers are worse than others. A sore head alone can sometimes be a good result.

He walked back up the beach to the road.

The woman was full of surprises. He had expected to see her white with fury or shambling with shame. But her face was perfectly composed. She came towards him, regal as a queen, and slapped him once, very hard, across the face.

'So. You've had your revenge on my father. How does it feel?'

'Kate . . .'

She was fighting for breath. He looked her in the eye and waited for her to do her worst.

'I feel sorry for you, Cameron McKenzie. I do not believe that you truly understand what you have done.'

He was surprised to find himself quite numb as he looked at her. He had hardened his heart for this moment. He experienced an overwhelming sense of shame, quickly replaced by belligerence. Wasn't this what he wanted, the chance to end this, quickly and cleanly?

'How do I know the bairn does not belong to George?'

There was a look in her eyes, sadness and pity rather than anger. 'You fool. I would have loved you until my last breath and followed you to the very ends of the earth just to be with you. I would have given you my very last drop of blood. Was any pearl worth as much?'

She gave him time to answer but when he did not she turned and allowed her Chinese servant to help her up into the sulky. It bounced away down the rutted red road. Kate Flynn did not look back.

15

The *China Cloud* beat back for another drift under jib and mainsail. They were on good shell, in less than ten fathoms of water. The afternoon passed to the monotonous click-clack of the air pump where two of his Malays, their brown skins shiny with sweat, toiled under the canvas awning. Wes fed out the lifeline, while Assan, the Malay, tended the air hose. Curry-Curry was bent over the firepot.

The new diver sent up another bag of shell from below, big grey oysters covered with green and brown seaweeds and ferns. The Koepangers set to work with their toma-hawks, chipping away the coral and plants from the shells and tossing them into a wet, slippery pile in the middle of the deck.

Cam took out his knife and began to cut open the shells. After a while he threw his knife, point down, into the decking. He went to the scuttle.

'You hokkay, skip?'

'I've no mind to do the shell right now.'

'Mebbe only one hour to sunset, skip.'

'Aye, well, tomorrow then. I'm away to my bed. I don't feel well.'

Wes frowned as Cam disappeared down the scuttle to his cabin. The skip never left unopened shell on board overnight, it was too much of a temptation for the crew. But the skip had not been himself since they left Broome. It was that woman.

Wes knew all about women. He had never had any trouble getting them; it was getting rid of them that was hard. During lay-up time Wes fell in love at least once a week. His Christmas had been marred when a Chinese girl became jealous of his attentions to an Aboriginal girl called Mary. A fight started and Mary picked up a broken bottle and attacked the little Chinese. Wes stepped in to stop her getting hurt and got a deep slash across the forearm for his pains. Women!

The skip had it bad. They had been at sea nearly three weeks and he had hardly spoken except to give desultory commands on the sailing of the *China Cloud*. They were on good shell and had nearly three tons in the hold, but if he was pleased, he had not let his face or demeanour show it. Now he wouldn't clean the lay and hardly touched his food. Jay-sus!

They worked until the sun dipped below the horizon. Wes staged the diver. He didn't understand quite how it worked but Tanaka was proof that the skip had some powerful magic.

When Cam did not appear on deck for dinner, Wes took two plates of curry and went down to his cabin. He found him lying on his bunk, staring at the planking above his head.

'Bring you some chow, skip.'

'I'm not hungry.'

Wes put down the plates of stew and sat on the end of the bunk. 'What is it, skip? Dat one white woman, I reckon.'

Cam did not answer. He sat up, took a tin of cigarettes from his shirt pocket and lit one. 'Dreamed about finding a pearl, Wes. Dreamed about that one moment when your luck changes and you have everything you ever wanted in your grasp. You tell yourself when that moment comes, everything is going to be okay.'

'Was a fine pearl, boss. Never seen finer.'

'Goddamn my luck to hell.'

Wes rubbed at the caulking between the planks with a calloused toe. There were things had to be said here, and they were things he had no place saying to a white boss. But the skip was different to most.

'Why you do this, skip?'

'He stole my pearl!'

'Mebbe.'

'No maybe! He drugged me and thieved it!'

'You throw yo' pearl away, skip.'

Cam exhaled a long and impatient stream of tobacco smoke. 'What are you talking about, Wes?'

'A pearl is just a pearl, skip. Mebbe you have sometin''

better and you throws her away. Woman like dat, harder to find than any damned pearl.'

Wes thought the skip would get into one of his rages, but he didn't. He just threw the stub of his cigarette angrily out of the porthole and hung his head.

'I never planned for this to happen.'

'What you plan fer, skip?'

'I came here to make my fortune, not to fall moon-eyed for some woman.'

'So da good Lord send you a surprise an' you throws it back in His face. You got stole dat one pearl, for sure. Ask me, you found another, and you done *throw* dat one away.'

Cam sighed. 'I got my revenge though, right? I paid him back for stealing the stone off me. What a fine man that makes me.'

'Damn right, skip.'

'You see, Wes, I grew up poor, and I grew up hard, I thought if I was rich, if I was proud, I could own the world. No one was ever going to cross me or they'd pay. My da' taught me that.'

'Taught you damn good.'

Cam felt a droplet of sweat make its way down his cheek and drip onto the decking.

'Did you know what you is goin' to do, skip, from the start?'

Cam shook his head. 'No, Wes. That is the frightening thing about men like me. We don't even know ourselves what we are capable of until it's too late.'

When Wes looked up from the deck he saw an extra-ordinary thing. The skip had tears on his cheeks. Wes had seen men fight and bleed, and he'd seen men die. But there was something fearful about seeing another man cry.

'What sort of man would do something like this, Wes? What sort of man did my father make of me?'

'I doan know you long time, skip. We sail together mebbe one season. But I seen you brave, I seen you save a man's life for no good damn reason, I seen you dive day 'pon day when you nuts is shrivelled up you is so damn scared.'

Cam stared at him. He didn't think anybody else knew.

'You got balls, skip. But one day mebbe you get a heart too. One day.'

Cam ran his hand through his thick black curls. 'Christ!'

Wes scratched his head. 'You done some mighty bad evil, skip. You know dis?'

'Yes, Wes, I know it.'

'If a woman love you, skip, she forgive you anythin'. God make 'em that way, or there be no man got no woman at all.'

Cam nodded. 'We sail back to Broome first light. I have to get back there and undo what I've done. I have to!'

16

A horned moon. The night was chill, and the heady aromas of the garden were muted by the cooler weather and long weeks without rain. Kate put a hand to her belly and closed her eyes. The fleets would still be away at sea when the baby came.

Flynn came out onto the veranda, looking solemn and drawn. 'He's here to see you now.'

He said it as if he was a priest informing a prisoner that the executioner was ready. She took a deep breath. 'Well, don't keep the gentleman waiting, Father.'

George Niland looked resplendent in his whites. He took off his sola topee and gave a small bow. The victor could afford to be gracious.

Flynn excused himself and went back inside.

'Good evening, Kate,' George said. He lit a cigarette, without asking her permission.

'Hello, George.'

'I hear you've not been well.'

'Morning sickness, George. Let's not play games. You know very well I am shamed and in disgrace. I can just bear that, but I cannot bear being patronised.'

'I see you've lost none of your spirit.'

'Losing my pride is enough, don't you think?'

'I should have warned you about him. McKenzie has always been the same –'

'I don't want to talk about it.'

George drew on his cigarette. He threw back his head and blew out the smoke in a long, silken stream. 'All right.'

'Father said you wanted to see me.'

'I think we have a lot to talk about, don't you?'

Kate crossed her arms and leaned back against the veranda post. 'Have we?'

'You're going to have McKenzie's baby.'

Kate found her eyes were brimming with hot, stinging tears. She fought them back. 'Everyone in town knows that by now.'

'What are you going to do?'

'What can I do? The outcome of Nature is inevitable. I cannot stop it.'

'Your father says you are planning to leave Broome.'

'He sees no other way.'

'And you?'

Kate left the question unanswered.

'What would you say if I told you that I still wanted to marry you?'

'I would say that you had probably had a little too much sun.'

George slipped into his prepared speech. 'I don't deny that when I first found out about . . . about this . . . that I was shocked. Truly shocked. However, if you can promise me that you no longer love this man, that you have no intention of ever seeing him again, then I am prepared still to offer you marriage. I do not believe that one tragic error should cost someone their whole life. My mother and father stand against me on this, of course, but I believe they might yet be persuaded, once they see I am determined.' He paused and looked at her thoughtfully. 'Of course, we would have to marry immediately. Well?'

The humiliation burned in her throat. She swallowed hard. She had to do it, for her father, and for her unborn child. She was drowning and he was offering her a lifeline. It didn't matter to her anymore who was on the other end of it.

'Yes.'

'You accept?'

Kate nodded again, not trusting her voice. George swept forward and took her in his arms and kissed her. It was the first time he had ever kissed her on the lips. When he released her, his eyes were shining.

'I always vowed that one day I would make you mine,' he whispered. 'Let's tell your father the good news.'

✦　✦　✦

The house looked much the same; heavy purple blossoms of bougainvillea were draped across the veranda, Flynn's hammock was strung between two of the posts. But now there were signs of dissolution: empty bottles of square-face gin had been left uncollected by the steps, all the window shutters were closed.

He walked up the shell-grit path, knew his life would turn on what happened in the next few minutes. There was no answer to his knock. He went to the back of the house, saw Liddy watching from the servants' quarters at the bottom of the garden.

'I've come to see Miss Flynn,' Cam said.

Liddy's sulky expression changed when she recognised him. A sly smile formed on her lips. 'Missy not here,' she said.

'I have to see her. Now.'

'Not here,' Liddy repeated.

Cam tried the back door. It was unlocked. He pushed it open and went inside. 'Kate!'

Liddy ran in after him, outraged. 'You can't come along here! Missy not b'long here no more!'

'Kate!' Cameron went through the house, Liddy fussing behind him like an old hen trying to protect her eggs.

'Miss Flynn not b'long here!'

Cam turned on her, grabbed her by the shoulders. 'Where is she then?'

'I tell you! She not b'long here no more! She b'long Mista Nilan' now! All same marry 'im!'

Cam stared at her. 'Marry? She married George Niland?'

Liddy wore an expression of triumph. 'Father Murphy he say it all same sin. But she go longa white dress anyway. She go debil-debil one day!'

Cam slumped into a cane chair.

'Hey! You can't sit there! That chair b'long my masta!'

Married, already? He had been gone barely a month. But of course, the pregnancy changed everything. Christ, what had he done?

'You can't sit there!' Liddy screamed at him.

'Damn you,' Cam muttered. He got up, spilling the chair behind him, and stamped out of the door.

Liddy picked up the chair, cursing white men's manners, and got on with her work, feeling much better in herself for having seen sinners duly punished. Like Father Murphy said, God worked in mysterious ways.

❖   ❖   ❖

Kate was sitting on the veranda of the Niland house with George's mother. A jug of lemon squash lay on the wicker table between them. Together they were crocheting a baby's shawl.

Elizabeth saw him first. 'Oh, my goodness,' she murmured and sat bolt upright in her chair. He was striding up the path in his whites, a panama hat pulled down over his face.

Kate put a hand on Elizabeth's arm. 'It's all right. I'll talk to him,' she said. She stood up and went down the steps to meet him.

He stopped, and took off the panama. 'Hello, Kate.'

'What do you want, Cam?'

'Is it true? Did you marry George Niland?'

'I don't see what business that is of yours.'

He spread his hands in a helpless gesture. 'Am I too late?'

'Too late for what?'

'To say I'm sorry.'

Kate's lips compressed in a thin, pale line. 'Is that what you came here for?'

He passed a hand across his face. 'I was crazy with hate. I must have been out of my mind. Will you forgive me? I love you, Kate.'

She felt the rage inside her boil over. The force of it took her breath away. He was sorry. *Now*. He loved her. *Now!*

'Get out of my sight.'

'Kate?'

'Just go.'

He stood there. Did he think his charm, his sorries, his regret would ever be enough?

'You used me to break my father's spirit, Cam, and I can never forgive you for that. Then you let me marry a man I detest and then you come back here and tell me you love me – God damn you to hell!'

'You're married?'

'Four days ago. Now for God's sake, just go!'

She turned on her heel and a moment later the screen door slammed behind her.

✦   ✦   ✦

The *China Cloud* was moored alongside the jetty. Cam was standing in the shade of the storage shed with a clipboard supervising the unloading of the shell when he saw George Niland stride along the boards, the white tails of his jacket flapping behind him. His cheeks were flushed beet red.

'I want to see you!'

'Well, here I am.'

'Alone!'

'Anything you have to say, you can say as well here as you can in my cabin.'

George was panting hard. He took a silk handkerchief from his breast pocket and dabbed at the perspiration on his forehead. 'You went to see my wife.'

'I did.'

'I want your word you'll stay away from her from now on.'

'I'll do as I damned well please.'

'You've harmed that girl enough! Now she belongs to me! So stay away from her!'

Cam stepped onto the jetty, his thumbs in his belt. 'I don't like being told what to do, George. I'm not on your payroll now.'

'Get out of Broome.'

'You're not threatening me, are you?'

'You're a bully and a charlatan. You always have been and you always will be. This town doesn't want you.'

'Aye well, no doubt you're right about me. I'm not afraid to use my fists, I admit. As for being a charlatan, I can't deny I'm damned for all time for what I did to Kate. I dare say she'll never want to see my face again. But if I ever get the chance to make amends to her, George, I swear to God, I will!'

'Now let me tell you something, McKenzie. My father owns this town, he's on every committee and is chairman of the Roads Board. There's not a dog sleeps on the street here without our blessing.'

'You and your damned father don't scare me.'

George smiled, as cold an expression as Cameron had ever seen. 'You underestimate me. You always did.' He turned to go, hesitated. When he turned back, his voice was no more than a whisper. 'When I found out about you and Kate, I wanted to kill you. But I'll have the last laugh. The baby will be a boy, I know it. If you choose to stay here in Broome you can watch your son grow up to be a Niland. And he'll hate your guts, I promise you that.'

He spoke the last words like a benediction. 'He'll–hate–your–guts!'

17

Nineteen fourteen was a good season. The price of shell was at record highs and the harvest was good. But the news from Europe sent a thrill of unease through the community. The major powers, Britain, France, Germany and the Hapsburg Empire, were sparring with each other and threatening war.

The cable superintendent out at Cable Beach kept the town informed by telephone of each new communiqué, and small groups started to gather around the post office to discuss the latest developments. The assassination of a little known dictator in Sarajevo passed without comment, but a few days later came the news they had all dreaded. Britain had delivered an ultimatum to Germany. It was war.

And overnight the price of shell plummeted.

✦   ✦   ✦

Cam made his way from the foreshore to the Pearler's Rest in the Continental Hotel. Frank, the barman, was leaning on the countertop.

Cameron reached into his pocket and slapped some coins onto the bar. 'I can't pay my chits, Frank. I'm cleaned out. I don't think I'll even be able to cover my costs.'

Frank held up the chitty jar. It was full of ash. 'Everyone's in the same boat, Cam. You just missed the ceremony. I burned everyone's chits at the same time.'

'It's the end of the town.'

'Maybe, maybe not. As they say, it's an ill wind . . .' He nodded towards the far end of the bar. Patrick Flynn was reeling towards them, dead drunk. He stopped, swaying, in front of Cameron.

'Well, well. Cam, my boy! You're looking glum. Can I buy you a drink now?'

'I'd not drink with you if I were dying of thirst.'

Flynn threw back his head and guffawed. 'Well, I'll have one anyway. And you can put it on my chitty, Frank, you'll not have to burn mine.'

'Stole another pearl, Flynn?'

Flynn grinned. 'Pearls! What do people want with pearls when there's bullets whizzing round their ears? Seems Patrick Flynn was the only man who could see what was coming. That's why I can pay my chitties and the rest of you are using your pearls for bottle stoppers!'

'What are you talking about?'

'Wool, my boy! You're looking at the major shareholder in the Niland–Flynn Pastoral Company. War means uniforms and uniform means wool! My luggers may be useless to me now, but my sheep station is going to make me a fortune!'

'Well, good luck to you, then. If your flock runs short, I suppose you can always try your hand at sheep stealing. It might make a nice change for you.'

Flynn downed his gin and slammed his glass on the bar. 'Get out of Broome, McKenzie! Get out with your tail between your legs and leave the *China Cloud* to rot at the pilings! You're finished here now!'

Cam spat on the floor at his feet and left.

✦　✦　✦

Two days later he stood on the deck of the *Koolinda* and watched the white roofs and rust-red hills merge into the blue horizon and drop out of sight. Perhaps, he tried to tell himself, things had worked out for the best. Even if he had married Kate, he could not have stayed in Broome while his country was at war. This way, at least, she would have a husband by her side when the child was born. She would have a secure future for herself and the baby.

No, that was a deception. He knew that however he explained it to himself, he had made the most terrible mistake of his life. He had come to Broome with nothing; he was sailing away with much less.

There was no way of knowing how long he would be away, or even if he would ever see Broome and Kate Flynn again. But as he stared at the white foam under the bows he made a silent vow to himself that if it ever fell again within his power, he would win her back and try to erase the terrible wrong he had done her.

He might yet have his pearl.

18

Broome, 1920

Simeon Espada wanted the girl more than he had ever wanted anything in his whole life. Her name was Anna. She was fair-skinned and blue eyed and she flounced around the camp like she was a princess, instead of the daughter of a poor lugger boss. She had blazing red hair and a soft, rounded figure and the muslin dresses she wore clung to her, so that whenever he saw her his mouth went dry and he felt a terrible cold ache in the pit of his belly. She was as irresistible as she was unattainable.

Her father owned two luggers now at rest out in the mud of the bay. They had made him not nearly wealthy enough to afford a house in the town so he and his wife and two daughters had to live on the stinking, muddy beach with his Manilamen and Malays and Koepangers. But he was still a white man, and he wasn't about to allow any coolie near his daughters.

Unless.

The beach was empty, the sky still grey, like oyster flesh. Simeon sat down on a rock, picked up his guitar and strummed softly. It was a pre-arranged signal. A few minutes later Anna appeared at the doorway of the corrugated iron shack, her hair still tousled from sleep, carrying a basin of water. When she saw him the edges of her mouth turned upwards in the secret whore-girl smile. He knew what she was thinking, what she might do if ever they were alone.

She put the basin of water on a wooden crate, turned her back towards him and washed her face.

Simeon Espada was a strikingly handsome boy, a velvet-skinned Filipino with hair as black and shiny as coal, a hard, whipcord body and a smouldering and sulky expression that drove girls crazy. He had always had his pick of the girls in Manila, but he did not want just any brown girl. He wanted what was impossible; he wanted to touch the white and freckled skin of Anna Lacey.

All the girls he had ever had were dark and small and slender, with hard little breasts and taut behinds like a boy's. He dismissed them now in his memory with a sort of casual contempt. A white girl like Anna would be a real prize. She was so pale, it made him think of the moon. Her breasts were swollen and stretched the muslin of her dress when she walked, made him think of ripe fruit, fragrant, easily bruised. He watched her wash and almost groaned aloud,

106

seeing the shape of her through the muslin, imagining her bent over like that, naked.

He had to have her. Had to.

Anna dried her face and arms and walked slowly away from him, down to the water's edge. She threw the contents of the basin into the mud.

She came back then, that taunting smile still playing around the wicked little mouth. 'Good morning, Simeon.'

He put down the guitar. 'You look beautiful,' he whispered.

She seemed pleased when he said that. She put a hand on her hip. 'You're up early. It's only just light.'

'I wanted to see you.'

'Why?'

'You know why. I can't sleep thinking about you.'

'You know that isn't allowed,' she said.

She wants to torture me, he thought. She enjoys the game. Perhaps she doesn't want it to end. She started to walk away from him but he caught her by the wrist. She gasped and Simeon was delighted to see the look on her face, a hint of fear. He wanted to make her kiss him but he did not dare.

Suddenly her mother appeared in the doorway. 'Anna? What are you doing?'

'Nothing, Mama,' Anna called, and ran back to the hut. Molly Lacey frowned at the young Manilaman and then she, too, went back inside.

✦　✦　✦

'You're crazy,' his friend Huey Fong said to him later. 'Forget it. Stick to the whores in Sheba Lane.'

'I'm going to marry her.'

The others laughed. 'If you touch his daughter, Lacey will feed you to the sharks!' Huey told him.

Simeon glowered. 'You'll see.'

'She just likes seeing you suffer! She does it to all the crews! She's a little whore!'

Simeon rounded on him and suddenly there was a knife in his fist.

Huey stepped back, surprised and alarmed. 'All right, all right. Calm down.'

'Take that back,' Simeon said.

'I'm sorry. There. Okay?'

Simeon put the knife back in his belt.

Huey shook his head. 'You'd better be careful, old friend. If Lacey finds out you've got lover's balls for one of his daughters he'll find himself another number one diver!'

'Where will he find himself another diver at this end of the season?' Simeon asked him.

But Huey Fong was right. Later that day Lacey came down to the camp and found Simeon sitting on his cot strumming his guitar. He was a big, bluff man with mutton-chop whiskers and a big belly. He stuck his thumbs in his belt and stood there in the doorway, blocking out the light.

'I hear you were bothering my Anna this morning.'

Simeon got warily to his feet. 'I just said hello, boss.'

'That isn't how I heard it.' Lacey reached into his pockets and threw a roll of notes onto the bed. 'That's the money for your lay and the commission I owe you on pearls. I want you out of the camp by tonight.'

Simeon looked at the money, then back at Lacey. 'But

I've been taking a lot of shell, boss. Nearly three tons, last trip.'

'I want you out by tonight,' Lacey repeated and walked out.

Simeon stared at the wad of money on the bed. He couldn't believe it. These white bosses, treating him like a bit of trash. Well, he wouldn't be put off so easily. Perhaps there was one way he could get what he wanted. Money.

And in Broome money meant just one thing. A pearl.

      ✦   ✦   ✦

Nosiro Tanaka had come a long way in six years. His store and his gambling den had supported him through the lean years of the First World War but his ambitions went beyond mere survival. He was an intelligent man and he had set about acquiring an education. During the Kaiser's War he had learned to read English and had also set about learning commercial law. When the pearling industry began to recover he intended to be well placed to take advantage of it.

When newly indentured Japanese divers arrived in Broome he advised them on their rights and privileges and was able to negotiate better wages and commissions on their lay than they could have done themselves. Having won their trust, he persuaded them to bank with him. He in turn invested their earnings for them, and although scrupulously honest in his dealings, he was able to use these deposits to finance other business ventures.

He quickly acquired a substantial interest in Chinatown,

including a laundry, a brothel, two gaming parlours and a lemonade shop. He was elected to the committee of the Japanese Club and within two seasons had become one of the most influential foreigners in the town.

He had also put on a lot of weight. This corpulence was a matter of great pride, an ostentatious display of his growing prosperity. He started to dress in white linen suits, like the pearlers, which he sent away each week to be laundered in Singapore, as they did. He had even taken to wearing a fob watch. He had arranged for his nephew, Siosuki Hanaguchi, to come from Japan and help him run the store. He had come a long way from the little fishing village in Wakayama prefecture. That day in the Lacepede Islands had not been his day to die.

One afternoon he was making up accounts in the office at the rear of the store. The fleets had returned briefly for the Bon Matsuri Festival and business had been unusually brisk compared to the rest of the season, when Chinatown was virtually deserted. Hanaguchi pushed aside the curtain and told him there was a white gentleman wishing to speak with him.

Tanaka got to his feet, consulting the gold fob watch in his waistcoat pocket as he came out of the office to demonstrate to his caller that he was a busy man.

'Yes, sir, what I do for you?' he said pleasantly.

'Good God almighty, but you've grown fat, man. And where in the name of heaven did you get that suit?'

Tanaka's jaw dropped. 'McKenzie-san!'

'Aye, it's me. I didn't expect to see you dressed up like a pox doctor's clerk. Did you find yourself a pearl, Mister Tanaka?'

Cameron had changed very little. His face was a leaner, and there was something in his eyes that hinted at a weariness that had not been there before. But in his whites and his panama hat he reminded Tanaka of some English lord. It was only the soft Scottish brogue that spoiled the effect.

Tanaka led him into his office and sent Hanaguchi out to fetch iced lemonades from the shop next door.

Cameron loosened his tie. 'I forgot how hot it is in this infernal place.'

'You are away long time, McKenzie-san.'

'Aye. I hear you've been busy in my absence. They tell me you own half of Chinatown now.'

Tanaka bowed his head to accept the compliment. 'I have very humble business. But now, you tell me news. I don't think I see you no more. I think maybe this Kaiser mens shoot you.'

'Aye well, the bastards scuppered me at Jutland but I didn't take it personally.'

'Am most happy to see you, McKenzie-san.'

Cameron shook his head. 'If it wasn't for the sign above the door, I would not have recognised you. If you got on board a lugger now, you'd sink the damned boat.'

Tanaka grinned. 'Gods have smiled at me.'

'If you say so, Mister Tanaka. But when I asked after you at the hotel, they told me you were a conniving little bastard with your fingers in more pies than the town baker.'

Tanaka smiled.

Hanaguchi entered with two tall glasses of lemonade, thick with shaved ice. He bowed and went out.

Cameron sipped his drink gratefully. 'It's strange to be back here again.'

'Why you come back?'

A moment's hesitation. 'The pearls.'

'Pearls. Not so many, no more.' He lowered his eyes. 'Broome change very much.'

'In what way?'

'Henry Nilan' die this four year. Son now big boss at Nilan' Company. Own cattle and sheep station as well as many lugger. Last year he buy big red Buick motor car. He is number one man in Broome now.'

Cameron nodded. He took out a silver cigarette case and offered one to Tanaka. After he had lit their cigarettes, he said: 'And what of his family?'

Tanaka smiled to cover his embarrassment at this question. 'Has fine son now. They call him Jamie. They say he is very clever. Very dutiful to his mother and father.'

'Aye. I heard.'

'So what you do now, McKenzie-san?'

'I intend to get myself another boat. My pearl is still out there, waiting for me.'

'May gods bring you success,' Tanaka said, and added delicately: 'You have seen boat you wish to buy?'

'I've no money for purchase or lease. That's my problem.'

Tanaka smiled again. 'I see.'

'I've not come here to beg, if that's what you're thinking. I've no doubt the banks will extend me a line of credit.'

'Of course.' They both knew that without collateral the banks would do no such thing. 'But I not forget that if not for you, I will be in Japanese cemetery. Maybe you do me honour, let me pay back this great debt.'

'If that's what you wish, Mister Tanaka.'

'To owe another man life is great burden. This way I pay back. You have crew?'

'Wes as bosun, and a young Manilaman called Espada as number one diver. I dare say the rest of the crew will not be that hard to find.'

'You will dive yourself?'

'Aye, why not? I'll not get another good diver this end of the season.'

'With respect, white mens not dive no more. Too dangerous. Let proper dive man take risk.'

'It's too expensive. I was lucky to get Espada.'

'Perhaps Tanaka can help you. Have nephew here in Broome, perhaps you try him as number two dive man. He is good boy, very keen to learn.'

Cameron shrugged. He could hardly refuse a request from the man who had just bankrolled his boat. 'Aye, why not?'

Tanaka nodded. 'Good. Tonight you come to my house and we make celebration. May gods smile at you, McKenzie-san!'

'Aye. It's about time they did.'

19

So he's back in town, Kate thought.

There was a twist in her belly, a breathlessness still, when she thought about him. It was a mix of anger and longing, a curious emotion she had never felt for anyone else.

The smell of dust in the air, warm and rotten with the ripening of the season, the clamour of the crickets in the gathering ochre twilight.

'I have missed you,' she said aloud, knowing that no one else could hear. She bit her lip, felt a teardrop of sweat start its long march from her temple to her cheek.

She wished he had not come back. She wished he had never left.

The stars blinked on one by one, a morse twinkling across the sky, telling her her fate, but she had no key for their cipher.

◆　◆　◆

That evening Cameron was sprawled in a sulky on his way to Tanaka's whitewashed house in Chinatown. There were still only a few cars in Broome and Cameron immediately recognised Niland's red open-topped Buick from Tanaka's description.

As it roared past along the rutted red dirt of Dampier Terrace, Cameron glimpsed a pale, beautiful face beneath a wide-brimmed bonnet, and a small, sombre-looking boy with dark curls. He saw Niland too, imperious beneath his sola topee. He had a moustache now, and looked plump and prosperous.

Cameron turned for another glimpse of her but the Buick had disappeared in a cloud of fine red dust.

'Must take care now,' Tanaka told him later, when he recounted the incident. 'A man can live only now. Not possible to go back. I don't think so.'

'Aye, I know that. But I can't forget either.'

Tanaka's daughter, Fumiko, brought them green jasmine tea and they spoke about the war and pearls and the future. While they talked Fumiko served them sashimi – strips of raw tuna marinated in soy bean sauce, a delicacy – and wild rice. Afterwards they got drunk together on Suntory whiskey.

As Cameron was leaving, Tanaka whispered: 'Be careful of Nilan'-san. You make enemy too easy.'

Cameron thought about this as walked back to the Continental Hotel. He was not frightened of Niland, but he was frightened of himself. For six years he had been racked with guilt over what he had done to Kate; had he come back to seek his own absolution or because he really loved her? How much more injury was he prepared to mete out just to salve his own conscience?

Well, his moment would come. Meanwhile he was broke. He had left the Royal Navy with next to nothing and spent the little he had on his passage back to Australia. Unless he could find some good shell quickly, he would end up sleeping on the beach.

Six years. As the sulky bumped along Dampier Terrace he looked over the night sea and wondered whether his pearl still lay out there for him somewhere in his future.

✦ ✦ ✦

Siosuki Hanaguchi had been born on the island of Taiji in Wakayama prefecture, a narrow neck of land southwest of Tokyo. When he was ten years old the men of his village had rowed out to the bay where a whale was giving birth. They had caught the calf in their net, but the enraged mother had charged the whaleboat, tipping the men into the water. They had all drowned in their own net, along with the whales. Among those drowned on that cold, grey morning were Hanaguchi's father and his three older brothers.

The village lost most of its menfolk on that one day, and Hanaguchi and his mother and sisters were reduced to begging to stay alive. His uncle in Broome had sent back money to support them, writing glowing accounts of the opportunities for a young man to make money beneath the ocean. Hanaguchi resolved that when he was old enough he, too, would go to Broome.

So far it had been a bitter disappointment. He had been in the town for nearly two months and he was still helping out in his uncle's store in Chinatown. The closest he had come to the sea was at the end of the long jetty. He hated Broome, and was miserable with homesickness. Taiji was mountainous, and green; Broome was flat and red. Taiji's hills were covered with ash, sugi pines, elms and larch; Broome was surrounded by an endless desert of pindan scrub and monstrous elephant trees. Taiji had cool, misty waterfalls and hidden valleys; Broome was dry, dusty and suffocatingly hot.

But Hanaguchi was determined to stay and learn his trade as a pearl diver. He did not want to be his uncle's lackey forever. He would make his own fortune and he would never have to beg again.

Finally he had his chance. He was to start as try diver on the *Roebuck*, for a white pearler called McKenzie. He would get four pounds a month, plus a lay bonus for shell and a commission on any pearls he found. It was not much, but it was a beginning. He received three months' wages in advance before they sailed. His uncle knew that McKenzie was pressed for money, so on Uncle Tanaka's advice, he offered to loan it back to him at ten per cent interest.

He was surprised when his new employer accepted the offer. The next morning the *Roebuck* left Broome and set sail for the pearling grounds.

20

Hanaguchi prepared for his first dive, tried not to let his fear show on his face.

It would be cold on the sea floor and the divers wore as much insulation under their diving dress as they could. Hanaguchi had put on two suits of flannel pyjamas and two pairs of thick woollen socks. He had wrapped another piece of wide flannel, almost four yards long, around his abdomen. Over all this he had put on a pair of woollen drawers and a heavy woollen sweater that reached almost to his knees. By the time he was dressed he was gasping in the tropical heat. It would be a relief to get into the water.

Wes helped him into the tough canvas diving dress, the cuffs at the ankles and wrists well greased. Then came the heavy lead-soled boots and the great copper corselet that fitted over the top of the suit, attached to the canvas with butterfly nuts.

'Hokkay?' Wes said.

It was as much as he could do to stand up. Faint from the heat, his knees buckling under the weight of the corselet, he panted from fear. His throat was too tight to answer. He nodded and by effort of will went to the side of the lugger, knowing Cameron and Simeon, his number one, were watching him. He was determined not to fail. It was his chance to go back to Japan rich. No more begging.

He stepped over the rope ladder and waited as Wes hung the heavy lead weights down his back and over his chest, then checked and rechecked his air pipe and lifeline. Finally he picked up the heavy sea-greened copper helmet and placed it over his head. Wes screwed the face glass into place.

And suddenly he was no longer part of the world of light and clear sound. The hissing of the air filling his suit echoed inside the cavernous helmet, and with it came the sharp smells of salt and diesel and fish. He balled his fists tighter around the rope to stop them trembling and steeled himself for the coming ordeal. He must not fail.

He stepped off the ladder and into the ocean.

For a few minutes the air in his suit held him upright in the water. Then he remembered he had to adjust the large air valve screw on the outside of his helmet. He used his right hand to close it down and sank with an explosion of bubbles into another world.

Hanaguchi stood on the sandy bottom mesmerised by the beauty of what he saw around him. He was standing on a wide underwater plain, the seagrass waving with the current

– the underwater wind – like grass in a field. Ahead, a cliff loomed from the murky green, clusters of sponges in soft pinks and aquamarine clinging to the vertical walls.

He started to walk towards it. Red and white angel fish darted in and out of the shadowed grottoes, and the tiny yellow eyes of a sentinel fish peered out, protected by the waving tendrils of an underwater plant.

He didn't know how long he stood there, transfixed by this alien world. Suddenly the fear returned in a cold rush of panic. He felt as if he was standing in the fog, alone, surrounded by thieves and murderers. The dismal green light of the sea and the impenetrable black shadows below the underwater cliffs horrified him. His hand tightened around the lifeline. One tug and they would haul him up, back to the warmth and the light.

For a long time he stood perfectly still, paralysed with fear. I must force my way past this fear, he thought. Unless you want to spend the rest of your life being laughed at, standing behind the counter in your uncle's shop! You must think only about the shell. Shell!

He took a few faltering steps and, finding nothing, tugged on the line and gave the command to drift. But finding shell was not as easy as he had thought. His fear was forgotten as he searched the reefs in growing desperation without finding a single oyster. Soon Wes signalled that it was time to come up and when he reached the surface there was not a single shell in the string bag at his waist. No one said anything to him as Wes helped him out of his suit and he sat down by the mast, smoking a cigarette, alone.

Simeon was on the bottom and had already sent up his first full bag of shell.

Twice more Hanaguchi went to the bottom and twice more came up empty-handed. Meanwhile Simeon's pile of shell grew higher on the deck.

The sun was low in the sky when he went down for his final dive. He was oblivious to the scenery around him now, his fear obliterated by rage at his own failure. He must at least find one shell. Just one!

He drifted from cliff to cliff, searching desperately. Suddenly he saw something glinting among the weed to his right. It was there for only a moment, like a mirror flashing in the sun, and then was gone. He lumbered towards it.

It was a pearl oyster, a big one. It had opened its shell to feed from the passing tide and what Hanaguchi had seen was the mother of pearl sheen inside the shell. But the outside was so encrusted with weed and seaplants that if it had not opened for that instant he would never have spotted it.

He prised it from the reef with his knife and placed it almost reverently in his net bag. Suddenly he realised there were oysters all around him. Where a moment ago there had been only coral and rock and weed, he could now see a harvest of shell. He felt like a blind man who had suddenly regained his sight.

His heart pounding with triumph and relief, he started to fill the bag at his waist.

✦　✦　✦

Simeon watched as another bag of shell was brought up from below and thrown on Hanaguchi's pile. Their new try diver was becoming more expert every day. Soon his pile would match, or even surpass, his own. It was only experience that

121

separated them now. Hanaguchi was going deeper, and staying down longer, than he ever could. How much longer would he be number one diver? The little yellow bastards would take over the whole industry one day.

He got up from his stool and strode towards the edge of the boat. 'I'm going down for another spell,' he told Hassan, his tender.

'You're still on your break.'

'I'm going down! Do as you're told!'

Cameron looked up from his shell-opening. 'Your shift's not due for another half an hour, Mister Espada.'

'I'm all right, boss. I want to go back down.'

Cameron smiled. 'He's keeping you on your toes, isn't he?'

Simeon turned away and lowered himself over the coir ladder. A few minutes later he was descending through the dark green water into the deep.

It was a neap tide, and the water was crystal clear. When Simeon reached the bottom, he could see Hanaguchi quite clearly, almost fifty yards away. He was on good shell, his fingers busy among the weed and sponge. In his suit and helmet he lumbered along the sea floor like some ancient monster, the red rubber air hose and the thick manila lifeline snaking up through the mists like enormous tentacles. His air bubbles spiralled upwards in sparkling silver clouds.

Simeon started to walk towards him even before he had decided what he was going to do.

✦ ✦ ✦

Hanaguchi worked feverishly, stripping the oysters from the rock. As he put the last oyster in the bag, he looked down to see if the bag was full. It was almost empty. He grabbed at the bag and held it in front of his face, looking for a hole.

Suddenly the comforting clack-clack of the pump from the lugger above was silenced. His air hose! His air hose was cut! He grabbed for his air valve to close it and stop the water rushing into his helmet. It was already shut off.

Air bubbles roared out of his helmet in a frothing mass, and his suit started to collapse under the pressure of the water. He groped desperately for the valve, adjusted it, and as his suit repressurised, the crinkles in it smoothed out again.

What was happening?

He planted his feet firmly on the seabed, taking deep breaths to control his breathing. He could feel his heart hammering against his ribs. He tried to fathom what could have happened. All he could think of was that the valve must be faulty. Should he go back to the surface? If he was wrong they would all laugh at him.

But what about the shell bag?

Something hit him hard from behind. A shark! He grabbed for his lifeline and tugged hard. 'Pull up!' he shouted into the cavernous emptiness of his helmet. 'Pull till your backs break!'

As soon as Hanaguchi was on the rope ladder beside the *Roebuck*, Wes deftly removed the helmet and started to unscrew the corselet. 'What is it? Mebbe shark look out for you? Mebbe puss-fella?'

Hanaguchi did not respond to Wes's and Cameron's urgent interrogation. His legs were shaking so hard, Wes had to help him to the little stool by the main mast. He wiped the sweat from his face with a towel and took a proffered cigarette with trembling fingers.

'Water spirits steal my shell,' he said finally.

There was a silence and then the crew – mainly Koepangers – started to laugh. Cameron was the only one who did not seem to find it funny.

'There's no such thing.'

Hanaguchi snorted and drew deeply on the cigarette. Of course there were water spirits. Even the smallest child in his village knew that. 'Water spirit steals my shell, turn off my air valve, then attack me.'

'Oh aye, and what did this water spirit look like?'

'Green,' Hanaguchi said, improvising. 'Green, all rotten. Just skull for face. Perhaps dead diver. Maybe ghost.'

'Get back down, Mister Hanaguchi. Mister Espada's sending up good shell. You should be down there with him.'

'Not here. Another place more better. Dead diver here for sure.'

Cameron swore and turned away. He knew the Japanese; they were good divers but superstitious beyond belief. It would be futile to try and persuade him. And working at depths sometimes did this to a man. After a while even the best diver began to imagine things. Well, Simeon would have to dive alone until they had exhausted the shell bed. The crew rolled their eyes at each other and chuckled among themselves on the foredeck.

Simeon finally surfaced nearly two hours later. When he was out of his suit, he accepted a cup of coffee from the cook-boy and sat down on the bulwark.

'A good haul, Mister Espada,' Cameron said, surveying the Manilaman's pile of shell. 'By the way, you didn't happen to see a dead diver down there?'

Simeon pursed his lips thoughtfully and shook his head.

'Mister Hanaguchi thinks a skull with a green body stole all his shell.'

'Well, I know I stole some of his shell. But I didn't see no ghost. Perhaps I frightened him off.'

All the crew were staring at Simeon now. 'I thought so,' Cameron said. 'Did you turn off his air valve also?'

Simeon grinned. 'Then I gave him a good kick in the pants with my boot. You should see him jump!' He threw back his head and roared. Soon the rest of the crew were laughing too. The only ones who did not laugh were Cameron, who had lost an afternoon's work from one of his divers, and Hanaguchi.

'It was just a joke,' Simeon said.

Hanaguchi picked up a marlin spike and came at him. He would have cleaved the Manilaman's skull but Wes intercepted him, pinning his arms. He held him while Cameron prised the heavy iron from his fist, then hefted him, screaming curses at Simeon in Japanese, downstairs to his bunk.

Cameron turned to his diver. 'I ought to break your head myself for that little prank,' he said, and threw the marlin spike across the deck where it lodged in the scuppers. He went below decks to help Wes calm the little Japanese.

There was a shuffling silence. Simeon winked at the Koepangers. That should give the little yellow bastard something to think about. Never mind that he had just made himself a mortal enemy. He was too vain to realise it.

✦　✦　✦

Simeon lay on his bunk in the darkness, listening to the sounds of the night. The *Roebuck*'s chain groaned and

125

trembled as she faced the tide, her timbers creaking as she came about. He heard the Japanese, Hanaguchi, whimpering in his sleep, wrestling with the sea demons again. Something scurried across the floor – a cockroach, or perhaps a rat.

The symphony of snores from the crew satisfied him that it was safe. He eased himself gently out of his bunk and padded barefoot across the deck to the scuttle.

It was a hot night, a bright three-quarter moon throwing the shadows on the planking into stark relief. The deck was deserted, except for the Koepanger crewman asleep on his watch at the tiller. He eased out of the scuttle and waited, hardly daring to breathe. If the skipper caught him now he would never get a job on these pearling grounds again. For a prize like Anna Lacey, he would take the risk.

A small pile of shell lay unopened on the deck, by the main mast. That afternoon the skipper had sent him back down, as punishment for the trick he had played on Hanaguchi. The sun had set by the time he got back on deck, and so Cameron had been forced to leave the shell.

The oysters had almost suffocated in their shells during the evening and now some of them had opened on their gristly hinges to gasp in the cooler air. Simeon approached them cautiously; he knew that at the slightest touch or vibration they would snap shut. On the few occasions that shell was left on deck overnight, in the morning they sometimes found dead rats with their tails protruding from a half-open oyster they had tried to eat alive.

Simeon got down on his knees, a cork and a piece of twisted wire held in his fingers. He crawled forward, looking for the dull gleam of an open shell. When he found one he thrust the cork between the lips of the shell to hold it open and hooked the wire inside, feeling for the telltale hardness of a pearl.

A dozen times he tried, knowing the odds were almost hopeless. But he had heard the stories in Chinatown. This was how it sometimes happened. Why shouldn't there be a pearl for Simeon Espada? Still, he was on the point of giving up after an hour or so. Then, on what he promised himself would be the last shell, the twist of wire encountered something hard. He scooped it out and heard it plop gently onto the deck. He held it up to the moonlight and stifled a gasp. It was a pearl, a huge pearl!

He wanted to shout with joy; instead, he wrapped the precious stone inside the fold of the red kerchief he wore at his neck. His fingers were trembling so hard with excitement he almost dropped his prize into the scuppers. He returned the cork and the wire to his pocket and crept back down the scuttle to his bunk.

Sleep was impossible. He imagined he must surely wake everyone on the boat with the hammering of his heart. He was a rich man! His new-found wealth would be his passport to the plump, creamy secrets of Anna Lacey.

His fingers constantly worried the pearl concealed at his throat, to reassure himself that it was really true, not some fevered diver's dream. As he lay awake with his dreams and plans, another soul joined him in the long and secret pre-dawn vigil.

A baby humpback had become separated from its mother and had adopted the bulky shape of the lugger in its pitiful desperation. Simeon could hear it swimming alongside, and its mournful keening made him shiver with dread. It was as if the Fates had seen what he had done and were preparing suitable punishment even as they mourned his fall from grace.

21

By the afternoon of the next day, Simeon's lay was well down. He couldn't concentrate. They were in twelve fathoms, on good shell, but he had brought up only about half of his usual shell. It didn't matter to him anymore. The only thing that mattered was the pearl, which was now carefully knotted in the folds of the kerchief at his neck. All he could think of was being back in Broome where he could find a buyer for his secret treasure.

Distracted, he did not see the danger until it was much too late.

On the *Roebuck* Wes was standing by the air compressor, his eye on the gauges, while one of the Koepangers, Hassan, sat on a platform out from the port shrouds, feeding out the lifeline. Hanaguchi was sitting by the main mast, smoking a cigarette.

'Do you know what's wrong with Mister Espada today?' Cameron asked Wes.

'Mebbe he scared of Hanaguchi, skip.'

'I would not have thought a man like him scares that easily.'

Wes shrugged. Who knew how a man would react until presented with danger? Men who were fearless when faced with a shark could be cowards when they saw a bared knife. He had been on the pearling grounds for over ten years now and had long stopped being surprised by anything a man might or might not do.

It was late afternoon, and the sun was low over the water. The sea was flat and oily. The glare hurt the eyes, lulled a man into fatigue. Boredom took over and it was the hardest thing, sometimes, just to stay awake.

Suddenly there was a puff of mist less than a hundred yards off the starboard bow and a huge grey body broke the surface.

'What was that?' Cam shouted.

It was a gnarled old humpback. It wallowed in the swell, stared right at them with one small, cow-like eye. It snorted water from its blowhole with a giant *whoo!* and water sprayed high into the air. Then it disappeared, its tail flukes exposed for a moment as it finished its dive.

'Bring up the diver!' Cameron shouted at Hassan. 'Quickly, man!'

Cameron felt a juddering vibration through the hull as the great beast scraped its body along the keel, trying to rid itself of the barnacles and sucker fish that tormented it. Several of the crew lost their footing and were thrown across the deck.

Then the humpback rose out of the water on the port side, almost standing on its tail to look down at the scampering figures aboard the *Roebuck*. It was close enough that Cameron could see the ancient scars on its flanks, spray streaming from the slate-grey body. Then it shook itself like some huge, wet dog and a shower of sucker fish plopped into the water in all directions. Then it plunged on its back in a gigantic explosion of spray.

The crew scampered for kerosene tins and coffee mugs, beat them frantically against the side of the hull to try and scare the monster away. Cameron waved his marine almanac in his right fist.

'It's not the season!' he yelled at it. 'You're a month too early! Go away, I've got a man down there!'

He flung the book at it in helpless rage.

'Get that diver *up*!'

Simeon felt the urgent tug on his lifeline and the morse message – *come up quickly!*

He looked up, saw the copper hull of the *Roebuck* to his right and then, almost directly above him, a massive white belly, almost as big as the lugger itself.

'*Ikan paus*,' he murmured. 'A whale! Mary, Mother of God, help me!'

One lazy flick of its tail and it was right alongside the slender red tube of his air pipe. Quickly Simeon adjusted his air valve, filling his suit with air, ready to ascend. Then he looked up again and watched in horror as his red air tube slid right along the whale's body seventy feet above him. As it neared the tail he pulled down hard, trying to drag it away from the flukes.

Too late. The humpback cow felt the hose tighten

131

around her body and panicked. She bolted, dragging Simeon along in her wake.

The lifeline hissed over the port gunwale. Wes grabbed a coil of the heavy rope and made a turn around the halyard rack to secure it. Then Cameron threw his weight on the line and shouted for the rest of the crew to help. The Koepangers scurried across the deck and braced themselves against the line; even Curry-Curry rushed from the galley to lend a hand.

The air pipe reached its limit, trembled for a moment and then snapped with a bang.

'Jesus, he's gone!' Cameron shouted.

The lifeline was played out. The *Roebuck* gave a shudder and started to move forward, towed in the wake of the whale. Cameron, his hands raw and bleeding from rope burns, ran to the bow. He saw the whale surface, the line still wrapped around its body. For one surreal moment, he saw Simeon Espada sprawled across the great creature's back. Then the lifeline snapped too, with a crack like a gunshot, and the rope snaked high into the air and fell into the sea.

Simeon rolled off the whale's silvery back and followed it down.

✦   ✦   ✦

Simeon's eardrums had burst. It felt as if red hot needles had been thrust into his ears and nose and brain. His head smashed against the copper helmet, his body spreadeagled by the weight of his boots.

Even through the red mists of his agony he kept a desperate hold of his air pipe. He knew that while the fragile rubber hose stayed intact he could survive.

Air spurted intermittently into the helmet as the pipe was twisted and squeezed. Knowing it must soon burst, he closed off the valve on the side of his helmet. Seconds later it tore apart in an explosion of bubbles. It was the last thing he remembered before the world went dark.

'Anna,' he said, and blacked out.

Cameron picked up a tomahawk that lay beside the pile of shell. He slashed away the lashings of the whaleboat. It thumped into the water and he leaped into it, nearly capsizing it.

'Wes! Hassan! Ramus! To the oars! Move!'

Cameron pushed the dinghy away from the *Roebuck* and the others jumped in alongside him. They grabbed the oars. A dozen quick strokes and they were clear of the *Roebuck*. Now Wes could see what Cameron had spotted from the bows. Simeon's partially inflated suit had been holding him up in the water.

But already he had started to dip out of sight below the oily swell.

'Faster!' Cameron shouted at the others, straining at the oars. 'Put your backs into it!'

Simeon's helmeted body was two fathoms down, sinking slowly through the water. As they manoeuvred the whaleboat above him, Cameron tied a slip knot into one end of some coir rope and dived fully clothed into the water. He arrowed straight down, towards the blurred image of the copper green helmet. He looped the rope over Simeon's legs.

They were nearly three fathoms deep. Would the rope be long enough?

Cameron's lungs were bursting for air. He struck for the surface, clutching the other end of the rope. He broke the

133

water, gasping, and threw the rope to Wes, who made the end fast round the thwart of the whaleboat while Ramus and Hassan pulled Cameron aboard. He vomited seawater into the scuppers; Wes and the two Malays hauled Simeon back to the surface.

Trying to lift him clear of the water, with the heavy helmet and corselet on his shoulders, would have been impossible. Instead, they lashed Simeon to the stern and Wes jumped into the water and unscrewed the face glass. It was smeared with Simeon's blood. Wes peered inside, wiping away the mask of blood with seawater. Simeon was not breathing and his face was swollen and black.

'Mebbe too late,' Wes muttered.

Cameron crawled to the stern on his hands and knees. 'I'll not let him die after all this trouble. Back to the *Roebuck*, quick!'

✦ ✦ ✦

Simeon remembered nothing of the *Roebuck*'s run for Broome. When he came to, he was lying in a Heinke re-compression chamber, a sterile steel cylinder in which the nitrogen gases could be slowly dissipated from his body's tissues. He saw faces peering at him through a glass at the end of the chamber. He tried to move but every joint in his body screamed in protest. It was as if there was something trapped inside his brain, trying to force its way out through the top of his skull. His face pulsed with pain and the joints in his groin and his shoulders felt as if they had been prised apart with a blunt instrument.

But he was alive. How? Must have been the white boss.

Wes had told him that the boss had never lost a man at sea. Somehow he had found a way to save him.

He remembered his pearl and his fingers clutched at his throat. It was still there. His swollen lips broke into a grin and fresh blood oozed out, staining his teeth. Anna!

'Sorry, Mister Boss,' he whispered into the silence of the empty chamber. 'I owe you my life. But I still must have your pearl!'

22

It was sunset. From the foreshore came the smell of cooking, the aromas of curry and *belachan* mixed with the taint of the nearby mangroves and the saltwater tide.

Out on the bay two ancient Malay fishermen, dungarees rolled up to their knees, rowed a dinghy back to the beach, the click-click of the oarlocks resonant on the still evening air. They beached the dinghy and padded back to their hut, carrying a yard long barramundi strung on one of the oars.

Anna Lacey went to the rainwater tank to fill her bucket. A hand reached out and grabbed her wrist, pulling her into the shadows.

'Simeon!'

He pulled her towards him and kissed her hard on the

lips. But when he tried to explore the hot, sweet mouth with his tongue, she pushed him away.

She stared at him, wide-eyed with outrage and excitement. 'What do you think you're doing?' she hissed, throwing an apprehensive glance at the doorway of her family's shack.

'I love you,' Simeon whispered.

'You're out of your mind.'

'I'm on fire for you, Anna. I burn every day.'

Anna shook back her hair and studied him. 'I heard you were in the hospital.'

'You didn't come and see me.'

'Of course I didn't come!'

He could feel her eyes on him and leaned back into the shadows.

'What happened to your face?'

'It's nothing.' He was mortified that she had noticed. He had always been vain about his looks and his ordeal with the whale had crushed his nose and cheek. His boyish looks were blurred now.

She took a step towards him and ran her fingertips along his cheek. He snatched her hand away. 'Don't be cross,' she said. 'I don't care.'

Simeon looked towards her family's shack. 'Where's your father?'

'He's at sea.'

'Come here then.' He tried to pull her towards him but she skipped away.

'I can't.'

'Don't you like me?'

'You know I like you.'

So it was true, she wanted him as well! She stood there, her arms crossed, like the little tease she was, watching him burn. Another toss of the head.

'Then why won't you let me kiss you?'

'You know why!'

'I'm going to marry you,' he whispered.

'You can't.'

'I have a pearl.'

She stared at him. 'What are you talking about?'

'It's beautiful, it shines like the moon. I'm going to be rich. Then your father won't treat me like I'm nothing anymore.'

'Let me see this pearl.'

He beckoned her closer. But instead of showing her the pearl Simeon pulled her towards him and crushed his lips against hers. This time she did not struggle so much and she let him put his hand on her plump, round breast.

A voice shouted out her name from the nearby shack. 'Anna!'

She threw herself away from him. 'Coming, Mama!'

And then she was gone, leaving him angry and frustrated, the ghostly memory of her breast and her raw scent his lovesong to the twilight.

Anna came out of the shadows, hoping her mother would not notice the flush of her cheeks in the darkness. But Molly Lacey was neither stupid nor blind. She saw the silhouette of a man slip away between the straggle of shacks on the beach.

'Who were you talking to, Anna?'

Anna went back to the rainwater tank and started to fill her bucket. She pretended not to hear.

Her mother didn't need an answer. It was that swarthy Manilaman who had been making eyes at her daughter while he was in their camp.

'Come inside now, girl. I want to speak to you,' she said. She would talk to her husband when he got back from sea.

◆　◆　◆

In his tiny room in the Canton boarding house, Simeon locked the door then went to his mattress and took the pearl from its hiding place. He unfolded the red handkerchief it was wrapped in, and held the stone in his palm. It was a perfect round, perhaps a hundred and fifty grains in weight, and tinted rose, like a blood moon. They called them roseate pearls, the most precious pearls of all.

Simeon knew he could not trust a snide like this with any of the Chinese storekeepers. They would cheat him for sure. But there was one white man in town who bought snides. It was common knowledge that he purchased them for Niland and Company; he would go and see Patrick Flynn.

◆　◆　◆

Her father had aged, Kate thought. His nose was laced with the pink tributaries of broken blood vessels, a legacy of his drinking, and the flesh on his face hung in pouches under his eyes and his chin. The long strands of silver on his head were getting thinner.

Now he settled himself into a cane chair on the veranda and took a swallow from the large gin and tonic water that Junzo, the houseboy, had placed on the table in front of him. Kate sipped her lemonade and watched Jamie playing with Liddy in the garden. He was attacking her with a wooden sword.

'Jamie! Gently please!'

'He's a fine boy,' Flynn said. 'He's going to be a handful when he grows up.'

'He's a handful already,' Kate said. The boy knew no fear. Once she had found him preparing to launch himself off the top of the water tank; on another occasion he had cornered a taipan and was about to try and kill it with a stick when Flynn found him. He was energetic and aggressive; quite unlike her taciturn husband.

Just like his father, Kate thought, and experienced again the familiar ache of regret and loss.

She turned to Flynn. 'How's the station?'

'Couldn't be better,' Flynn lied. Within a year the boredom and isolation had started to drive him out of his mind. So he had hired a manager and returned to Broome. He leaned forward. 'Any news for me?'

'News?'

'Any more happy events to report?'

Kate stared at him. As subtle as a kick in the shins with a boot. 'I'm sorry. I'm going to disappoint you.'

How could she tell him that she and George hardly ever made love anymore? The marriage had been a disaster from the start, born of spite and convenience.

She guessed that George still loved her. But she did not love him; she never had. George had at first seemed satisfied with the arrangement he had engineered; but now even he realised that there was a terrible difference between possessing a thing and having it freely offered. These days he showed Junzo, their houseboy, more deference than he showed her.

'How's the business doing?'

'I've no idea. George never discusses it with me.'

'If you ask me, pearling won't ever be the same again. The Japs are taking over, it's as plain as the nose on your face. I wonder if George might not think about getting out.' He finished his drink and looked up at his daughter. 'What's the matter, girl? You don't seem very happy. Is he not treating you right?' There was sudden and unexpected tenderness in his voice.

'He treats me well enough.'

He reached across the table and gripped her hand. 'It's not still that other business, is it? I thought you would have been over that by now.'

Kate looked away.

'I should have killed him.'

'And what damned good would that have done?' Flynn leaned back in his chair, offended. 'Mind your language, girl.'

They sat for a time in silence after that, staring out over Roebuck Bay.

'I don't know how things got to turn out this way,' Flynn said. 'Everything I did, I did for you. You mean the world to me. I just wanted you to be happy.'

Happy. What on earth was that?

◆　◆　◆

Kate drew the tortoiseshell brush through her hair and studied her reflection in the mirror. The green eyes that stared back at her were etched with sadness and recrimination. She thought again, as she had a thousand times, about the day that Cameron had come back to see her. She had been married just a few days then; George had been too busy to take her on the promised honeymoon.

What was it that Cameron had said? *I was wrong. I love you.*

She threw the brush on the dresser. *Wrong!* Cameron had been wrong, they had both been wrong. She had been wrong to marry George Niland. Her father had told her she should be eternally grateful. 'There's few men that will look at a girl when she has a baby, now. I'd call it the grace of God that has moved him!'

The grace of God! It was pride. He had always wanted to own her and life had punished him by giving him what he wanted. What a bitter harvest they had both reaped from their mistakes.

Now Cameron was back. She had given him up for lost, swallowed by the Great War like so many others. Instead he had returned to haunt her, and the knowledge that he was walking these same streets made her travesty of a marriage that much harder to bear.

◆　◆　◆

After breakfast Kate left the house with Jamie to take him to a Christmas party. Flynn had been invited to stay at the house so after his daughter and grandson had left he took an ancient copy of the *West Australian* out to the veranda and settled into one of the wicker chairs with a bottle of Niland's square-face gin and a glass.

It was lay-up time, and the Wet was close. The poincianas were in bloom, and the bougainvillea creepers that
shaded the verandas were a mass of purple and crimson.
Clouds were forming into billowing white mountains over
the sea, and even this early in the day the air was stifling.
Flynn scratched irritably at the prickly heat behind the
creases of his ears. Impossible to stay dry and comfortable in
this godforsaken country. He poured himself another gin.

The bottle was half empty when the white-jacketed
Junzo appeared on the veranda.

'What is it?' Flynn said.

'Someone wish to talk with you, Flynn-san.'

'Who is it?'

'He no say. Manilaman, I think.'

A Manilaman? In the European quarter? Damned
nerve! 'Send him away.'

'He say, tell you is very important.'

Flynn threw the newspaper on the floor. 'Well, all right.
But it had better be important or I'll kick his black arse
right out the door again!'

◆　◆　◆

Simeon Espada bowed and introduced himself. Flynn
studied him with distaste, his thumbs hooked into the broad
leather belt at his waist. The man looked like he had been in
a fight.

'What do you want?' Flynn growled.

Simeon reached into his pocket and took out a red handkerchief. He unfolded it carefully and removed something
which he held between his index finger and thumb.

Flynn took his thumbs out of his belt and stood up. He swallowed hard, his Adam's apple bobbing in his throat like a cork in a high sea. 'Christ, where did you get that?'

'Is it not a beautiful pearl?'

Flynn held out his hand for it. Simeon dropped it in his palm. Holy Mother of God. He had only ever seen one pearl bigger than this and that was the one he had taken from Cameron McKenzie.

'Why did you come to me with this?'

'They say you are an honest man, boss.'

'How much do you want for it?'

'A thousand pounds,' Simeon said.

Flynn shook his head. 'Five hundred, that's it. Take it or leave it.'

Simeon held out his hand for the pearl.

The boy had more nerve than he had bargained for. 'Look, my boy, it's just not worth a thousand.'

'No, boss, worth a lot more. A thousand pounds.'

'A thousand pounds is a lot of money.'

'A lot of money is what I want.'

Flynn shook his head. Impudent little greaser. He tried a more conciliatory tone. 'I'll see what I can do. I can't promise anything, mind, but I have a few friends who may be interested. You leave it with me.' He started to put the pearl in his waistcoat pocket.

Simeon took two quick steps forward. 'When you have the money, you can have the pearl.'

'It will be safer with me. There's a lot of thieves in this damned town.'

Simeon grinned. 'There's two of them standing on this veranda right now.'

Flynn calculated the odds of the Manilaman pulling a knife if he tried to bluff him out. They were pretty damned good. Never knew with these greasers. He sighed and handed back the pearl.

'If you want to do business with me you'll have to trust me more than that.'

'I never trust anyone.'

Flynn chuckled. 'All right. So how much do you really want for that pearl?'

'I told you. A thousand pounds.'

'And what if I can't raise that sort of money?'

'You will, or you won't get the pearl.'

Little bastard. Needed teaching a lesson. But the pearl first. 'I'll see what I can do for you.'

'I'll come back tomorrow.'

'No, you can't come back here, my boy.'

'Where then?'

Flynn thought a moment. 'The beach. By Niland's store.'

'Tomorrow night?'

'Whoah, my boy, I've got to get my hands on the cash first. I'll need two or three days. Make it Wednesday night, ten o'clock.'

Flynn watched him leave. A thousand pounds. He could make four or five times that profit from a pearl like that. Perhaps more. It would solve a lot of problems.

He finished his gin, had Junzo fetch his hat and cane, then walked into town to cable his bank.

23

Cameron rose naked from the bed. He lit a cigarette and offered one to Rosie. She felt his eyes studying her and she pulled up the sheet, embarrassed.

'Now that's a strange thing to do when we've just made love.'

'I think you're picking out all the faults.'

'You haven't got any faults. You're as slim as a nymph and the shape of you would make a bishop kick a hole in a stained glass window.'

Rosie folded her arms across her breasts anyway and drew up her knees. 'I've never had any man talk to me like you do.'

Cameron grinned. 'Do you mind?'

Rosie smiled in spite of herself. No, she didn't mind at all. 'Sometimes,' she said.

Cameron started to dress. Rosie turned her eyes away, heard him chuckling at her modesty. It was something he didn't understand about her. Rosie had been brought up to be a good girl. She was deeply ashamed of some of the things she had done since she had come to Broome. But a girl had to survive.

'How much do you charge, Rosie?'

'That's none of your business.'

'I'm a customer, lass.'

Rosie glared at him. 'Don't say that. I do it because . . . because I want to.'

Cameron slipped his shirt over his head and sat down on the edge of the bed, stroked an errant lock of hair away from her cheek.

'You're not a customer,' she repeated.

'Tell me anyway. I'm interested.'

Rosie pulled up the sheet. 'Ten shillings.'

'Ten shillings!'

'It's more than I get working a whole day in the bar!'

'A pound at least. And five for the ugly ones!'

'I don't go with ugly men. What sort of girl do you think I am?'

Cameron laughed again. He pulled on his boots and stood up, tucking his white shirt into his trousers. 'You're a beautiful-looking woman, Rosie. I mean it. You've got the face of an angel and the rest of you . . . a pound and not a penny less. You're spoiling these heathen.'

Rosie looked away. There was a lump in her throat. Cameron had the knack of making her feel like a queen;

then he would tip his hat, grin and walk away.

What hurt her was that she had loved him desperately. He came three or four times a week and he always treated her gently, even with respect. Sometimes she wondered if she hadn't put herself up for hire when she first came to Broome, whether she might not have got him for herself. But why would a man like him want a barmaid and a whore? Well, except for the obvious. A man's a man.

Rosie hadn't been a prostitute before she came to work at the Continental Hotel. But men being what they were, they often dropped more coins in her tips jar than was necessary, then whispered their propositions to her. At first she had slapped their faces, but a girl needed money to live, and one day the idea of doing it with a man for money appeared less outrageous and she started taking a few of the pearlers to her room to supplement her income. Now she was making more money in a month than her mother ever made in a year of working below stairs as a scullery maid in London. It was easier to live with shame when there were only strangers to witness it.

Cameron slipped a panama on his head and turned to leave. 'Don't forget, a pound,' he said, and walked out.

Rosie swung her legs over the side of the bed. There was a ten pound note on the bedside table. He had scribbled across it: *Merry Christmas!*

She crumpled it in her fist and started to cry.

◆　◆　◆

The Canton boarding house was in John Chi Lane, next to a barbershop. Cameron passed two Chinese in black pyjamas on the stairs, their wooden slippers clop-clopping on the steps.

Simeon's room was on the second floor. He opened the door, dressed only in white shorts and a singlet. When he saw Cameron he took a step back, startled.

'Mister Espada. May I step inside for a moment?'

'Sure, boss.'

Cameron closed the door behind him. The room smelled of sweat and boiled cabbage from the cookshop across the lane. Chevrons of light from the shutters angled across the dusty floorboards and an unmade single bed.

'How are you feeling?'

Simeon put a hand to his battered face. 'Hokkay, boss.'

'You have a new profile, by the looks of things.'

'You saved my life,' Simeon said.

Cameron reached into his jacket pocket and produced a large envelope. 'Here's the money for your lay.'

Simeon took it and looked inside. 'It's too much,' he said.

'The doctors say you'll not dive again. Maybe this will help you when you get home.'

Simeon stared at him. What could he say? The white boss had saved his life and now he was giving him money. And there was his pearl lying just a few feet away, concealed in his mattress.

He held out the envelope. 'Can't take this, boss.'

'Aye, you can. It's Christmas, man. If you're still in Broome come the season, Mister Espada, maybe I can find you a job as crew.'

He turned and left.

Simeon slumped onto his bed, staring at the money in his hands. The notes slipped from his fingers onto the floor.

Too late for conscience now. He had the pearl, and he wasn't going to give it back.

24

Joseph Lacey was shown into George Niland's office by one of the clerks. George looked up from his papers and silently indicated that Lacey should sit.

Finally George put down his pen and called to the *binghi* outside the window to start the *punkah*. The air was thick, like moist treacle, and the faint movement of air the fan provided was small relief. Tiny blisters of sweat formed on George's forehead and he patted them away with his handkerchief.

'What can I do for you, Lacey?'

'I've got some information for you, Mister Niland. I thought you might be interested.'

'Go on.'

'There's a big snide in town.'

George raised an eyebrow. 'Who has it?'

'One of my Manilaman divers. Or he used to be one of mine. Name of Espada.'

'How did you find out about this?'

'He was bragging about it. My daughter . . . overheard him.'

George pulled on his wispy blond moustache. Finally he took his cheque book from his drawer and picked up his pen. He wrote out a cheque and handed it to Lacey. 'The usual fee.'

Lacey blew on the ink, folded the cheque carefully and put it in his pocket. He stood up to leave. He detested George Niland and his fancy airs but his money was as good as anyone's.

'Not a word please, Lacey. This is private business.'

'Yes, Mister Niland,' Lacey said, and went out. Why would he tell anyone Niland was buying snides? He wasn't going to kill the goose.

♦ ♦ ♦

Later that afternoon a Chinese Manilaman called Huey Fong was ushered into George Niland's office. He was a squat, ugly man with hooded eyes and bad teeth. He sat opposite George wriggling on the hard, wooden chair, his eyes darting restlessly around the room.

'Do you know who I am?' George said finally without looking up from his papers.

Huey nodded.

'You are one of Lacey's divers, aren't you?'

'Yes, boss.'

'Do you know a man named Simeon Espada?'

'I know him.'

'Is he a friend?'

George looked up, noted the indecision on his face. 'Maybe,' Huey said finally.

George leaned forward, his elbows resting on the desk. 'Some men say you can't put a price on friendship. What do you think?'

✦ ✦ ✦

Simeon lay sprawled face down on his cot, drunk. He was snoring. He did not hear the rattling of the door as the flimsy lock was prised open. Holding the jemmy above his head, Huey crept over to the bed and hit Simeon on the back of the head. The sleeping figure jerked and the snoring stopped abruptly.

Huey set to work. He searched the sparse furniture in the room; a flimsy chest of drawers, half eaten by white ants, a sailor's trunk in one corner. Nothing.

He rolled Simeon onto the floor and tore at the bedding. He found a hole in the mattress, shoved two fingers inside and found the cotton handkerchief stuffed into the kapok. He pulled it out, felt the hardness of the pearl in the knotted folds.

He dropped the pearl into his palm. Mother of God, it was huge! He looked down at Simeon, his body crumpled on the floor, limbs all twisted. He hoped he hadn't killed him. Still, a man loses a pearl like this, he'd wish he was dead.

When he woke up he would be just another poor, crippled diver. Broome had its share. But that couldn't be helped. The pearl was too good for the likes of him anyway. He would only have spent it all on drink and women.

25

Simeon opened his eyes. A cockroach scuttled across the wooden floorboards, just in front of his face. He tried to remember what had happened last night. He couldn't lift his head. Worst hangover he had ever had. Perhaps he hadn't managed to make it as far as the bed.

He tried again to get up, and the world started to spin. He vomited on the floor, retching until there was only bile in his stomach.

He felt as if he was covered in cold grease. His head was drumming with pain. He touched the back of his head. There was a lump there, the size of an oyster shell. He must have fallen over last night. No wonder he felt so ill.

He dragged himself to his knees and clung to the edge

of his bed. The acid stench of his vomit was overpowering. He looked around the room. The lock on his door was smashed and the door hung ajar.

'My pearl,' he shouted, and plunged his fist into the torn mattress.

It was gone.

Simeon staggered into the corridor. Two old Malays, Ri and Mahmud, were on the stairs, smoking.

He grabbed Ri by the throat. 'Where is it?' he screamed at him. The old Malay just stared at him, terrified.

Mahmud jumped to his feet to run away, and Simeon grabbed him and dragged him down the stairs by the shirt.

'Where is it? What have you done with it?'

Billy Ng, the owner of the Canton, came out into the hall. 'What name?' he shouted in his hacking, high-pitched voice. 'What name you? Who fighting up there?'

Simeon was sitting on Mahmud's chest, pummelling him with his fists. Old Ri, still clutching at his throat, came staggering down the stairs. 'Get Sergeant Clarke quick time!' he shouted at Billy. 'Simeon too much humbug! He killim Mahmud finish!'

Billy ran out of the door.

Huey Fong ran out and came piling down the stairs. He wrestled Simeon away from the old Malay. He was just in time. Mahmud looked half dead.

◆　◆　◆

Later Huey Fong watched Sergeant Clarke and two constables take Simeon away. He was still screaming threats at everyone and drooling like a lunatic. Poor bastard.

156

Huey went back to his room and put on a clean white singlet and trousers. Then he walked down John Chi Lane to Dampier Terrace and the offices of Niland and Company.

This time George Niland did not keep him waiting. He was ushered into the main office immediately on his arrival. Like an important man.

As the door shut behind him George Niland held out his hand. 'You found it?'

Huey smiled and handed Niland a matchbox from the deep pockets of his pants. 'Right here, boss.'

George examined the contents. He smiled, went to the safe and put the matchbox inside. He took out his cheque book. 'Well done, Mister Fong.' He wrote out a cheque and handed it to him. 'I believe you will find that more than adequate compensation for your services.'

◆　◆　◆

Hanaguchi had had a good season. In one year with McKenzie he had made more money than he had ever seen in his whole life. He had bought himself a new white suit with gold sovereign buttons and a Malacca cane with a carved ivory handle to show that he was now a number one diver.

Last night he had lost a lot of money gambling, but this morning, when he heard what had happened to Espada, his spirits lifted once more. The news had spread around the town like wildfire; the Manilaman had gone crazy and tried to murder some of the tenants at the Canton boarding house. Everyone was saying that his tussle with the whale had made him crazy.

Hanaguchi didn't care about that. He had a score to settle with Simeon. That afternoon he and two of his friends waited in John Chi Lane for Simeon to return from the lock-up. He knew he wouldn't be in gaol long. If Sergeant Clarke kept all the crazy divers in his gaol he would have no room for anyone else.

◆　◆　◆

This lay-up there was a lot of tension in Chinatown. Some Koepangers had come ashore talking about how a Japanese master had keel-hauled one of their comrades on his lugger. There had been some loose talk about a vengeance knifing.

Damn them, Hanaguchi thought. They were just cattle anyway. None of them were good enough to be divers. They had no courage, no face. How did they expect anyone to treat them any differently from animals?

The heat had exacerbated the tension. Today, all the air seemed to have been sucked out of the atmosphere, and seabirds crouched in the shadows of the mangroves, their beaks agape, too exhausted by the heat even to fish.

Hanaguchi dabbed at his forehead with a white linen handkerchief. As he replaced his panama he saw Simeon shuffling along John Chi Lane, his shirt bloodied and torn. He looked dazed, as if he had been smoking opium.

Hanaguchi nudged one of his companions and said, loud enough for everyone around him to hear: 'McKenzie-san's number one diver! These Manilamans all same! Two seasons and all they are good for is cooking rice!'

Simeon looked up, saw Hanaguchi and his two friends dressed in their best white suits with their white men's hats and their canes, all swagger and arrogance. He realised they were mocking him.

He lurched towards them. 'What did you say?'

Hanaguchi's eyes sparkled with amusement. 'They say you see ghost in your bed last night. You dive too long. Steal too much shell. Make you go crazy in the head.' He made a face at the other man, showing the whites of his eyes.

All day Simeon had thought about nothing but his lost pearl, and about Anna. Now this Jap was taunting him. It was too much. He would have liked to cut him open but Sergeant Clarke had taken his knife. Instead he grabbed Hanaguchi by the throat and started to squeeze. The ivory-handled cane clattered into the dirt as the Japanese tried to prise the strong brown fingers from his throat.

His companions rushed to their friend's aid, slamming their canes into Simeon's ribs. Simeon screamed and retreated, his arms over his head to protect himself from the rain of blows.

Hanaguchi picked up his own cane and raised it two-handed, like a *kendo* sword. He smashed it down on the back of Simeon's skull and the Manilaman fell to the ground. As he lay there the three Japanese continued to thrash him with their canes.

Several Koepangers, crew from the *Roebuck*, were watching from the steps of the Canton. They had crewed with Simeon for two seasons and they would have helped him anyway, but they had been talking about the Japanese and the stories of the keel-hauling, and this only made them more eager to get involved.

Hanaguchi and his companions had their backs to the Koepangers, their attention focused on Simeon, his writhing and screaming encouraging them in their efforts. The Koepangers took them by surprise, wrestling Hanaguchi and one of his companions to the ground. The other Japanese managed to shrug off his attackers and flailed wildly about him with his cane. One of the Koepangers fell back screaming, his eye hanging down his cheek.

A knife flashed in the sun. The Japanese dropped the cane and sat down on the steps of the boarding house, gasping like a beached fish, bright blood frothing through his clean white shirt.

Simeon, almost blinded by his own blood, threw himself at Hanaguchi. The Japanese tried to run. But two of the Koepangers caught him and threw him against the iron wall of the boarding house. Simeon staggered back to his feet, his fingers gripped around a broken wooden paling. He smashed it into Hanaguchi's face, and as the Japanese slid down the wall he hit him again.

He raised the stake to strike once more, heard police whistles, saw Sergeant Clarke and his constables racing into John Chi Lane for the second time that day. Simeon dropped the paling. Hanaguchi lay at his feet, red dirt and dark blood staining his white suit, his face a pulpy mess, like stewed eggplant.

I've killed him, he thought.

The Koepangers started to run. He followed them.

✦　✦　✦

Rosie lay on top of Cameron, their naked bodies slick with sweat. Her long hair fell across his face. She began to move her hips, slowly, in time with his.

Cameron groaned, arching his back. She felt his body tremble violently. Then he closed his eyes, his breath coming in gasps, and he relaxed. She felt his arms encircle her. She lowered her head onto his chest and started to cry.

Cameron felt the slight trembling of her body. He tried to turn her face towards him, but she resisted.

'Rosie? What is it?'

She did not answer.

'Rosie?'

'For God's sake, stop it. I feel like such a fool.'

'But what is it?'

She pulled away from him and he gasped in disappointment, feeling himself slide out of her. She pulled a silk kimono around her shoulders. She took a tin of cigarettes from the bedside table and lit one.

Cameron put a hand on her shoulder. 'What is it, lass?'

'It's none of your damned business. You had what you came for. Just go.'

'Rosie . . .?'

'Just go!'

Cameron sighed, bewildered. He got up and started to put on his clothes.

'Where are you going?' Rosie said.

'You told me to go.'

'For God's sake, I didn't mean it. What's wrong with you?'

She got up and went to the window. She leaned against the sill, watching the smoke from her cigarette spiral to the rafters. 'I'm going to have a baby,' she said.

Cameron said nothing for a long time. 'Is it mine?' he asked her.

'I'm two months gone, according to Doctor Halloran. You haven't been back in port more than four weeks.'

'Then whose is it, Rosie?'

'I don't know. If you sat on a bull ants' nest, would you know which one of them bit you?' Cameron tried to put his arms around her but she shrugged him away. 'Don't.'

Cameron stood there, feeling as useless and as ashamed as he had ever felt in his life. He thought about Kate. He imagined how she would have felt when she discovered the trick he had played on her body.

'What are you going to do?' he whispered.

'I don't know.'

'If I can help . . .'

'What can you do?'

'If you need money . . .'

Rosie hung her head. 'Look, it's not your fault. I'm a whore. It's what happens to whores who aren't careful.'

'Don't talk like that!'

'It's true.' She went to her dresser and pulled a tobacco tin from one of the drawers. 'Here.'

'What is it?'

'It's money.'

'What do I want with your money?'

'It's yours. Every penny you've ever left on the dresser from every time we've been together. I've not touched it, Cam. Not a penny of it.'

'I don't want it.'

'Take it! Take it so I won't be *your* whore! The rest of them, I won't even let them kiss me. But I don't want to be a whore with you. Take it!'

She thrust the tin at Cameron. He took it from her. 'I don't understand.'

'All you can think about is that Niland woman.'

'What I did to her was wrong. I told you.'

'You still love her, Cam.' She wiped away the wetness on her cheeks with the back of her arm.

Rosie turned to the window and threw the remains of her cigarette into the street. She stood there for a long time, her arms folded. 'What's that noise?' she said finally.

'Lass?'

'Can you hear it?'

Cameron went to the window. He could it hear it now too, a faint murmur, like distant thunder. It was coming from the foreign quarter. Cameron leaned out of the window and now he could see crowds spilling onto Dampier Terrace.

'Christ,' Cameron murmured.

He threw on the rest of his clothes and rushed out of the door.

◆　◆　◆

The Christmas ball had been a subdued affair. Broome was unusually quiet for a Christmas Eve. There had been trouble in Chinatown that day and a Japanese had been killed in a knife fight with some Koepangers. It was why a lot of the Europeans had decided to stay home while others, like the Nilands, had left the ball early.

George and Kate sat in the back of the Buick, Jamie between them, Junzo at the wheel, driving carefully through the deserted streets. As they turned onto Dampier

163

Terrace a mob appeared in front of them, blocking the road. Junzo slammed his foot on the brake.

'Koepangers!' George muttered.

Kate put her arm around Jamie.

'What's wrong?' Jamie said, trying to peer around Junzo for a better view.

'Hush,' Kate said. The mob had clubs and knives. Their leader pointed at Junzo.

George fumbled with the door of the Buick and jumped down onto the road. He walked among the Koepangers, shooing them with his hands as if they were a mob of unruly sheep. 'That's enough, bimeby! Me big white Niland boss! You go now!'

The mob fell silent but did not disperse. George tried to push one of them out of the way but he stood his ground.

George wagged a finger in his face. 'You! You tell all everybody go now or there be big trouble! You savvy?'

The man stared sulkily back at him. He rubbed the long blade of his knife against the fabric of his khaki shorts and looked at Junzo.

Junzo turned round in his seat and pointed. There were more Koepangers behind them now.

Kate put a hand on his shoulder. 'It's all right, Junzo. No one's going to hurt you.' She got out of the car, pulling Jamie after her. She opened the driver's door. 'Now stand directly behind me,' she said to Junzo. 'No one will hurt you but you must do precisely as I say.'

Junzo did as he was told.

'You go!' George was shouting. 'Bimeby you get damned big trouble!' Kate heard fear in George's voice now.

The Koepangers were edging closer. Their leader, a

lean, surly man in a white singlet and khaki shorts, took a step towards George. George retreated. Emboldened he kept advancing.

George turned and ran. The mob parted to let him go.

Kate stared at the ring of dark, angry faces. The only sound was the hissing of the kerosene lanterns that several of the mob held above their heads. Junzo was babbling something in Japanese, perhaps a prayer to his ancestors. She hoped they were listening.

Jamie suddenly tore away from her and aimed a kick at one of the Koepangers. Kate caught his arm and pulled him back. But the man retreated a few steps, astonished.

Kate wrapped her arms around her son, torn now between her need to protect Jamie and her stubborn refusal to abandon Junzo. He was her houseboy, the Niland house-boy no less, and she would be damned if she was going to leave him to this mob. She looked around for George; he could not have gone far.

'Go home!' she shouted. 'Junzo b'long me!'

Where was George? Surely he hadn't just run off? He couldn't have, it was unthinkable. She looked around desperately for other whites to come and help her. No one.

The Koepangers closed in again.

'That's as far as you go, boys,' a voice said.

A white man pushed his way through the crowd, one of the Koepangers held in front of him, a revolver against his head. When he reached Kate he shoved the man onto the ground in front of her and immediately trained the revolver onto the forehead of the mob's leader.

'Back off now, or I'll splatter your brains all over the road.' Cameron pulled back the hammer and the click of the safety release resounded in the silence like a rifle shot.

'Cameron,' Kate said.

'Where's George?'

'He's . . . he's not here.'

'I can see that. But where is he?'

'Darwin, by now, I should think.'

Cameron swore softly under his breath. 'Get into the car,' he said. Then he took a step forward and pressed the barrel of the gun into the Koepanger's nose. The man squeaked in fear and stepped back. 'Now you'll make way for the lady like a good gentleman or I'll blast a highway through the middle of your skull. Do you understand me now?'

The Koepanger nodded.

Junzo scrambled back into the driver's seat, while Kate pulled Jamie into the back of the car. Junzo's hands were shaking so violently he could barely grip the wheel. He revved the engine of the Buick, waiting for Cameron.

'Well, don't hang around here, man. It's dangerous!'

Junzo engaged the first gear with a teeth-jarring grinding of metal. The Buick jumped forward and the mob spilled back.

'Jump in!' Kate shouted.

'I'll catch the next tram,' Cameron said. He kept the revolver pressed against the leader's head. He waved his other arm and the Koepangers grudgingly backed away to make a passage for the Buick.

'Wait!' Kate shouted, but Junzo recognised his opportunity. The Buick sped through the crowd and was gone.

Kate twisted around in her seat. The figure in the white panama hat was swallowed up by the night and the mob of brown faces.

26

Patrick Flynn leaped from the sulky and ran up the darkened pathway. Sergeant Clarke and George Niland hurried behind him. 'Kathleen! Dear God, if anything's happened to my girl . . . Kathleen!'

Kate Flynn glided onto the veranda with the dignity of a queen. Flynn bounded up the steps and hugged her. 'Kathleen! Thank God!'

Kate pulled away. She turned to George, who could not meet her eyes. Sergeant Clarke looked away, embarrassed. He knew, of course.

She turned back to her father. 'How did you know where I was?'

'We didn't, we hoped . . .' Flynn stared at George. Then the words came out in a torrent. 'I was at the police station being sworn in. There's riots everywhere. Sergeant Clarke here's recruiting all the whites as special constables. Then George came in and said the Koepangers had knocked him down and carried you off. We searched everywhere, then we saw McKenzie —'

'Cameron?'

'He said you were all right. He said you were here.'

'Cameron's all right?'

'He was sitting by the side of the road smoking a cigarette, damn his eyes. Coward! And there we are needing every white man in town at the police station. Thank God you're all right. What happened, girl?'

'Cameron McKenzie saved my life.'

'How? What happened? George said that —'

She pushed past her father and went down the steps.

George still would not look at her. 'There was nothing I could do,' he said. Clarke turned away, inspected a piece of lint on his uniform. 'I knew you'd come to no harm. Calm down.' He had the temerity to try and embrace her.

Kate leaned close to his ear. 'If you had shown for just one moment that you possessed a grain of decency I think I could have forgiven you for these last six years.' She turned on her heel and went back up the steps. The screen door slammed behind her.

Flynn stared at him. 'George?'

He turned away and Flynn hurried after him.

'What was all that about?'

'I don't know. She's hysterical.'

George climbed into the sulky. 'Sergeant Clarke! We have work to do! Are you going to let them burn the town down around our ears?'

✦ ✦ ✦

Kate was trembling with rage. She wanted desperately to weep, to release the fear and tension of the last hours, but she was too angry. Damn him. What kind of man had she married?

She saw a cigarette glow in the darkness.

'It's me.' He stepped out of the shadows. He stopped at the top step, one foot on the veranda. 'I came to see you were all right.'

Suddenly there was a stone in her throat and she couldn't speak.

He mistook her silence for fear, or perhaps for enmity. 'Well, I can see you are. I should not have come. Good-night.'

'Wait.'

He hesitated. 'Truth is, I was not sure I would be welcome here.'

'I owe you my life. And my son's.'

'They would not have harmed you. They were after your houseboy.'

A long silence. He scuffed the step with his boot. She was afraid he might leave.

'I thought they were going to kill you,' she said finally.

'Would that have mattered to you, still?'

She didn't answer. She folded her arms, a part of her wanting to run to him, another part of her urging her to run inside and lock all the doors.

'As soon as you drove away I put the gun back in my pocket and told them all to go home. They're not a bad lot. The Japanese have been riding them hard this season and

169

a few of them have some old scores to settle. They've no quarrel with us.'

'I thank you anyway.'

'It's Junzo who ought to thank me. And he should thank you, as well. If you hadn't stood up to them they'd have spread his brains all over the road.'

Kate studied his face in the light of the kerosene lantern. He had hardly changed at all. 'For years I thought you were dead,' she said.

'Now why did you think that?'

'The war.'

'A lot of men went to the war.'

'And a lot never came back. I was afraid for you. Is that what you wanted to hear?'

'Aye, it is.'

She smiled. 'You haven't changed.'

'You have. You're another man's wife now, and I have no one to blame for that except myself.'

'Would you like to come inside?'

Cameron took off his panama and toyed with the brim. 'Sergeant Clarke is calling for volunteers for a special force to try and quell the riot.' He grinned, his teeth flashing white in the darkness. 'Seeing as I have my own revolver, he's certain to make me a field marshal.' He hesitated, suddenly serious once more. 'But perhaps just a moment. To see the boy. May I see the boy?'

Kate nodded and led the way inside.

Jamie was asleep, one fist tucked underneath his chin. Cameron moved the mosquito netting aside and stared. He felt his throat tighten. The dark blue-black curls, the long eyelashes, the square jaw. Christ, it was like looking at a smaller version of himself.

My son, Cameron thought. He let the netting fall back.

'He's like you, isn't he?'

Cameron couldn't find his voice. He nodded.

'I still hate you, Cameron. Whenever I look at him, it's impossible not to hate you.'

'I hate myself for it, too.'

'I'll never understand why you did it.'

Cameron shrugged his shoulders. 'My only value then was the weight of a pearl. I loved you too much, Kate, and it scared the life out of me. Back then I thought being rich and being happy were the same thing.' He sighed.

'Will you tell him?' Cam managed finally, nodding towards the sleeping boy.

'That he's your son?' She shook her head.

'I don't think it will be a help to him. Do you?'

She put a hand to his cheek. 'I've never loved anyone but you.'

Cameron pulled her towards him. The ashes he thought were dead and cold flared again, into a fire that consumed all reason and restraint.

✦   ✦   ✦

It was after midnight. Kate slipped out of bed and, dressed only in her nightgown, made her way to the bathroom at the back of the house. Their bore water came from the ground scalding hot, so they let it cool in the tub. She scooped the tepid water over her body, washing away the sticky residue of their lovemaking. She was tender and her breasts felt swollen and bruised. Their coupling had been urgent and violent, like animals. They had consumed the bitterness and recriminations of the lost years in an angry, clawing passion. The strength of her longing, after all this time, had frightened her.

She towelled herself dry and went out onto the veranda. It was too hot to sleep. In the distance she could hear the sounds of rioting in Chinatown. Despite Cameron's assurances she worried that it might yet spill over into bloodshed against the whites, and the fear gave an edge to the residue of guilt . . . and what else was it?

After all these years. It was hope.

She heard a board creak behind her and she spun around.

'Liddy! You gave me a fright. What are you doing creeping around here at this time of the night?'

'Liddy see whitefeller come. He go home now?'

She felt her cheeks flush hot. 'It's none of your damned business! Go back to bed!'

'Mister God He say –'

Kate got up and advanced on her, wagging her finger in her face. 'I don't want to hear one word about Mister God or debil-debil, do you hear me? Go back to bed!'

Liddy shuffled off down the path to the servants' quarters, muttering to herself.

Damn her! Kate put her head in her hands. First she had conceived a baby out of wedlock; now she was an adulteress. No good could come of it. Liddy was probably right, she was a bad lot. God would find some way to punish her, she was sure of it.

✦ ✦ ✦

As the rioting spread, Sergeant Clarke enrolled as many Europeans as could hold a rifle to act as special constables, to try and keep the people in the foreign quarter from murdering each other. The Japanese outnumbered the Koepangers four to one, and they were better organised, and more skilled in fighting with knives and clubs. The Koepangers would be massacred to a man if the Europeans did not intervene.

The fighting spread along Dampier Terrace, and the Koepangers in Ferguson's camp were attacked. As they fled past Moss & Richardson's store they saw a small group of Japanese who had not yet been involved in the brawling. Seeing an easy target for revenge they set upon them, and Kanawa, a diver, was murdered.

Meanwhile two hundred Japanese had swarmed towards Owen's camp. The Koepangers there barricaded themselves into the Roebuck and Continental hotels, just a handful of whites to protect them from the Japanese mob, who had gathered on Dampier Terrace armed with mangrove clubs and broken bottles.

When Cameron arrived at the Continental he found Flynn standing next to Sergeant Clarke on the steps of the hotel, his hands on his hips, like some relic of the British Raj. George stood behind him, ashen-faced.

'Got here just in time, my boy,' Flynn said when he saw him. 'Looks like the fun's about to start.'

'Where have you been?' George said.

'Attending to my own affairs, George.' Cameron stared at the mob of Japanese making their way towards the hotel. 'What do you propose, Sergeant? We can't shoot them, surely?'

'Not if we can avoid it, Mister McKenzie. If they've half a mind, they could massacre us as well.'

'Why did you issue us with guns if you don't intend us to use them?' George asked him.

'I think it's time for cool heads, sir,' Clarke told him. 'We must try and avoid any unnecessary bloodshed.'

Flynn checked the breech of his Lee Enfield rifle and loaded it. He turned to Cameron. 'By the way, my boy, I believe I owe you my thanks. My daughter says you looked out for her tonight. I'd like you to know I'm grateful.'

'There's no need to be,' Cameron said. 'I did it for her, not you. We still have a score to settle, you and I – and I'll see you in hell for what you did to me!'

◆　◆　◆

The Japanese were not afraid of the whites or their guns. Some of them ran towards the hotel, slapping their bared chests and shouting, 'Shoot! Shoot!' None of the whites availed themselves of this opportunity. Common humanity was only part of it; there were too many of them, even with their guns. And anyway, none of the Europeans wanted to harm the very men who controlled the industry on which their livelihoods depended.

Through the long and sweltering night the mob swarmed around the hotel, neither the Japanese nor the whites backing down or taking the fateful one step too far. Just before morning the mob drifted away and melted back into Chinatown.

For three days the running skirmishes continued. Isolated from the rest of Australia, the preservation of law and order in the town depended on Sergeant Clarke and six constables, and the handful of whites who had been pressed into service.

The Malays were itching to join in the fight and blood their *kris* knives on the hated Japanese; Clarke and the white bosses persuaded them to stay out of it. In the end, cooler heads prevailed. With the aid of some of the senior Japanese – including Nosiro Tanaka – the rioters were persuaded to put down their weapons.

But for a few others the trouble was only just beginning.

27

Flynn made his way purposefully along Sheba Lane. Dim lamps shone from the open windows and a bronze-muscled Manilaman crouched in one of the doorways strumming a guitar. Flynn heard the rattle of dice and the shouts and curses of the gamblers above the billiard saloon. He ducked inside, bumping shoulders with one of Clarke's constables on the way. The constable touched the peak of his cap and walked on.

The billiard room was thick with cigarette smoke, and crowded with coloureds and those whites that Flynn never met at any of George's cocktail parties. The men wore either singlets or went bare-chested, and beads of sweat shone on their arms and chests and foreheads.

Flynn looked quickly around the room. One pair of eyes returned his stare. Flynn nodded, almost imperceptibly, and made his way to the rickety wooden bar. He bought himself a tumbler of square-face, and waited.

Simeon sauntered across the room, still clutching his billiard cue, and bought a beer.

'Boss,' he said. He took care not to look at Flynn.

'You look like a bashed crab,' Flynn said.

Simeon flushed but said nothing. He still wore the scars that Hanaguchi and his friends had given him. They had broken his nose for a second time.

'Our business was interrupted,' Flynn said softly. 'Do you still have the pearl?'

Simeon hesitated only for a moment. 'I still have it.'

'Then I suggest we rearrange our meeting for tomorrow night. Same time, same place.'

'You'll bring the money?'

'I'll have the money, my boy. You bring the pearl.'

Simeon took his drink and wandered back to the billiard table. He continued the game. When he looked up again, Flynn was gone.

So far so good. After his initial panic, he had realised that losing the pearl was not so terrible after all. What had been lost by trickery could be regained the same way. A steamer, the *Gorgon*, was arriving the morning after his meeting with Flynn, and would sail within the day to catch the tide. He would be on it, and he would have Flynn's money with him. When he arrived safely in Singapore he would send a message to Anna and money for the fare. Everything would still work out as he had planned.

'What are you grinning at?'

Simeon looked around. It was Huey Fong. 'Nothing.'

'Then let's get on with the game.'

Simeon bent over the table and completed a successful cannon off the cushion into the corner pocket. He grinned at Huey. His luck was back. He could do no wrong.

✦   ✦   ✦

'So how are things between you and Kathleen?'

George stubbed out the remains of his cigar and picked up a glass of brandy. 'A rather personal question, old boy.'

'It's a personal matter, George. She's my daughter.'

They were on the veranda of George's bungalow. After a late dinner, Kate had complained of a headache and retired to bed.

It was almost a week since the riots and George and Kate had hardly spoken a civil word to each other during that time. Flynn had been the only one attempting any conversation at dinner.

'I'm concerned about the marriage, George,' Flynn said.

'I can sort out my own domestic affairs, thank you, Patrick.'

'Can you now?'

George poured himself another brandy. 'Drink?' he said.

Flynn wanted to refuse on point of principle – it was hard to lecture a man when you were drinking his brandy – but he could not help himself. 'A small one.'

George poured three fingers into a glass and handed it to Flynn. 'Your health.'

Flynn raised his glass. 'As I was saying –'

'Mind if we change the subject?'

'Look here, George –'

'Keep your voice down, old boy. She's only in the next room.'

Flynn leaned forward. 'What happened the night the riot started?'

'It's all in the past now.'

'Is it? What if she decides to leave you?'

'She won't do that.'

George leaned back, put his hands behind his head and yawned. 'Where would she go? How could she live?'

'I would think that's obvious, my boy.'

There was a long silence. 'You can't even support yourself,' George said, finally.

'What are you talking about?'

'I've been covering your debts for years, Patrick. You don't think I paid for your drinking and gambling for nothing? They were loans, Patrick, properly documented, as you know. You didn't think I intended to tear them up? If I choose to call them in now, how much do you think you'll be left with?' He paused, watching Flynn's face. 'You don't even know, do you?'

'I'll pay you back.'

'Of course you will. The trouble is, after you've sold your shares in the Niland Pastoral Company, it won't leave very much.'

Flynn gulped the rest of his brandy and mopped his face with his handkerchief. 'You've gone quite pale,' George said.

'You bastard.'

'Personally, I've no fondness for two-up and I never

drink to excess, either. But I don't condemn those failings in others. As long as I don't have to finance them.'

'I'll pay you back. And sooner than you think.'

George raised an eyebrow. 'You have another iron in the fire?'

'You'll get your money. All of it. And then I'll have you off my back forever.'

George shook his head. 'I'm not your enemy, Patrick. Besides, if she leaves me, she won't go running back to Daddy. She has someone else in mind.'

'What are you talking about?'

'McKenzie.'

'That bastard!'

'He's been seeing her. Here in this house. One of the servants told me.'

Flynn's face flushed the colour of raw liver. 'In your own house?'

'Calm down.'

'Calm down? What are you going to do about it?'

'What can I do?'

George's equanimity shocked and outraged him. Flynn jumped to his feet and the cane chair clattered onto its side on the veranda. 'Jesus, Mary and Joseph. Maybe she's better off without you after all! If you were any sort of man you'd call him to account!'

George gave Flynn a chill smile and sipped his brandy.

'I ought to deal with the bastard myself if you're not man enough!'

'Good luck.'

Flynn stormed away, his footsteps drumming on the wooden veranda.

'Where are you going?' George called after him.

'I've business to attend to!' he shouted, and then he was gone.

Between the slats of her bedroom window, Kate watched him go. The sound of raised voices had woken her. She had been unable to make out the conversation at first until the shouting started.

That bastard!

He's been seeing her. Here in this house. One of the servants told me.

In your own house?

Calm down.

Even in the hot and sticky room she felt a chill shiver of apprehension. Long after George had slipped into bed beside her she lay staring at the darkness. She was still awake when Sergeant Clarke knocked on the door, soon after midnight.

❖   ❖   ❖

It was a boisterous night at the Roebuck Hotel. The sound of fiddles sawing out an Irish reel echoed around Dampier Terrace, mingling with snatches of singing and piano music that drifted over the empty beach from one of the pearlers' bungalows. The solitary glow of a masthead light bobbed on the bay.

Simeon waited in the shadows below the Streeter and Male stores, his heart thumping in his chest. Many times he had climbed into a diving suit and gone below the waves but he had never been as frightened as he was now. The squeal of a flying fox in the trees nearby made him start.

Calm down, Simeon. If you are too nervous he will know there is something wrong.

He heard a footfall on the sand.

'Espada! Are you there? It's me, Flynn!'

'I'm here, boss.'

He moved out of the shadows. He was grateful that it was a dark night; the moon was no more than a sliver.

'You have the money, boss?'

'I've got it, my boy.'

'Let me see it.'

Flynn patted his jacket pocket. 'It's right here. Now show me this pearl!'

Simeon reached into the pocket of his trousers and brought out a large white handkerchief. Inside it he had wrapped a bottle stopper. It was hard and large and round. Convincing enough for his purpose tonight.

He handed it to Flynn.

Flynn unwrapped it carefully, squinting in the darkness. He couldn't see a damned thing. Cursing, he knelt down and spread the handkerchief on the sand. He reached into his pocket and produced a box of matches. He lit one.

'Wait a minute . . .'

Simeon felt for the iron crook he had hung on his belt at the back of his trousers. As Flynn looked up he brought it down hard on Flynn's head.

Flynn fell back onto the sand; to Simeon's horror he was still conscious. He tried to scramble to his feet but, like a punch drunk boxer, he couldn't coordinate his arms and his legs and flopped back on the sand. 'Help me!' he roared. 'Murder!'

Panicked, Simeon swung again, as hard as he could.

Flynn put up an arm to fend off the blow and Simeon heard a crack as the bones in Flynn's forearm shattered. Flynn screamed, writhing in pain. Simeon swung again. This time the blow connected with the back of Flynn's head. It made a sound like someone stomping on a cabbage in heavy boots.

Flynn lay still.

Simeon threw away the bar and knelt down, turning out Flynn's pockets. He found a thick envelope of money and shoved it into his shorts. He heard footsteps on Dampier Terrace. Someone must have heard Flynn calling out.

He jumped to his feet and ran.

✦ ✦ ✦

Cameron had been about to turn in for the night when he heard the commotion on the beach. The *Roebuck* had been dragged up onto the shore for lay-up, and he was sleeping on board while he had a camp built further along the beach, next to Ferguson's. When he heard the shouts he clambered down the coir ladder at the stern and ran along the sand towards the Streeter and Male jetty.

He tripped on something in the sand and fell headlong. In the darkness it took him some moments to realise that it was a man's body. He reached down, and his right hand came away sticky and wet.

A sickle moon appeared from behind the clouds and Cameron saw a man running, silhouetted against the pilings below Dampier Terrace. He started to run after him.

✦ ✦ ✦

By the time Cameron got back a crowd had gathered, some carrying kerosene lamps. Half a dozen men from the Roebuck Hotel had helped to carry the body back up to the street.

'Jesus, it's Flynn!' someone said

'Someone's caved his head in!'

One of the men – Cameron recognised him, it was the pearler Lacey – tore open Flynn's shirt and put his ear to his chest. He shook his head. 'He's dead.'

'Christ Almighty.'

'What a mess.'

One of the men looked up at Cameron. 'Where did you come from?'

'I heard someone call out. There was a man running up the beach towards Chinatown. I chased him.'

Lacey looked at Cameron's hands, then at his shirt. 'There's blood all over you.'

Cameron looked down, surprised. Lacey was right. 'I found him lying on the beach. I fell over him.'

There was a long silence. 'Someone better call Sergeant Clarke,' Lacey grunted. Cameron realised they were all looking at him. And he was in no doubt at all what they were thinking.

28

Simeon ran into an alley behind John Chi Lane and fell against the wall, trying to catch his breath. Chinks of light shone into the alley from the shutters of a second storey window. Holy Mary, there was blood on his hands.

He looked down at his shirt. There was a stain across the front, as if someone had squirted him with red ink. Simeon fought down his panic. This wasn't meant to happen. Who would have thought the old white boss would be so tough?

Simeon heard shouts from the end of the lane. People were streaming out of the boarding houses and shops and running towards Dampier Terrace. He heard someone shout 'Murder!' and his blood ran cold.

Murder. The word echoed in his brain. Murder, murder. Holy Mary, Mother of God, he hadn't meant to kill him! They would hang him!

He ran down the alley. When he reached the bathhouse next to the Canton he ripped off his shirt and dashed inside. He scooped up handfuls of water from one of the troughs and splashed it over his face and arms, washing off the blood. He would have to burn his shirt.

For now, he draped it casually over his shoulder, folding it up in a way that would cover the bloodstains. He went back outside and up the steps of the boarding house. A few moments later he was back in his room. He locked the door, threw himself down on his bed and sobbed like a child.

After a while he sat up, ashamed. He had to pull himself together. He had to think.

He reached into his pocket and pulled out the envelope of money. He tore it open and spilled the notes onto the bed. He counted them. Five hundred pounds. He had asked for a thousand! So the old bastard was trying to cheat him after all.

What should he do? The steamer would be leaving in the morning. No, that would be the first place Sergeant Clarke would look. If he found him it would be a virtual admission of guilt. No, he would have to stay in Broome and brave it out.

Five hundred pounds! It was still a lot of money. But it wouldn't buy him very much if he had a rope around his neck.

Holy Mary, Mother of God. How could things have gone so wrong so quickly!

✦ ✦ ✦

It was almost dawn before Cameron fell asleep. His dreams were black and disturbed. Every time he closed his eyes he saw Flynn's lifeless body spreadeagled on a table in the Roebuck Hotel, blood and brains leaking out of his skull.

'I didn't do it!' Cameron moaned in his dream, and the crowd of men gathered around the body all pointed at him, shouting: 'There's blood on your hands!'

He jerked awake. There were footsteps on the deck above. He jumped out of his bunk and hurried up the scuttle.

It was Sergeant Clarke. Two of his constables were climbing up the coir rope at the stern to join him on the deck.

It was just light, the sun low over the flat horizon. It could not have been much after six o'clock.

'Good morning, Sergeant,' Cameron said. He felt an ominous chill of apprehension. 'You're calling very early.'

'Morning, Cam.' Clarke looked uncomfortable. He waited until his two constables were in position on either side of him and then he said: 'I'm sorry about this.'

'Sorry? What are you sorry for?'

Clarke smoothed the wings of his ginger walrus moustache with his fingers. 'I've a warrant for your arrest.'

'My arrest?' Cameron put his hands on his hips. 'On what charge?'

'The murder of Patrick Bernard Flynn.'

'You're not serious?'

Clarke coughed, embarrassed. 'Like I said, I'm sorry, Cam.' He held out the handcuffs, then decided against them. Where would Cam run to? 'You didn't really do for him, did you?'

187

Broome, March 1921

The courtroom was packed. The fans laboured slowly overhead, barely stirring the air. The heat inside was stifling. Cameron stood in the dock between two of Clarke's constables and looked across the sea of faces, searching for just one.

Kate would not return his gaze.

Lacey was on the stand. Barrington, the Crown Prosecutor, consulted his notes through his pince-nez. 'Mister Lacey, in the statement you made to the police, you said you were the first to see the body of the deceased. Is that correct?'

Lacey squirmed in his chair. 'Deceased?'

'The dead man,' Barrington said, his patience sorely tried. 'Mister Flynn.'

'That's right. It was terrible, you could see his brains.'

Barrington adjusted his spectacles. 'Thank you, Mister Lacey, we may safely leave the anatomical details to those qualified in medical matters. Could you just tell us, in your own words, how you happened to find the body?'

'We was in the Roebuck, having a few drinks, me and Jack and Tom.'

'That is Mister McDonagh and Mister Gibson?'

'Yeah.' Lacey loosened his collar and leaned forward. 'We heard someone shouting: "Help me! Murder!" Like that. So we ran outside. The yelling was coming from the beach. When we got there we found Flynn lying face down with his brains –'

'Thank you, Mister Lacey. Was anyone else present?'

'Ay?'

'Did you see anyone else?'

'Nar, there weren't no one.'

'I see.' Offended by the double negative, Barrington consulted his notes. 'And when did you first see the accused?'

Lacey glanced at Cameron. 'It was later. After we hauled Flynn up to the street. He was breathing hard and there was blood all over him.'

'Can you be more precise. Where was the blood, Mister Lacey?'

'Everywhere.'

'On his hands?'

'Yeah, on his hands. On his trousers. On his shirt. Everywhere.'

'Did Mister McKenzie give any explanation why he was covered in blood. He cut himself shaving, perhaps?'

Cameron's lawyer, a local solicitor by the name of Whitehouse, was on his feet in an instant. 'Objection!'

The magistrate looked down his nose at the Crown Prosecutor. 'Mister Barrington . . .'

Barrington bowed. 'I withdraw the remark, Your Honour.'

'Strike it from the record,' the magistrate said to the clerk. Then to Barrington: 'I don't expect to hear any more of that.'

Barrington accepted the rebuke with equanimity. He had made his point. He smiled at the jury. 'I'll repeat the question. Did Mister Cameron give you any explanation as to why he was covered in blood?'

'He said he'd found Flynn lying on the beach before we had.'

Barrington looked puzzled. 'I see. But you say you were the first to find the body.'

'Well, there weren't no one else there when we got there.'

'So where was Mister McKenzie?'

Lacey shrugged. 'I dunno. He said he was chasing someone.'

'Chasing someone?'

'The bloke who did it, he said.'

'I repeat, Mister Lacey, when you found the body, did you see anyone else on the beach?'

'No, I didn't.'

Barrington took a deep breath and looked across the courtroom at Cameron. 'Curious.' He scratched his wig, a fine portrayal of bewilderment. 'One more question, Mister

Lacey. Did you ever hear the accused threaten the deceased
– Mister Flynn?'

'Once.'

'Please tell the court about it.'

'It was the night the riot started. Some of the Koepangers had barricaded themselves into the Conti.'

'The Conti?'

'The Continental Hotel. Anyways, Sergeant Clarke had
recruited a load of us blokes as special constables. We was
standing on the steps when I heard him say it.'

'Say what?'

Lacey cleared his throat, like an actor preparing for a
speech. 'He said to Flynn: "I'll see you in hell for what you
done to me."'

Barrington considered this for a moment, allowing the
dramatic impact to be absorbed by the jury. 'And what do
you suppose he meant by that?'

'It was common knowledge. Flynn stole a snide –'

Whitehouse jumped to his feet immediately. 'Objection,
Your Honour, this is just hearsay!'

'Sustained.'

Barrington smiled at the jury, all long-term residents of
Broome, save three. They all knew the story too, but it
didn't hurt to remind them. 'Thank you, Mister Lacey,
you've been most helpful.'

✦　　✦　　✦

Cameron sat on the edge of his cot and stared at the floor.
He still could not believe the nightmare that had overtaken
him. It was like being trapped in quicksand. At first the

191

danger had seemed absurd, but the more he struggled, the deeper he had sunk. Now he was completely and hopelessly trapped in a morass of half-truths and misleading perceptions.

He put his head in his hands and tried to think. The prosecution had established a clear motive. What did he have? The one thing that could have proved his story – footprints in the sand – had been obliterated by the crowd of people who had been drawn to the beach by Flynn's cries, and even they had been erased by the morning tide. His only hope was to find the real murderer. And that was no hope at all.

He heard footsteps on the stone floor and looked up. It was Sergeant Clarke. 'You've got a visitor.'

Kate! Cameron jumped to his feet.

A woman swept into the cell behind Clarke. She was slim and fair-haired. 'Five minutes, ma'am,' Clarke said to her. She waited patiently while he went outside, locking the door behind him.

'Cam.'

'Rosie! What are you doing here?'

She put her arms around him and buried her face in his neck. Cameron, embarrassed, tried to disentangle himself. 'You didn't have to come,' he said.

Rosie clung on grimly. He felt her trembling. 'What have they done to you?'

She fumbled for a handkerchief. 'I'm sorry. You don't need me blubbing all over you.' She tried to laugh, but it was a hollow effort that quickly turned into tears again.

Cameron put an arm around her. 'It will be all right,' he said. 'Don't take on so.'

She shook his arm away and suddenly her eyes were

blazing. 'How can it be all right? They're going to hang you, Cam!'

Cameron shrugged again. 'But I didn't do it.'

'Tell them you were with me!'

'What?'

Rosie shot a glance towards the door. 'Don't you remember, Cam? When it happened I was with you. On the *Roebuck*.'

'You can't do it, Rosie. Not for me. It's perjury. They'll crucify you.'

'Who cares what really happened? You've told the truth until now and what good has it done you? If you're innocent then you'd better start lying!'

He stared at her. She was right, they were going to hang him, and it didn't make one bit of difference that he didn't do it. As far as the law and everyone else was concerned he looked guilty, and that was an end to it.

'Rosie –'

'I won't let them do this to you,' she whispered. 'Sergeant Clarke!'

He unlocked the door for her. Rosie turned back, kissed Cameron quickly on the mouth and left.

30

The Crown Prosecutor called four other witnesses, including Sergeant Clarke, who had been present the night Cameron made his threat to Flynn. McDonagh and Gibson and several others corroborated Lacey's story of how Flynn had been found on the beach.

Finally George Niland was called to the stand. He looked cool and affluent in his white linen suit and pearl tiepin. He crossed his legs and leaned back in the bentwood chair, studying Barrington down the length of his nose.

After the preliminaries, Barrington asked: 'Mister Niland, you were, I believe, the last person to see the deceased alive?'

'I assume so – apart from the murderer, of course.'

There was a ripple of amusement in the court.

'Of course,' Barrington agreed. 'The deceased was your father-in-law, that is correct?'

'Yes.'

'And where was the deceased living at the time of the murder?'

'He was staying with us at our home. He had just come up from his station in Geraldton. He had been living there.'

'And you were having a discussion with him about this on the night of the murder?'

'Yes, we were on the veranda, I recall. My wife had gone to bed.'

'And what did you discuss?'

George hesitated for the first time. 'Personal matters.'

Barrington frowned and consulted his notes. 'Did you not say in your statement that the accused's name was mentioned?'

George glanced at Cameron, then at the jury.

'Mister Niland?'

'I believe I was mistaken.'

'But you said in your statement that the deceased appeared to be angry with Mister McKenzie and said he was going to look for him?'

George appeared flustered. 'I'm not sure now.'

'But in your statement –'

George tugged at his moustache. 'I may have been mistaken! The matters we were discussing were of a highly personal nature. I cannot repeat them in court.' He looked across at the jury once more. 'I think the statement may have been misleading.'

Barrington was furious. 'Well can you then explain to us in your own words what did happen?'

'I cannot disclose the substance of what we discussed . . . only to say that Mister Flynn was angry with Mister McKenzie would be inaccurate.'

'But his name was mentioned?'

'Yes, but –'

'In what context, Mister Niland?'

George sighed. 'It was a subject of a highly trivial nature. I cannot see that it has any relevance.'

'Perhaps you would let the court decide that.'

'As I said, it was personal.'

Barrington was sweating now, angry and flustered that one of his star witnesses had turned on him. 'Personal enough to make him angry?'

'Yes . . . no . . .'

'Mister Niland, were you at the Continental Hotel on the night of the twenty fourth of December?'

'Yes.'

'And did you hear the accused make a threat against the deceased?'

'If he did, I don't remember it.'

Barrington straightened, the muscles in his jaw rippling. 'Thank you, Mister Niland.'

Cameron stared at George Niland, almost as bewildered as Barrington. It had been an admirable performance from a man with whom he had barely spoken for six years and whose last words had been a warning to get out of town. It appeared that George had just done everything in his power to protect him.

He wondered, then, why he had just felt the noose tighten around his neck.

✦   ✦   ✦

Simeon watched Anna leave Lacey's foreshore camp, and followed her along Dampier Terrace into Chinatown. She looked radiant, wonderful, her red hair cascading down her back from under her bonnet, her creamy arms bare, one pale hand clutching a parasol against the sun, the other clutching a wicker basket.

He watched her go into Tanaka's store. When she came out, he was waiting for her.

'Anna!'

She gasped and took a step back. 'Simeon!'

'I have to talk to you.'

She tried to wriggle past him but he grabbed her wrist. 'What's the matter?'

'My father will kill me if he sees me talking to you!'

'He won't see us here. What did you buy?' He reached into her basket and pulled out a bolt of silk. 'Pretty. A dress for you?'

She snatched it away from him and put it back in the basket. 'Please, Simeon, I can't see you anymore.'

He ran after her. 'Why? What have I done?' He stood in front of her, blocking the way. 'I have money now. I can buy a lugger and be a pearling master!'

'How can you? You're not –'

'I was born in Manila, that makes me an American citizen. I can buy a lugger if I want.'

'You're crazy.'

'Crazy for you.'

She tried to push past him.

'We don't have to stay here,' he said, desperately. 'We can go to Singapore or Malaya.'

Anna studied him, frowning. 'Where did you get the money from?'

'I had some luck with the dice.'

She knew he was lying, of course.

He took her by the shoulders. 'Come with me, Anna.'

'I can't.'

'Why not?'

She took a deep breath. 'Because I'm marrying Herbert Gibson.'

She twisted away and walked quickly in the opposite direction. For a moment Simeon was too shocked to react, but then he took off after her. 'Please, Anna! Stop!'

'Go away!'

'I thought you liked me!'

She stopped and squared her shoulders. On her face was a look he had never seen before. 'I do but . . . you're not . . . you're not white. So don't be so stupid. I could never *marry* you.'

Then she turned and ran, holding her skirts, her red hair bouncing under her bonnet – pretty, pale, unattainable, *white* Anna. This time he let her go.

A fathomless rage bubbled up inside him, bringing with it the cold, unbearable pain of his humiliation. His Madonna was just another white boss in a skirt. He was just a coolie she wanted to torture with her sex. It had all been for nothing – the pearl, Flynn, Cameron . . . All for nothing.

He walked slowly down the street towards the Roebuck Hotel. He needed to get drunk, very, very drunk. He had murdered one man and sentenced another, to whom he owed the debt of his life, to a hangman. And for what? Huey Fong had been right all along.

✦ ✦ ✦

George Niland entered the bedroom dressed only in his nightshirt. Kate thought he looked ridiculous but she never broached the subject with him. After all, she had no desire to see more of his body than the nightshirt afforded her. Indeed, she had not seen him naked in almost seven years of marriage; he always dressed and undressed in another room.

It was late. George sometimes worked until nine or ten o'clock in his office, and Kate made sure she was asleep by the time he got home. Tonight, he seemed intolerably pleased to find her awake and she noticed a bulge under his nightshirt that betrayed the reason for his pleasure.

'Still awake?' he said needlessly. He lifted the mosquito netting and slipped into the bed beside her.

'I wanted to talk to you,' she said.

'Just talk?'

'Yes. Just talk.'

'What about?'

'About why you lied in court today.'

'Lied? I didn't lie. I was under oath.'

'Then you told less than the truth.'

'Did I?'

'I heard you two talking on the veranda the night it happened. I heard Papa call Cameron a bastard.'

'Language, please.'

'Don't be such a prig. That was the word he used.'

He folded his arms across his chest. 'And?'

'You didn't say that in court.'

'No, I didn't.'

'Why not?'

George sighed. 'I know you still love him,' he said. He waited for her to protest, but she didn't even have the shame to pretend anymore. 'I would do anything to get him out of your mind, except . . . except put a rope around his neck.'

Kate stared at her hands. 'You really think he killed Papa.'

'I don't know.'

'You have a duty to the law.'

'You want to see him hang?' Now here was an interesting question, he thought.

Kate's fingers twisted the edge of the sheet into a knot. 'I don't know what I want.'

'There's no proof, as such.'

'You *do* think he did it.'

George reached across to the bedside table and turned off the lamp. 'Go to sleep now.'

Kate sat there in the darkness, worrying the sheet. 'Why did you lie in court?'

'I told you. I have good cause to hate him, but I don't want to see any man hang. Also, my sweet, I will not have his blood on my hands and give you another reason to despise me.' He plumped his pillow and rolled over onto his side, away from her.

But George could not sleep. He heard Kate weeping softly into her pillow and felt a cold satisfaction. *Your turn to suffer. I wish you well of your secret and unholy desires. See where they have got you, my girl.*

31

Whitehouse threw his battered brown leather briefcase on the table and sat down. 'Mister McKenzie,' he said. 'I must know one thing. Did you do it?'

'You've asked me that question before, Mister White-house. The truth does not change with the season.'

Whitehouse nodded. He was a short, brusque man in his middle years, his hair thinning to reveal a pale and freckled skull. The wisps of grey hair that sometimes protruded from beneath his wig in the courtroom were unruly and appeared comical when he was out of his robes. He wore brown wire-rimmed glasses and an expression of Protestant severity. He still retained a faint Welsh accent though he had been in Australia for most of his life.

He drummed on the table with his fingertips. 'George Niland is no friend of yours,' he said. 'He did you more damage with his testimony yesterday than half a dozen Joseph Laceys put together. Right now that jury is wondering why he was trying to protect you.'

'Every man on that jury knows my past. They know he has cause enough to hate me.'

'And they were expecting him to gild the lily. Instead he does just the opposite. George Niland came across as a decent man who doesn't like you but doesn't want to see you hang. If anyone in that courtroom had their doubts, he just about convinced them you had something to hide.'

Whitehouse reached into his briefcase and pulled out three handwritten foolscap sheets. 'I have here a deposition from a Miss Rose Thompson. The question is, what shall I do about it?'

'Rosie?'

'She is willing to swear under oath that she was with you the night of the murder. That she was on the *Roebuck* and heard Flynn's screams.' He pushed the papers across the table to Cameron. 'If the jury believes her, you're off the hook.'

'And if they don't believe her?'

'A good question.' He tapped the deposition with his forefinger. 'This is a fabrication, isn't it?'

Cameron stared at the papers on the table in front of him. Sergeant Clarke stood at the door of the remand cell, his hands folded behind his back, watching. Had he overheard Rosie's whispered conversation when she visited him here in the gaol?

Cameron leaned towards Whitehouse. 'What if I have to lie to tell the truth?'

Whitehouse lowered his voice also. 'Do you swear on your mother's life that you didn't do this, Mister McKenzie?'

'As God is my witness, I'm innocent of this, Mister Whitehouse.'

Whitehouse picked up the deposition and put it back in his briefcase. 'In that case, we'll give Miss Thompson a try.' He stood up.

'Mister Whitehouse, will you do me one favour?'

'Well, that all depends on what you wish me to do.'

'Will you go and see Kate Niland for me?'

'You want me to go and see Flynn's daughter?'

'I want you to tell her I didn't do it. Will you do that for me? Tell her I swear I didn't do it.'

Whitehouse sniffed and tucked the briefcase under his arm. 'I'll have to think about this,' he said and went out.

◆ ◆ ◆

Simeon was propped on a stool in a corner of Hagen's Billiard Room. His head was lying on the counter in a pool of beer and one arm hung uselessly at his side. There was dried vomit on the front of his shirt.

Huey Fong shook him roughly. 'Come on, Simeon. Time to go home.'

Simeon shoved him away. He lost his balance, fell off the stool and onto the floor. Some Manilamen started to laugh. Huey tried to get him back on his feet.

'Wasn't worth . . . cheated me . . .'

'What are you talking about?' Huey laughed. 'Who

cheated you?' He put one of Simeon's arms around his neck and lifted him to his feet.

'Flynn.'

Mother of God, Huey thought. Keep your voice down.

'Cheated . . . Anna . . . cheated . . .'

'Shut up,' Huey said.

'Cheated . . . didn't mean . . . kill him . . .'

'*Shut up*!' Huey hissed at him. He dragged Simeon towards the door.

'Pearl . . . not . . . worth . . .'

Huey staggered under the weight of Simeon's body and crashed into one of the jarrah posts. The Manilamen cheered and shouted encouragement. Huey dragged Simeon outside into the alley. But he was too heavy for him and Huey landed on top of him in the gutter.

'Cameron die . . . mustn't . . . my fault.'

Huey put his hand over the other man's mouth. 'Shut up, idiot!' He hauled him to his feet. They weaved along John Chi Lane towards the boarding house.

The Canton's owner, Billy Ng, helped Huey carry Simeon up the narrow wooden steps to his room. They threw him face down on the bed and Billy retreated. 'Smell like bloody pisshole!' Billy said. 'He too much sick in room, clean it up, bloody quick time!'

'It's all right,' Huey said. 'I look after him.'

'Smell like bloody pisshole!' Billy shouted again, and went out. Huey closed the door after him.

'Cameron . . . save my life . . .'

Huey sat down on the edge of the bed and rolled Simeon over onto his back. His breath reeked of cheap arrack. 'What's this about Flynn?' Huey said.

'Cameron mustn't die . . . save life . . .'

'What about *Flynn*?'

'Not worth . . . cheat me.'

Huey shook him by the shoulders. 'Did you try and sell Flynn your pearl?'

'No mean . . . kill him.'

Mother of God. Simeon had killed Flynn! Huey wiped his hands on his trousers as if Flynn's blood was now somehow smeared on his own hands. What should he do about this?

'Anna . . . love you, Anna . . . Anna . . .'

Huey went out, shutting the door carefully behind him.

So Simeon had murdered a white boss! He wondered what he should do with this interesting piece of information. There had to be some profit in it for an intelligent man. He was too drunk and too tired to think about it properly tonight. In the morning he would find a way to turn this to his advantage.

A few minutes later he too was snoring in his bed.

✦   ✦   ✦

Whitehouse climbed out of the sulky and went up the white shell-grit path to the veranda of the Niland bungalow. Liddy opened the door.

'My name's Whitehouse,' he said. 'I'd like to talk to Mrs Niland.'

Liddy regarded him with suspicion. 'I'll go find the missus,' she said, and disappeared into the bungalow's dark interior.

A few minutes later she came back, opened the screen door and ushered Whitehouse inside.

Kate sat alone on the back veranda, in a cane peacock chair delicately patterned with strips of coloured cane and bamboo. He felt as if he was being received at court by some oriental queen. The effect was only spoiled by the restless fluttering motions Kate made with her hands.

'Please, sit down,' she said. 'Would you like a drink?'

He would have liked a stiff whiskey but he said: 'Just a lemonade, if you don't mind.' Kate nodded to Liddy, who glared at him as if he was a tax collector.

'I think I've offended her,' Whitehouse said.

Kate forced a smile. 'You're representing Mister McKenzie in court, aren't you?'

'Is that a crime?'

'Liddy thinks so.'

'I see.'

It was peaceful here in the garden, the flowers and plants heavy with scent.

Whitehouse took a deep breath. 'I imagine you want to know why I've come. I'd like you to know that I –'

Whitehouse was interrupted by Liddy, who placed the lemonade, glistening with shaved ice, on the table beside him. He waited until she had gone back inside.

'You were saying?'

'I am here at my client's request.' He paused. 'I'm sorry, I am not very comfortable with this.' He mopped his forehead with a handkerchief and sipped gratefully at the lemonade.

'Please go on.'

'Mister McKenzie has asked me to give you a message. He wants you to know that he is innocent.'

Whitehouse sat back in his chair and waited for some response. Kate continued to stare at him in silence.

'That was all,' he added.

'I see.'

Whitehouse fidgeted under the young woman's gaze. He sipped the lemonade and noticed how drawn Mrs Niland was looking. It had not been evident to him at first, partly because of the bright sunlight, and partly because of her clever use of cosmetics.

'Well, that's all. Perhaps I had better go.'

'No, wait. I'm sorry. I'm being very rude. I just don't know what to say.' She bit her lip and he realised with some horror that she was close to tears. He prayed she would not break down in front of him. What would he do?

'I'm very sorry about your father,' Whitehouse heard himself say, to cover the long silence. 'I have known him for many years. He was a fine man.'

Kate smiled at that. 'He was a rogue, Mister Whitehouse. We all knew that. But he was my father and I loved him –' Her voice cracked and she broke off. Whitehouse looked away and sipped at the lemonade. Ghastly stuff. Too sweet. He wished it was something stronger.

'What am I to do, Mister Whitehouse? What am I to believe?'

'As his lawyer, I am bound to say only one thing.'

'And when you are not being his lawyer?'

'I am always a lawyer,' Whitehouse said.

Kate stood and looked out over the garden. 'No doubt you have heard the talk about me.'

Whitehouse felt himself flush crimson. Really, this wasn't proper. 'This is a small town. One hears things over the years,' he said. 'One pays no attention.'

Kate gave a tight, bitter smile. 'Well then, let me tell you this. George Niland's wife I may be, but I believe I know Cameron McKenzie better than anyone in this town. I know his capacity for spite and revenge. More than anyone else, I want him to be innocent, but . . .'

'In my mind, there is reasonable doubt.'

'Don't misunderstand me, Mister Whitehouse. I don't for a moment believe that he killed my father in cold blood. What I think . . . is that my father went looking for him on the *Roebuck* and Cameron defended himself a little more energetically than he might have done. That is what I believe. At the same time I have no desire . . . to . . . to see him hang. I just hope I never have to see him again. He has turned my life into . . . a nightmare.'

Whitehouse picked up his hat from the table beside him. It had been a mistake to come here. The poor woman had been through enough. 'I really do apologise for troubling you.' He rose to leave. 'I'll go out this way if you don't mind,' he said, and went down the back steps.

He paused in the garden and looked up at her. She seemed so fragile just then, like a china doll. Not at all like the spirited young girl who had once thrown her father's clothes on the street.

'Shall I convey any message?'

Kate shook her head. 'No,' she said, 'no message.'

32

Sergeant Clarke rapped on the cell door. 'Cameron, it's Mister Whitehouse.'

Cameron jumped to his feet. He peered through the barred window in the cell door. The top of Whitehouse's head barely reached the bars.

'Have you been to see her?' Cameron said.

'I did as you asked.'

'Will you not come in and tell me what she said?'

'There's nothing to tell.'

'What did she say?'

'Nothing, Mister McKenzie. Nothing at all.'

Cameron turned away and slumped down on the edge of his bunk. He put his head in his hands.

'Jesus Christ,' he muttered, knowing he was damned.

✦   ✦   ✦

The window of George Niland's office overlooked the sullen mangroves and endless grey of Dampier Creek. Niland always sat with his back to the window so visitors had to squint against the glare of the sunlight to look at him. It immediately put him at an advantage.

Huey Fong had a dull, depressing headache and his mouth was gummy and dry, the result of too much arrack the night before. The light hurt his eyes. He wiped the sweat off his face with his hand.

George leaned back in his chair. 'You wanted to see me?'

'It's about that white boss. Flynn.'

'Really. What about him?'

'I know who do for him.'

George got up and locked the door. Huey Fong stared at the floor.

'The police seem to think McKenzie murdered him,' George said.

'No, boss. Not him.'

'Who then?'

'Simeon Espada.'

George sat down again. 'How do you know this?'

'He drunk too much arrack last night. He told me.'

'Did he tell you why?'

'Something about a pearl.'

'He was trying to sell Flynn a snide?'

Huey shrugged. 'That's what he said.'

George tugged at his moustache. So McKenzie had been

telling the truth after all. Not that it mattered, for there wasn't a soul in Broome who believed him. But now this chink could ruin everything.

'Has your friend told anyone else about this?'

'Don't know, boss.'

'You're absolutely sure he's telling the truth?'

'Why would he say he done it if he didn't? Have to be something wrong in his head, right?'

'So why did he tell you?'

'Like I said, boss, he was drunk. Maybe he doan feel too good about this now.'

'Flynn won't be missed.'

'Not him. That McKenzie save his life on the *Roebuck*. When that whale broke his lines.'

George thought about this. Fong was a shifty little blighter, one of those chinks that could never look you in the eye. But he didn't think he was making this up, it was too unlikely. 'Why didn't you go to the police, Fong?'

'Police doan pay so good,' he said and grinned.

George reached into the drawer for his cheque book. He laid it on the desk in front of him. 'I need a number one diver on the *Ilsa* this season, Fong. I'm sure I can offer you more than Lacey ever paid you.' He tore out a cheque and handed it to the Manilaman. 'Here's your advance plus a bonus for your loyalty.'

Huey bobbed his head appreciatively.

'You can hire your own crew,' George told him. 'Just make sure one of them is your friend Espada.'

'Doctors say he can't dive no more, boss.'

'He'll dive. If you offer him enough.'

Huey reached for the cheque but George slapped his

hand down on it before he could pick it up. 'Make sure Espada doesn't come back and I'll double your bonus.'

Huey looked up into George Niland's eyes. George could read the question there but he had no intention of explaining himself to this dirty little chow. His money was every answer he needed.

'Do you understand?'

Huey nodded. 'Dangerous business, diving for pearl.'

He picked up the cheque and went out.

✦　✦　✦

Wes looked around the tiny cell and shook his head. 'Bin hyar mebbe thousand time. You?'

'It's my first time, Wes.'

'Coppers, dey put me in hyar for drinkin' and carryin' on, and dat one time for puttin' dat Mary in de fambly way. So dey says. Coulden prove nuttin'. It was twins anyway. None of my women has twins. Never has done befo'.'

He eased onto the cot beside Cameron, resting his massive hands on his knees. 'So what they goin' to do wid you, skip?'

'They intend to hang me, Wes.'

Wes blew out his cheeks. 'You? No, dey doan wanna hang you, skip. Dat crazy.'

'I don't think we'll ever go pearling together again, Wes.'

Wes shook his head. 'Ain't right.'

'You'd better find yourself another lugger, Wes.'

'Mebbe I get on board dat *Ilsa*, I reckon.'

'Who's sailing her?'

'Huey Fong.'

'Fong? Be careful. Don't trust him. They say he once cut a diver's line when the *Donna* was caught in a storm.'

'De money's good.'

'Just be careful, man.'

Wes looked at Cameron. 'Yo' a good man, skip. Ain't right.'

He seemed about to say something else and changed his mind. He got up and stood there, shuffling his feet.

'Spit it out, Wes.'

'Ain't nothin',' Wes said finally. He banged on the door. When Sergeant Clarke opened it, Wes glared down at him, hands on his hips. 'Ain't right,' he repeated.

Clarke shrugged his shoulders. 'I don't make the law.'

Cameron shook his head. 'He's right, Wes. It's not his fault.'

Wes shrugged and brushed past the policeman. 'Bye, skip.'

'Goodbye, Wes.'

The door slammed shut behind him.

33

Chinatown was quiet. It was midday, siesta time. For nine months every year, between April and December, Broome slept. It was only when the crews came in for lay-up that the town came alive. Tomorrow the *Ilsa* and the rest of the Niland fleet would also set sail, heading south for the Condon Banks.

Huey Fong had taken Niland's money but he had no intention of killing Simeon Espada himself. If the opportunity presented itself, he would take it, of course; if a storm blew up while Simeon was underwater, or if his line snagged on a coral, or . . . well, there were a thousand fates waiting for any diver. As master of the *Ilsa,* he might well hold Simeon's life in his hands at some stage.

But he would not put a noose around his own neck for George Niland. Simeon still had friends and relatives among the crews on the other boats; the white boss's money was no good to him if he ended up with a knife in his ribs. There was a better way.

He wandered through the clutter and singsong chatter of Sheba Lane to Tanaka's store. A squat Japanese in a snow white singlet and shorts was bending to pick up a bundle of silks from the shop front.

Hanaguchi's pug features were now hideously disfigured. A broad scar ran across his nose and down his cheek and the skin over one eye was smeared pink, like melted wax.

'What you want here?' Hanaguchi growled at him. His voice sounded like the honking of a goose. The Koepangers and the Malays – even the Aborigines – laughed at him behind his back now.

'I wanted to see you.'

'What about?'

'You want to get even with Simeon Espada?'

Hanaguchi hawked the phlegm from the back of his throat and spat in the gutter. 'More better you come inside. We talk then.'

Huey waited in the little office at the back of the store while Hanaguchi closed up the shop. A few minutes later he pushed the beaded curtain aside and sat down.

Holy Mother, Simeon had done a job on him, Huey thought, staring at the livid pink scar on the other man's face. 'You don't dive no more?'

Hanaguchi leaned forward so that the terrible face was inches from Huey Fong's. 'Your friend do this to me. Smash

216

nose, smash cheeks, all smash up inside. Doctor say me –
you finish. But I try, just one. One fathom and head feel like
it will burst open, like melon. So no more dive. Have to
work here in shop.'

'You want to get even?' Huey whispered.

Hanaguchi's eyes narrowed. 'Why you come here,
Manilaman?'

'Got my reason.'

'You his friend, right?'

Huey shrugged. 'Maybe. Maybe not. Up to you,
Japanese. You want to see him pay for what he do to your
face, your whole life?'

'How?'

'I am number one diver on *Ilsa* now. Simeon is number
two. I need crew.'

'Crew?' Hanaguchi said contemptuously.

'Anything can happen at sea. Up to you.'

Hanaguchi thought about this. 'What crew?'

'Cook-boy.'

Hanaguchi jumped to his feet. 'Cook-boy? You want me
be cook-boy?' A fleck of spittle hung from his bottom lip.

'Well cannot be his tender,' he went on, trying to be
reasonable. He got to his feet. 'Like I say, up to you,
Japanese.'

He turned to go. A bluff, because he was desperate, but
it worked. Hanaguchi grabbed him by the arm. Huey
watched the play of emotions on the other man's face.

'How?' Hanaguchi said at last.

'I'll tell you how. At sea.'

'Must be slow.'

'Slow, quick, I doan care.'

'Cook-boy?'

'*Ilsa* sail first light.'

Hanaguchi looked like a man who had just tasted poison. 'I be number one diver this season, if not for Manilaman.'

'We can watch him die together,' Huey promised. He went out into the bright March sunshine. The money was as good as in his pocket.

34

The red mud was bare. Not enough time had passed to even lay the headstone. This afternoon it would rain again, lightning flickering over the ocean behind slate grey clouds. One of the last storms of the season was moving in, for the Wet would be over soon, the fleets would head back to sea, leaving the town silent again, leaving Kate to her grief.

'You're hurting me,' Jamie whined.

'Sorry, Jamie,' she murmured, bringing herself back to the present and relaxing her grip on his hand.

So Cameron had done it in the end, that famous temper of his had got the better of him. His temper, and his taste for revenge.

'Is Granpa down there?' Jamie asked.

'Yes, darling, he is.'

'Doesn't it hurt?'

'He can't feel pain anymore, darling. I told you, his spirit's gone to heaven with the angels.'

The last place she would have expected to find her father. No doubt it was straight to the hot place for the likes of Flynn. He'd be welcome there and much more at home, playing billiards with the devil and finding some way to cheat money from him.

'How can he be here and in heaven?' Jamie asked.

'He just is,' Kate said impatiently.

She could not believe what Cameron had done. How could she ever have trusted a man like that? Her heart had turned to stone, just coldness inside now; it was only ever Jamie who made her feel alive. Damn Cameron McKenzie, damn all men to hell.

'So what bit of Grandad is down there?' Jamie said.

'His body's there, Jamie, his soul's in heaven.'

'What's your soul?'

Ah, her son would ask a question like that. And how to answer him? What should I tell him, and what should I tell myself? What she had felt for Cameron, what she now felt for Jamie, something that could not be touched or seen or even explained, well she supposed that was the soul.

'It's the part of you that doesn't grow old and that never ever dies,' she said.

Jamie frowned at her. He had a logical mind, like George, and besides, he was only six years old. How could he understand what a soul was? Some of us, she thought, live our whole lives and never learn. Some, like George and like Flynn, never even think about it.

But Cameron had been part of her soul; which was why his betrayal and this, this unspeakable act, had murdered her very spirit. When it was her turn to die, they would put her in the ground here next to her father, but at this moment it felt as though there would be nothing left in this heavy ochre mud to either rise to heaven or descend to hell.

35

The luggers raced for Entrance Point, vying with each other for the honour of leading out the fleet. Simeon stood at the stern on the *Ilsa* and watched as the white bungalows of Broome disappeared out of sight behind the mangroves.

He wondered even now if he had made the right decision. He had been on the point of surrendering himself to Sergeant Clarke but Huey Fong had persuaded him out of it.

'You crazy! They won't hang a white boss! Putting your head in a noose for nothing!'

What if Huey was wrong? How could he let McKenzie die? He owed him his life; it was enough to have one man's death on his conscience, he would have not a moment's peace for the rest of his life if he let McKenzie pay for something he had done.

That pearl, it had brought him nothing but despair. Why did Flynn have to die? Anna! She had torn his heart out and now he had Flynn's ghost dogging his every footstep. At the thought of her his fingers tightened around the rigging. He would like to choke the life out of her, as she had choked the life out of him.

You're not white. Don't be so stupid. I could never marry you.

He made up his mind. He should confess everything. His life was not his anyway; it belonged to the white boss, McKenzie. He would tell everyone how it was all an accident, how he had done it all for Anna. When they hanged him, she would be sorry then.

He heard the clatter of pans and put his head into the cramped and stinking galley. Hanaguchi was busy with his pots and bowls. 'So at last you find a job you are good at!'

Hanaguchi didn't answer. Ayeee, it was hot in here! He wiped away the sweat from his face with the back of his arm and lit the little mangrove-wood stove. He ignored the Manilaman *kichibu.*

'Too scared to dive no more?' Simeon persisted.

Hanaguchi eyed a bone-handled knife on the galley bench. How he would have liked to stick it in the Manilaman's guts. 'Cannot dive no more.'

'You talk like a duck.'

Hanaguchi bobbed his head, like a good cook-boy. 'Yes, boss,' he said.

Simeon was disappointed. He had hoped the little Japanese would give him an excuse to throw him into the water, as Hanaguchi's friends had done to the Koepanger last season. Perhaps it would lighten the black mood he was in. But it looked like the beating he had given him had made the Japanese a little simple.

When he had gone Hanaguchi picked up the knife and plunged it into the timber bulwark. He did not know if he could wait a few more days for the Manilaman to die.

+ + +

Rosie looked out of the window from her room at the Continental Hotel towards the shanties of Chinatown. She put a hand on her belly.

She had been to the courthouse every day, knew Cameron was doomed unless someone stood up for him. He could not have done what they accused him of; she knew at least that much of him. If he said he was innocent, that was enough for her.

She knew he did not love her. The truth was in his eyes. She had no illusions of that. But he was a good man, even if that spoiled bitch Kate Niland could not see it, and she would not let him die.

36

'Can you tell the court your name, please?'
'Rosemary Kathleen Thompson.'

Barrington adjusted his gown. 'Your occupation?'

'. . . Barmaid, sir.'

Barrington wrinkled his nostrils as if he could smell the stale hops. 'And where do you reside, Miss Thompson?'

'At the Conti – at the Continental Hotel.'

'At the Continental Hotel.' Barrington organised his notes on the table in front of him. 'At the hotel,' he repeated, giving her a chill smile. 'Now then, Miss Thompson, you say in your statement that you were with the defendant, Mister McKenzie, on the night of the third of January.'

'That's right, sir.'

'But the murder did not take place until the next night. The fourth.'

Rosie looked flustered. She looked up at the magistrate. 'Well, whatever night it was Mister Flynn was murdered, sir. I don't remember the date exactly.'

'You don't remember when you were there.'

'I don't remember the date. But it was the night poor Mister Flynn was murdered.'

Whitehouse got to his feet. 'I object, Your Honour. In her statement the witness has clearly stated she was with the defendant on the night of the murder. My learned friend is badgering the witness.'

'Sustained.'

Barrington bowed to the magistrate. 'My apologies to the court.' But he had achieved what he had set out to do.

'What were you doing on the *Roebuck*, Miss Thompson?'

Rosie looked at her hands. 'I have already explained that to the court, sir.'

Barrington shuffled his papers again, as if he was checking his notes on Whitehouse's examination of the witness. 'Ah yes, I'm sorry. You stated you were on intimate terms with the accused.' He paused to look at the jury. 'How many men are you on intimate terms with, Miss Thompson?'

A murmur spread around the court. Whitehouse jumped to his feet. 'I object, Your Honour.'

The magistrate peered at Barrington over his spectacles as if he was trying to see through a thick fog. 'Mister Barrington?'

'I intend to establish, Your Honour, that the witness is unreliable.'

'The girl's morals have no bearing on this case!' Whitehouse shouted.

The magistrate made a careful note. 'Proceed with caution, Mister Barrington.'

Whitehouse glared at Barrington, then slumped down into his seat, the chair legs squeaking on the wooden floor.

'Thank you, m'lud,' Barrington said. He returned his attention to the witness. 'Miss Thompson, is it true that you are going to have a baby?'

Rosie looked desperately at Whitehouse.

'Miss Thompson? Are you or are you not with child?'

'Yes.'

It was suddenly very still in the tiny courtroom. Rosie counted the slow revolutions of the brass fan above her head. One-two-three-four . . . she looked at the jury. Two of the men had been to her room above the saloon bar in the Continental.

'Who is the father of this child?'

Rosie did not answer.

'Is it the accused?'

'No,' Rosie said quickly. 'It's not hi –'

'Then who is the father, Miss Thompson?'

She could feel her heart beating in her chest.

'I'm sorry, Miss Thompson, would you like me to repeat the question?'

'I don't know.'

'I beg your pardon? I couldn't hear you.'

'I said, I don't know!' The unspoken 'Damn you!' hung at the end of the sentence.

227

'You don't know . . .' Barrington consulted his notes again, as if confused by some intricate, mathematical puzzle. 'I see.' He pursed his lips. 'Why don't you know, Miss Thompson?'

Oh God, she thought. I've only made things worse for Cam.

'Is it not true that the accused is the father of the child and you would do anything in your power to try and protect him?'

'He's not the father.'

'Then who is, Miss Thompson?'

Rosie looked at Cameron. His knuckles were white around the rail of the dock.

'Miss Thompson, is it not true that you have been working as a prostitute since you came to Broome?'

Rosie nodded her head.

'Please answer yes or no.'

'Yes.'

'You realise that it's illegal to engage in immoral acts for money?'

'. . . Yes.'

Barrington shuffled through his papers again. 'You say you were on intimate terms with the accused, Miss Thompson. Would it be fair to say you were in love with him?'

Rosie looked at Cameron. He shook his head.

'Yes,' she said.

'Could you speak up, please.'

'Yes!'

'May I put it to you that any young woman who is willing to prostitute her body might also be willing to prostitute her testimony for someone she thought she loved?'

Rosie shut her eyes. She realised now the enormity of her error. In trying to save Cam, she had only dug his grave for him.

As she left the dock Cameron looked at the jury. He could read their faces plainly. There was now only one man in Broome who knew he had not killed Patrick Flynn; it was the man he had seen running from Flynn's body that night on the beach.

Rosie walked with as much dignity as she could muster past the silent spectators. The men's eyes were turned away, some in embarrassment, some in private shame. The women stared her down, their eyes blazing with scorn or hate.

Oh Rosie, Cam thought. You deserved better.

37

Morning over the Condon Banks. A wisp of smoke rose from the *Ilsa* and buckets splashed into the pearly water to collect water for the crew's morning baths. The Koepangers and the Malays in their sarongs chattered in singsong voices while they drank their coffee.

Simeon leaned on the rail and smoked a last cigarette before getting into his diving dress. Hanaguchi approached him cautiously, holding a cup of coffee.

'Here, boss.'

Simeon knocked the enamel cup out of his hand. It clattered across the deck and bounced into a pile of unopened shell. 'Take it away!'

Hanaguchi hissed under his breath, wiping the scalding coffee off his hand onto his shorts.

'The food's shit! Your coffee's shit!'

Hanaguchi bowed and backed off. 'Yes, boss.'

The crew watched this exchange, shrugged their shoulders and got back to work. Divers were notoriously bad-tempered when they were working. Most of them had permanent 'rheumatics' – mild but chronic cases of the bends. It gave them terrible cramps in the shoulders and constant headaches that often kept them awake all night. Usually the pain did not subside until they went below again. There was nothing to be done except stay out of the diver's way and get on with the work.

The tenders checked the coils of manila rope of the diver's lifeline and the red rubber hose of his air pipe. Simeon climbed into his diver's dress and sat down on the stool next to the main mast to wait for the lugger to set into its drift. When he had finished his cigarette he crushed it out and threw the remains into the scuppers. He wanted another, badly, but in a moment he would be going over the side.

He had not slept last night but it was not the rheumatics that had kept him awake. The white boss's ghost had visited him again. Even now, when he closed his eyes, he could see him. His face was grey in death and the white bones of his skull glistened among the sticky mass of matted and bloodied hair. Flynn had hovered at the end of his bunk all night.

Soon the ghost would be joined by another, the white boss McKenzie. The previous afternoon Niland's schooner, the *Ada*, had brought them provisions and their 'slop chests'

231

– tobacco and drink. The *Ada* also brought news from Broome – Cameron had been found guilty. He was to be put on board the next steamer south and hanged in Fremantle Gaol.

The white boss had free-dived nearly four fathoms with a rope to save his life. He couldn't let him die.

Wes, naked except for a pair of white cotton shorts, padded across the deck.

'You shiverin'. You got da rheumatics dis mornin'?'

'I'm all right. Where's Huey Fong?'

'He still be in his bunk. Reckon you go down first.'

The breeze had settled into an easterly. The crew hauled on the halyard and the anchor chains rattled and groaned as the *Ilsa* got under way. Simeon ordered the crew to hoist mainsail and jib and the Koepangers started up the air pump. The *Ilsa* began its beat to windward towards the outer edge of the patch of shell they had worked the day before. Already the sun was rising over the red cliffs along Eighty Mile Beach. Simeon lowered himself down the rope ladder. The front of his corselet rested on the rail.

Wes lashed the heavy leads onto Simeon's suit and then screwed on the heavy sea-greened helmet. He checked the line and hose and then went to the bucket of water that was lying in the middle of the deck. He took out the face glass, dried it, and screwed it into position. He tapped on the glass and nodded.

Hanaguchi watched Simeon float for a moment on the glassy surface of the ocean and then sink out of sight in a foam of bubbles. He grinned. Within the next hour – perhaps in just a few minutes, with luck – Simeon would be dead. A horrible death, too. He touched the jagged cicatrice that snaked across his nose and cheek. Yes, a horrible death was only fitting.

He went back into the galley and waited for the first shouts of alarm from the deck that would signal the beginning of his revenge.

✦　✦　✦

Through the narrow bars of his cell Cameron watched the moon rise over the mangroves. It was rust-red, like Kimberley dirt. Blood on the moon, they called it. It rose higher in the sky changing from pink to silver until it hovered over the bay like a fat pearl.

He had encountered death many times, during the Navy diving experiments in the Scottish lochs, on the *Dreadnought* at Jutland, and in the warm green waters of the pearling grounds. But he had never really believed that the sea would conquer him and in the end, he supposed, he had been right.

It wasn't death he feared right now. But he had always thought he would one day set things to rights with Kate; even after he was arrested, he hoped at least to see her once more, to protest his innocence, to say his goodbyes, to try and make his peace. But he had betrayed her trust once, and trust, they said, was like a woman's virtue; you could only lose it once, and then it was gone forever.

He regretted what had happened to poor Rosie, and that he would not be able to repay her for what she had tried to do for him. They were wrong about her, those men in the courtroom who had sat in judgment of her. She may have been by some lights a whore, yet she was also an innocent.

For himself he had lost his innocence when he betrayed Kate Flynn. Now, it seemed, there would be no redemption. Perhaps he did not deserve it, anyway.

And then there was the pearl.

He would die, as he had lived, a poor man. He had vowed since he was a boy that he would make something of his life, that he would rise above the destiny his Maker had carved for him in the slums of Glasgow. It would have taken just one good pearl to change his fate.

A pearl moon poured silver through the bars and he reached out his hand, thinking he might touch it. So far away but so close. He withdrew his hand, empty, but its ghost light still beckoned him, like a promise unkept.

38

Simeon signalled bottom, adjusting his air intake valve to the water pressure, the bubbles rattling through his helmet close by his right ear. The only other sound was the reassuring clack-clack of the air pump ten fathoms above him on the deck of the *Ilsa*.

He was on a weedy plain and the seagrasses bent and swayed with the green tide. He walked slowly forwards, kicking up little puffs of sand with the shiny brass toes of his boots. A coral cliff loomed out of the sea mist ahead of him, dotted with the bright reds and yellows of rubbery sea vegetables.

A turtle flashed past him not ten yards away, its long neck straining, swerving left and right. The lithe grey shape of a tiger shark followed it, snapping at the turtle's fins like a dog chasing a rabbit. Simeon ignored the shark. He had spotted the telltale sheen of nacre from an oyster shell on the cliff and he lumbered towards it.

Suddenly he stopped, alarmed. Something was coming towards him from the shadows underneath the cliff, gliding out from under a ledge. At first he thought it was a large fish, a grouper perhaps. But then he saw silver hair waving dreamily with the movement of the sea and its eyes were luminous in the murky water.

'Flynn,' he murmured, his voice echoing in the cathedral chamber of the copper helmet.

Flynn was smiling and there was blood on his teeth. Simeon knew it was impossible, for the blood would dissipate in the water, but somehow it was there, oozing down his face. He was dressed in the white linen suit he had worn that night on the beach and he was holding a large handkerchief.

He wanted to signal Wes on the lifeline: *Haul up, quick!* But then his reason returned. *Don't panic, it's just your imagination. Close your eyes and it will disappear!* Simeon knew the effects that water pressure had on the mind. Hadn't he seen a score of other divers, Malays and Manilamen like himself, come up from the deeps wide-eyed and babbling about sea ghosts and green-eyed monsters?

But when he opened his eyes again Flynn was still there, floating in front of him. He stopped and unfolded his handkerchief. Flynn took out the object he had concealed there and held it up, dangling from his left hand. A noose. It was impossible, of course, but he heard Flynn say: 'Here is your payment for the pearl, my boy!'

Simeon clenched his eyes shut. *Just a phantom. It isn't real.*

When he opened his eyes again, Flynn was gone. He had been replaced by something far worse. It was the tiger shark, the pattern of bars on its flanks clearly visible. It swam slowly towards him, its short, blunt snout thrust out like a dog sniffing at raw meat. The sickle mouth revealed rows of razor-sharp cockscomb teeth.

Simeon was shaken from his torpor. He held out his arm towards the shark and pulled back the cuff at his wrist, letting loose a stream of bubbles. He had done it countless times to over-inquisitive fish. Sharks were cowards at heart, and the tactic had never failed to scare them off before.

The tiger twisted away through the water. But then, to his horror, it came back and started circling again, edging closer. He loosed another stream of bubbles at it.

The shark turned away but in a moment it was back once more, still curious. Simeon knew the shark would not attack him straight away; it would be wary of his menacing shape and the mysterious jets of bubbles. But it would take just one tear from its jagged teeth to his suit and the water would rush in, and he would drown in moments. He had to get to the surface.

Simeon bent down and scrambled in the sand, his hand closing gratefully around a large stone. Then he gripped the lifeline with all his strength and gave the signal: *Haul up until your backs break!*

He looked round once more for the tiger and was deafened by his own screams. The shark's hinge-like jaws gaped opened and he could make out the blood-red gills beyond them.

237

The shark's teeth snapped shut on the copper helmet. Mother of God! It was as if he had been trapped inside a cathedral bell and someone had struck it with a sledge-hammer. He felt as if his eardrums had been pierced with red hot needles. Mother of God! He could not think of anything now but to get out of the water. The shark was from the devil.

Wes and the crew had started to haul on the line. He looked up. Twenty fathoms. The copper hull of the *Ilsa* seemed so far away, it might as well have been the moon. He opened the air valve on his helmet wide. The air rushing into his suit would help speed him to the surface.

As he was jerked up through the water the big fish began to follow. He felt warm piss streaming down his leg inside his suit. He wasn't going to make it!

The shark nosed forward again. Simeon kicked at it in desperation, his heavy lead boot connecting with its sensitive nose. It wheeled away, furious and confused; for a moment Simeon thought it had gone. He jerked his head around inside the helmet, searching the murky green water.

He saw it coming at him again, a dark shadow, just out of his vision, behind him and to his left. He looked up. Another couple of yards. So close! *Pull harder, damn you, pull harder!*

The shark flashed towards him. Simeon released the heavy stone he had been holding in his right hand. The tiger shark instinctively swerved away and gobbled it up.

Then Simeon's head was out of the water and even through the helmet he could hear the shouts of the crew as they tried to scare the monster away, slapping at the water and the side of the hull with their coffee tins and gaffs.

The sea reluctantly gave Simeon up, his boots streaming seawater. He was safe.

Suddenly the tiger rose out of the sea, its jaw agape. Its teeth clashed shut like a steel trap and Simeon thought he had lost his legs. He screamed and blacked out.

The shark bit the toe of Simeon's lead boot clean off, and disappeared into the depths.

✦　✦　✦

Junzo brought two plates of bacon and eggs from the kitchen and put one on the table in front of George. Kate held up her hand and shook her head.

'Missy not hungry?'

'No, thank you, Junzo. Please take it away.' Junzo nodded and retreated to the kitchen.

'Are you all right, my dear?'

'Yes, thank you, George. I'm just not hungry, that's all.'

'You've hardly touched your food lately. Perhaps you should see Doctor Halloran.'

'It's the heat.'

'You're looking quite thin.'

Kate threw her napkin on the table. 'For goodness sake, stop fussing over me!'

George frowned. He didn't like Jamie to witness such scenes at the table. 'Have you finished your porridge?' he said to the boy.

Jamie pushed his empty bowl away. 'Can I have some bacon and eggs?'

'Not this morning. Go outside and play.'

'But I'm still hungry.' Jamie turned to his mother for

support against this injustice. 'I want some bacon and eggs. I'm starving.'

'Go and play,' George repeated.

'When I'm dead of starvation you'll be sorry,' Jamie muttered. He ran out of the house, slamming the screen door.

George sighed. 'That boy is unmanageable.'

'He's a normal little boy.'

'He has far too much to say for himself.' George wiped his mouth with a linen napkin and put down his knife and fork. 'Will you please tell me what's the matter?'

'I don't want to discuss it.'

'It's this business about McKenzie, isn't it?'

'What do you expect of me? I loved that man.'

George clenched his fists in his lap. Dear God, if only from common decency she might at least keep such thoughts to herself.

'Ever since the verdict you have been walking around like the price of shell has doubled overnight,' said Kate. 'Don't expect me to share your triumph.'

'I did what I could for him.'

'I'm sure he's very grateful for that.'

Her mocking tone enraged him. He reached across the table and caught her wrist. She tried to pull away but his strength surprised her. 'What do you want from me? I've given you everything! I made you a queen after he left you in the gutter! Is this how you repay me?'

'Let me go, George.'

'You vilify me and castigate me for every little fault and you refuse me my conjugal rights –'

Kate jumped to her feet but still he held her.

'Well?'

She had never seen him like this before. He had always been so aloof, so dispassionate about things. Now, as she looked into the soft grey-flecked eyes, she found that she could not hate him, not really. If she hated anyone, it was herself.

'I'm sorry.'

'Sorry?'

'I should not have married you. It was selfish, and it was a mistake.'

He let her go. His anger evaporated as quickly as it had come.

He checked his gold fob watch and stood up. 'I must go. I'll be late for the office. Junzo!'

He went into his study to get his briefcase. 'Junzo!' he called again, and swept towards the door. He kissed her on the forehead. 'I'll see you at lunch,' he said.

He went down the veranda steps to the Buick. Junzo was already stooped in front of the motor, turning the crank handle. George glanced up at the veranda and saw Jamie pushing an empty yolk-stained plate back through the kitchen window to Liddy.

They were all set on defying him, it seemed. Well, he might stop by the gaol on the way to the office and say goodbye to McKenzie. It would lift his spirits.

✦ ✦ ✦

For two hours Simeon lay on his bunk and sobbed like a baby. He had lost a lead boot to the shark; but there was not a mark on him. The shark continued to dog the *Ilsa*, its

241

dark body arrowing through the crystal blue water off the stern. There would be no more diving that day.

Wes got a cup of steaming black coffee from the galley and went down the scuttle. Simeon was curled up on his side, his knees tucked into his chest. Wes held out the coffee.

Simeon's eyes flickered. 'Mister Flynn?' he whispered.

Wes frowned. 'It's me, Wes.'

'Wes?'

'Dat shark plenty humbug, hey? Here, you drink dis, feel better.'

Simeon shook his head. 'That was no shark. That was Flynn. Never going to let me rest, I reckon.'

'What yo' talkin' 'bout? Jay-sus!'

'I saw him, Wes. That shark's got Flynn in him.'

'Mebbe you bin dive too long, boy.'

'He came straight for me. Like no shark I ever saw before.'

Wes put the coffee down and leaned in close. 'You check yo' suit befo' you dive, huh?'

Simeon shook his head.

'Dere was stains on yo' suit. Look like blood to me.'

'Flynn?'

'Will you shuddup 'bout dat Flynn? I'm tellin' you dey was bloodstains, true. Mebbe somebody puts dat turtle blood on yo' suit.'

Turtle blood! Just a drop in the water would turn a shark crazy. The previous afternoon, the crew had seen a turtle in the water. Three of the Koepangers had jumped over the side and captured it with ropes and knives. They had cooked it and eaten it for supper.

'Hanaguchi!' Simeon whispered.

'Mebbe.'

'I'll kill him!'

Wes grabbed him by the shoulders and pinned him to the bunk. 'You want kill 'im, dat yo' business. But not while you is on dis boat. Dere four mo' Japs on dis hyar crew, we doan want no war.'

'I'll kill him,' Simeon repeated.

'Mebbe you better, boy. Looks like he ain't ever goin' to let you be for messin' up his face. Till then, mebbe you better stay crazy. I tell dat Huey Fong better we go back to Broome. Hokkay?'

Simeon nodded. The big man was right. 'Okay,' he said.

◆　◆　◆

Huey crouched over the doorway of the galley, whispering to Hanaguchi. 'Wes saw the bloodstains on the suit!'

'What prove?'

'Have to find some other way! Maybe Simeon won't go down no more.'

'You help me.'

Huey looked around to make sure none of the crew was eavesdropping, but they were all too busy watching the shark, which had reappeared off the port side. 'Your fight, Japanese. Nothing to do with me.'

Hanaguchi picked up the bone-handled knife, the one he had used to cut up the turtle the night before. He held it under Huey's nose. 'You help! Or maybe you next!'

'Maybe I tow you behind the boat like your friends did to that Koepanger!'

'You not dare!'

Huey knew he was right. With four other Japs on board, there would be a mutiny.

'You help me, Manilaman!'

Wes came out of the scuttle and Huey scampered away from the galley. Jay-sus! A feud between Hanaguchi and Espada was one thing. If the skipper was involved, God help them all.

He remembered what Simeon had said about Flynn and he touched the ju-ju on his neck for luck and made the sign against the evil eye.

39

Simeon lay on his bunk, waiting for the dawn. It was deathly silent save for the creaking of cordage and the lap of the waves against the hull. He heard the padding of feet on the deck above as the night watch changed shift. He was drunk with exhaustion but fought against sleep. Whenever he closed his eyes Flynn's ghost was always there.

Huey Fong tossed and turned in his sleep, grinding his teeth. The diver's rheumatics. Simeon had suffered with it often enough himself. Finally he heard Huey roll out of his bunk and slide to the floor. He felt the other man's hot breath on his face.

'Simeon? You awake?'

'What is it?'

'I can't sleep. The pain's terrible.'

'You try cajeput oil?'

'Nothing help. Have to get back in suit and go down. Need you to help me.'

Simeon got up and slipped a sarong about his waist. Huey was in a bad way. He had to support him on his shoulder to the scuttle.

The deck was washed in silver from a three-quarter moon. As Simeon stepped out of the scuttle he sensed a movement behind him. He turned, instinctively raising an arm to protect his head.

The marlin spike crunched down on his forearm, snapping it like a dry stick. He screamed in agony and fell back among the loops of coir rope. Despite the pain he kept rolling. The heavy iron came down again, splintering the decking inches from his head. It stuck fast there.

He called to Huey for help but his so-called friend pulled his shattered arm behind his back. Simeon felt the jagged pieces of bone crunch and bend and almost passed out.

Through the pain he saw Hanaguchi's face above him in the moonlight. Hanaguchi managed to twist the marlin spike free of the decking and hefted it above his head. *Mother of God!* He was going to die.

◆   ◆   ◆

'Cameron, you've got a visitor.'

The door swung open and Sergeant Clarke ushered George Niland into the cell. Cameron lay on his bunk, his hands folded behind his head. 'I don't want to see him, thank you, Sergeant.'

George turned to Clarke. 'We're old friends, Sergeant. I want an opportunity to say goodbye.'

'He wants an opportunity to gloat,' Cameron said. 'Sergeant, I'd be obliged if you both left me in peace.'

'I understand you're bitter. But I did everything I could. You only have yourself to blame.'

'Get him out of here, Sergeant.'

Clarke hesitated. He touched George on the shoulder. 'If you wouldn't mind, sir.'

'My wife said to say goodbye also.'

Cameron leaped to his feet and lunged at him. Clarke stepped in and shoved Cameron back onto his bunk then bundled George quickly out of the door.

For just a moment, Cameron caught a glimpse of George through the cell door, standing behind Clarke. He was grinning.

'Bastard!' Cameron shouted and settled down to wait for his last, long day in Broome to end.

✦　✦　✦

Simeon pitched face forwards onto the deck. He put out his one good arm to break his fall, his head hitting the port bulwark, stunning him. He heard a bellow of rage and saw an enormous shadow throw Huey Fong head first into the scuppers.

Wes!

The Japanese still had the marlin spike. He backed away, in a fighting crouch. Then he raised it over his head and swung it at the big West Indian.

Simeon launched himself across the deck. He hit the

Japanese in the chest with his shoulder, knocking him off balance. He heard the heavy iron thud onto the deck, then he and Hanaguchi hit the starboard bulwark and toppled over the side into the water.

Simeon surfaced, choking. He flailed out with his right arm, trying to reach the *Ilsa*. His left arm hung useless in the water, like a dead weight.

He felt Hanaguchi's hands at his throat, choking him, pushing his head under the water. He fought desperately, but Hanaguchi held him fast from behind, and he had two good arms to fight with.

His chest was bursting. Water rushed into his mouth and his whole body writhed and contorted as he started to choke. He made one last feeble attempt to resist but then there was a buzzing in his ears and the world turned black. The bursting agony in his lungs receded and he saw the white boss Flynn's bloodied, grinning teeth, the black wound yawning at the back of his skull.

It was death coming.

✦   ✦   ✦

Next thing he knew, something hammered into him and threw him out of the water. He gasped at the air, water burning out of his nose and mouth. The copper-bottomed hull of the *Ilsa* was just a few feet away but he had no strength left. He started to sink under the water once more.

A huge hand closed around his and pulled him towards the ladder on the *Ilsa*. Other hands reached for him, dragging him aboard. He tried to scream as someone pulled on his shattered arm but no sound came, just a terrible gurgling that bubbled in his throat as he retched up the seawater in his stomach.

He lay on the deck like a beached fish, choking, his body racked with convulsions. He felt someone sit on his back, trying to pump the water out of his chest. He just wanted to die now. Why wouldn't Flynn let him die?

✦　✦　✦

Wes pushed again on Simeon's back and the Manilaman vomited up what looked like a pint of seawater and then took a long, shuddering gasp of air.

Wes went to the port gunwale. The crew were staring at the thing floating on the sea in the moonlight. It looked like a human limb, or part of one. Then something broke the surface and there was a snuffling sound, like a pig at a trough, and whatever had been floating there was gone.

'Shark,' one of the Koepangers muttered, and made the sign to ward off the evil eye.

'Flynn,' Simeon gasped, and then he passed out.

40

Huey Fong had split open his forehead on the capstan. He lay unconscious on his bunk, blood oozing from under a thick bandage. Wes was skipper of the *Ilsa* now. With the cook dead, their number two diver half crazy and crippled and the master badly injured, there was nothing to do but head back to port. The superstitious Malays and the four Japanese wanted to be off the lugger as soon as possible. The ship was possessed by bad spirits. Wes doubted if anyone could be persuaded to sail on her again.

Huey opened his eyes. He rolled onto his side and Wes held a bucket under his chin while he vomited.

'I ought to kill you now,' Simeon said to him.

Wes pushed him away. 'Mebbe, but you ain't.'

Huey groaned and looked at Wes. 'Where's the Japanese?'

'He be dead, boy.'

Huey shrugged. Well, thank God. One less knife in the back to worry about. 'He was crazy.'

'You tried to kill me,' Simeon said.

'What you talking about?'

Simeon grabbed him with his right arm; his left was strapped into a sling. Wes pushed him back.

Madre de Dios! Huey thought. Well, he wasn't going to be the white boss's scapegoat. Best try and get out of this any way he could.

'I'll tell you if you swear you won't come after me,' he said to Simeon.

Simeon hesitated. 'I swear.'

'On your mother's life?'

'On my mother's life.' Why not? She was dead anyway.

'That big white boss, Niland. He paid me.'

Simeon stared at him, bewildered. 'Why?'

'How I know why? He just tell me he don't want you to come back.'

Wes turned to the Manilaman. 'What's da big white boss want wid you, boy?'

'I don't know. He's lying.'

'It's true!'

Simeon drew his knife. 'Let me cut him up a little.'

Wes caught his wrist and squeezed. Simeon yelped and the knife dropped to the deck. 'Mebbe better you go topside,' Wes told him. 'There be 'nuff damn trouble, hokkay?'

Simeon's face was twisted with hate. Wes watched him

251

warily. The young Manilaman was like a wounded shark, unpredictable and dangerous. The broken arm could not be set properly until they reached Broome and the pain was making him crazy.

Wes gave him a push. 'Topside,' he repeated.

Simeon spat on the deck and disappeared up the scuttle.

Wes picked up the knife and stuck it in his belt. 'What 'bout dat Jap cook-boy?'

'He just does it for hate.'

Huey felt the sweat oozing out of him. The one thing he mustn't let Simeon know was that he was the one who took his pearl. If he did, he was dead for sure.

Wes shook his head. 'Dey got a special place in limbo for fellas like you, boy. Dey gonna fry you real slow.'

✦   ✦   ✦

Roebuck Bay shimmered like mother-of-pearl. To the north the gentle green slopes of Gantheaume Point slid beneath the sea. To the south lay Dampier Creek, the skeleton of an abandoned schooner rotting among the mangroves like the bones of some ancient dinosaur. A flight of pelicans wheeled gracefully overhead.

Wes rowed with his back towards the blood-red shore. Simeon sat facing him, his arm in a sling, whispering the story of Patrick Flynn's death.

After he had finished, Wes continued to row, saying nothing, the steady click of the oarlocks and the rippling of the water the only sounds. He did not want to think about death on such a still and beautiful morning.

'I doan know, boy,' Wes said finally. He heaved on the

oars again, the huge chest muscles rippling in time with each stroke. 'I doan know if I loves you or hates you ri' now. You gonna save de skipper, but it was you put his head in de noose.'

'Didn't mean for him to get the blame.'

Wes paused for a moment to lift his right hand from the oar and touch the ju-ju at his neck. 'Well I is glad I not de good God.'

'You do me one favour?'

'Mebbe.'

'Huey Fong. He gotta pay too.'

Wes shook his head. 'I doan know, boy, mebbe I bust his head when I get de chance, but Wes is a lover, not a killer.'

'Do it for me, Wes.'

'You got folk hyar in de town, boy. Let yo' kin do what has to be done.'

They beached the dinghy on the foreshore and Simeon waded into the ankle-deep water. Wes shook his head. Nothing more than a boy. That scared look on his face, like a kid just out of school. Jay-sus! But this was his day to die.

Simeon turned around. 'I'll see you.'

Wes nodded. What was there to say? A man about to sign his own death warrant had no use for good luck. Wes watched him pad bare-foot up the dunes towards the town. Simeon stopped once to stare down at the Lacey camp, hoping for a last glimpse of Anna. Then he disappeared over the rise and went to look for Sergeant Clarke.

41

The *Centaur*, with its familiar black hull and blue funnel, was moored at the end of the long jetty. It was just in from Singapore and would be leaving within the hour to catch the tide. The day before it was to be Cameron's death boat. Now he stood on the jetty a free man. After Simeon's confession, the Governor had immediately issued an official pardon.

Cameron searched the crowd for the one face he wanted to see. People were staring at him – he was a celebrity now, of sorts, and people treated him with either deference or suspicion – but he ignored the shouts of congratulation as easily as the cold stares of those still not convinced of his innocence. The crowd – government officials, clerks, pearlers, one of them a member of the jury that had declared him a murderer – parted to let him through.

'Rosie.'

She turned around.

'I heard you were leaving, lass.'

'Cameron.'

He looked at the battered trunk by her feet.

'I can't stay here,' she said. 'I hate this place now.'

They stared at each other, lost for the right things to say.

'I'm sorry. I let you down,' Rose said.

'You didn't let me down.'

'In court . . . I tried . . .'

'I don't understand.'

'Understand?'

'Why I'm placed so highly in your affections. I don't think I deserve it.'

'Cam, I –'

'Stay here with me.'

'What?'

'Stay here, Rosie. Don't run away. Abide here and marry me.'

She stared at him, her mouth open in surprise. She wanted desperately to say yes. But how could he love her? She had been his whore and he had left money by her bed. There could be only one reason for this sudden and unexpected declaration of love; it was gratitude, not desire. She knew he didn't really love her, at least, not the way he had loved the Niland woman.

'I love you, Cam. You know that. But I . . .'

'Then marry me.'

She had to refuse. It was the only right thing for

both of them. Yet if he loved her, only a little, it would be enough . . .

She nodded her head in assent.

He swept her up in his arms. She returned his embrace, all the while hating herself for her weakness. She hoped she wouldn't regret it.

✦ ✦ ✦

Junzo stared at the plates on the table with a look of sullen reproach. They had hardly touched their fish, a filleted barramundi with saffron rice. 'No good, missus?' he said to Kate.

'Thank you, Junzo, it was delicious. I'm just not hungry.'

George nodded, indicating that he should remove the plates.

Junzo busied himself clearing the dinner table. Something wrong here. The missus had been off her food for weeks, now the boss had lost his appetite too. At this rate they wouldn't need a cook much longer. Oh well, all the more for him and Liddy.

George waited until Junzo had left the room. 'You've heard the news?' he said to Kate.

She nodded.

'I would have thought you would be celebrating.'

'Let's not go through all that again.'

George toyed with his moustache. He moved his dessert spoon to the side, then tapped it back into place again. 'It's intolerable that this . . . greaser, whoever it is, should have kept quiet for so long. And I refuse to believe your father traded in snide pearls.'

'Everyone trades in snides, George.'

'I hope you don't include me among their number.'

Kate was too tired to argue.

He drummed on the edge of the table with his fingers. 'Well at least we know what happened.'

'I don't care what happened. My father's dead. Nothing will bring him back.'

'I blame Clarke personally. If he'd done his job –'

There was a commotion at the front door. Kate heard Liddy shouting and then the door banged open. There were heavy footsteps in the passage and then Junzo's voice was added to the affray. The third voice was a man's, deeper, and very angry.

'Cameron,' Kate said.

George went pale. He leaped to his feet and ran into his study. A moment later Cameron appeared in the doorway, Liddy still pulling at his jacket, Junzo trying to block his way.

Kate jumped to her feet. 'It's all right,' she said. 'He may come in.'

Terrified, Liddy fled. Junzo, who remembered Cameron as the white boss who had saved his life the night of the riots, immediately stood back, relieved. He bowed formally to Cameron and returned to the kitchen.

Cameron removed his panama. 'Hello, Kate.'

'What do you want, Cam?'

'I want to see your husband.'

'Why?'

Cameron ignored the question, cocking his head to one side. 'You look thin, lass. I hope you've not been worried on my account.'

At that moment George appeared in the doorway holding a revolver. 'Why, hello, George,' Cameron said.

'Get out of here.'

'Would you really shoot me now, George?'

'Get out.'

'It's all right, I don't intend to stay long. I just wanted you to know that I found out about you and Huey Fong. I cannot prove it, but one of my old crewmen told me the whole story.' He leaned forward, the muzzle of the revolver almost touching his chest. 'I just want you to know.'

The gun trembled in George's hand and for one dreadful moment Kate imagined she saw George's finger tighten around the trigger. But then Cameron turned away and strode out, the front door slamming behind him.

Kate ran after him. 'More revenge, Cam?' she called from the veranda.

He stopped on the path and looked back at her. 'With good reason.'

'There's always a reason, isn't there? Is there room enough in this world for all your vengeance and ambition?'

'Why did you not come to the gaol?' he whispered.

She didn't answer him. He walked away, the shell grit crunching under his boots.

✦   ✦   ✦

Laughter from the pearlers' bungalows echoed across the foreshore and a fish broke the surface of the water with a plop! somewhere out in the bay. The white finger of the Ghost Light, the beacon on Buccaneer Rock, searched the dark sea for unwary captains.

Huey Fong made his way through the shadowy dunes to the camps. He had quit Niland's fleet after the *Ilsa* and gone back to work for Lacey. One more good season and he would return to Manila, or maybe move on to Darwin and get a job on a lugger working the Arafura Sea. He had heard the pearls were not as plentiful but the shell was better. Not as much chance of a knife in the ribs either.

He jumped down on the sand and headed towards the cluster of shacks, where another dark-skinned Adonis was strumming a guitar. The sound of the plaintive chords made him think of Simeon. Poor Simeon. Put his head in a noose for some white boss. What a fool.

He stumbled. Too much arrack again. Well, why not? Tomorrow he would be back out on the pearling grounds and it would be a long time before the next big drunk. He would be glad when he was finished with this life.

He saw someone else weaving down the dunes towards him. He laughed. 'Too much arrack, huh?'

The man – a big man, too, as wide as he was tall – weaved again and bumped into him, knocking them both into the sand. Huey thought that was funny. He stopped laughing when a fat hand locked his throat in a vice.

He clawed at the hand clamped around his neck. What was happening? The man had him from behind, there was nothing he could do to break his grip.

He groped for the knife on his belt, but his attacker had anticipated him, and strong fingers closed around his wrist, twisting, until he lost all the feeling in his arm and he heard the blade that might have saved him drop onto the sand.

He struggled desperately, but the other man was too strong. And then he realised this was Simeon's revenge. He was waiting for him on the other side of the darkness, a rope dangling from his neck.

He did not hear the crack of his spine that signalled it was over. He was already unconscious when his attacker gave his neck the final twist that ended the struggle.

Nosiro Tanaka got slowly to his feet. This Chinese cockroach had been tougher than he thought. He brushed the beach sand from his clean linen suit and scrambled back up the dunes to Dampier Terrace. It was distasteful work, but it had to be done. His nephew had been avenged. He had never believed that story about the shark.

Hanaguchi's spirit could rest now. All debts had been paid.

42

Lacepede Islands, Broome, 1926

Cameron lay on his bunk and gritted his teeth against the pain of the rheumatics. He knew it better as caisson disease, the medical name they had given it in the Navy. It was called that after the illness that had afflicted men working in 'caissons', the watertight chambers used for excavating underwater during bridge construction. With the advent of the diving suit in the late nineteenth century, more and more divers had fallen victim. Then some boffin had discovered that the body absorbed more nitrogen at depth than it did on the surface, and that if a diver came up too quickly the gas did not have time to escape. It bubbled in the bloodstream like soda water, causing agonising pains in the joints, making elbows and knees spasm and bend – hence the diver's name for it: the bends.

The pain usually started in the shoulders, and was often followed by blinding headaches and chest pains. For Cameron it was like having a toothache in his whole body. It was not just the piercing agony of the attack, but the fear of how much worse the pain might get.

It started when he was in his bunk at night. The only real relief was to climb back into his wet diving suit and go below again. But he almost always preferred the pain to the darkness under the sea. If he could only hang on until the morning . . .

Wes rolled him a cigarette and handed it to him as he sat on the edge of his bunk, sweating and shivering. The pain in his shoulders was so bad he could hardly hold the cigarette to his lips. Wes splashed cajeput oil on Cameron's shoulders and started to rub it in, kneading the joints with his powerful hands.

'Mebbe time you give up,' Wes growled.

'I can barely afford to keep my ship at sea as it is, Wes, never mind the cost of another diver.'

'You doan pay nobody nuthin' if you is dead.'

'Spare me the homespun philosophy, you big bastard. Just try and get rid of this ache!'

Wes splashed on more of the oil. 'Man's a fool if he doan know when to quit.' He worked his fingers deeper into the joints and Cameron gasped with pain.

'Jesus!' Cameron groaned again. 'How long till morning?'

'Hour, mebbe. You hold on, skip?'

'Aye, I'll hold on, Wes.' He stared out of the porthole hoping for the first lemon stain of dawn over the sea, when he could get back into his suit and dive again, end this terrible pulsing pain.

♦   ♦   ♦

It seemed to Kate that they hardly ever dined alone anymore. Every night there were new guests to entertain; pearl buyers, bankers, accountants and office managers, George's acquaintances with their wives. One night George invited a man named Brierley back for dinner, to discuss the agency for the new airline link to Perth. He had with him a serious, silent man named Charles Kingford-Smith.

This particular night there were three guests. Dalziel, the manager of the Commercial Union Bank which had just opened a branch in Broome, ramrod-tall with a loud, braying laugh and ugly misshapen teeth. He smoked incessantly and his sole topic of conversation was banking. His wife was a curious woman, prematurely grey, with the sour expression of one who had just bitten down on a lemon. She rarely spoke.

The third guest was a Dutch pearler and buyer, Conrad van Heusen. He was a young man, perhaps just a couple of years younger than Kate herself, with very blond hair and a cowlick that defied his persistent attempts to brush it back into place. It hinted at a streak of rebelliousness beneath the very proper manners. Or perhaps she just imagined it.

He was handsome in a boyish sort of way, with deep, violet-blue eyes, and occasionally, when the conversation plumbed new depths of banality, she noticed him staring at

263

her, his lips curled into a smile. But when she returned his gaze he turned away and his smile was immediately replaced by a look of proper concern for the price of shell and the state of the roads.

'I'm convinced the price of shell will recover,' George was saying. 'The present hiatus is only temporary. Nothing can replace mother-of-pearl. And this talk of farming pearl shell is just so much hogwash.'

'Our bank takes the same view,' Dalziel said. 'That's why we've established a new branch here in the town. We want to give the industry the support that it needs. All the support it needs,' he repeated, making sure George had not missed the point. It was obvious he was pitching to wrest the Niland and Company account away from its present bankers.

'What do you think, Conrad?' George said.

The blond Dutchman shrugged his shoulders. 'I'm afraid I take a more pessimistic view,' he said quietly.

'Oh?' George glared at him as if he had uttered a personal insult.

'I am sure the industry has not reached a state of crisis just yet. It may continue as it is for many years. But I think the boom days are gone. It will never be like it was.'

'You have only been here for three years,' George flared. 'So how would you know how it was?'

It was rude, but Conrad accepted the rebuke mildly. 'I can read. I have seen the figures for 1912 and 1913. When I compare them to my fleet's returns for the last three years I can see that the profits are not there. Besides, mother-of-pearl may be more beautiful than this new plastic but it is nowhere as cheap. And a button is, after all, just a button.'

'Nonsense.'

'Perhaps, but it is my view.'

'Well as far as the Commercial Union Bank is concerned –'

'Besides,' George said, cutting Dalziel off in mid sentence, 'plastic can never fully replace mother-of-pearl. A properly run fleet will always turn a profit.'

'Then you may perhaps be interested in purchasing mine.'

'You're selling up?' George looked at him, incredulous. 'You're getting out of Broome?'

Conrad raised a hand. 'Not out of Broome. Just out of pearling. I will still keep an office here as a buyer.'

A white-jacketed Junzo came into the room and began to clear away the plates. 'Bring us the port and the cigars, please,' George said.

Kate knew this was her cue. With anyone other than Agatha Dalziel she would have been grateful to get out of the room. In the circumstance it was a case of the devil and the deep blue sea.

'Perhaps we should adjourn to the veranda and leave the men to their talk,' she said.

Agatha nodded and got to her feet.

'If you will excuse us, gentlemen,' Kate said.

Conrad and Dalziel half rose from their seats out of courtesy. George ignored them. 'If you're really serious about your fleet . . .' he was saying to Conrad.

Kate stepped out onto the veranda. It was June and the nights were cool and fresh. She took a deep breath, trying to clear her head. Her temples were drumming.

Agatha seated herself in one of the cane chairs. 'He's rather charming, don't you think?'

Kate turned around, surprised. 'I beg your pardon?'

'Mister van Heusen. A charming man.'

'Yes. Yes he is.'

'I wonder why he never married.'

'I believe he did. His wife died in Java. He managed a rubber plantation for a time.'

Agatha sighed. 'What a waste.'

Kate wondered what she meant by it. A waste that his wife had died so young; or a waste that Conrad did not have a wife?

The three men were still deeply engaged in their conversation about pearling. Kate heard George's voice raised above the others.

'I sometimes think they only marry us for the sake of appearance,' Agatha said. 'They would rather they didn't have to come home at all. They are much happier when they're at work, aren't they?'

Kate was surprised by her candour. 'Yes, it is the way it seems.'

'I should be accustomed to it by now. One cannot help but feel a little jealous sometimes.'

I would rather George never came home at all. Kate kept that thought to herself. They sat in silence for a while.

'How do you find Broome?' she asked her guest.

'It is rather a shock. After Perth. But I suppose one grows accustomed to the pioneer life. One has to mix with all kinds of people. You'll never guess who called on me the other day. The McKenzie woman.'

Kate tried to look indifferent. 'Oh?'

'Imagine. She used to be a barmaid.'

'Yes, before she married Cam – Mister McKenzie.'

266

'Quite a handsome man, I believe. Do you know him very well?'

Something in her tone warned Kate that this was not an innocent enquiry. Rather, the cat had decided to show her claws. 'He courted me many years ago.'

Agatha smiled, betraying the secret knowledge the gossips had no doubt imparted. 'A *very* handsome man. And a Royal Navy officer once. I wonder why he chose to marry a barmaid?'

'Perhaps he loved her,' Kate said.

'Love,' Agatha said. 'What a strange reason to marry, don't you think? What would ever happen to a woman if she did things like that?'

Kate looked away. 'I've absolutely no idea,' she said.

◆　◆　◆

The *Roebuck* drifted under mizzen and jib with its number one diver down. Cameron, who had finished diving for the day, sat on the hatch, cleaning shell. He threw the mother-of-pearl on the deck and the muscle in a bucket of saltwater. The rest of the fish he threw over the side as morsels for the copper fish.

'Dat Assan got him one gol' toof,' Wes growled as he slit through the oyster in his hand with his knife. He nodded at the Malay tender in his bright scarlet sarong. 'All de girls look out for 'im now.'

'That ugly bastard?' Cameron grinned. He slit open another shell, his fingers feeling inside the greasy sac for the miracle of a pearl. 'You do all right for girls, Wes,' he said.

'Nah, dey all look out for dat Assan now,' Wes repeated gloomily.

'Must have cost him plenty.'

'Mebbe I get me'self a gol' toof. Yeah, mebbe.'

Cameron threw his shell on the pile in the middle of the deck. 'And spoil those beautiful white teeth you've got –' Cameron stopped mid sentence. Wes's eyes had opened wide and his jaw gaped open. Cameron thought he was about to have a fit. 'Wes, are you all right?'

Wes slowly withdrew his thumb and forefinger from the shell in his left hand and held up a truly enormous pearl. 'My God,' Cameron whispered.

Cameron reached up to take it. But the pearl, still greasy from the shell sac, slipped out of Wes's fingers. He bent to pick it up but it rolled across the deck.

'Grab it!' Cameron screamed to Assan. But the Malay was too slow. Before he could react the pearl slipped through the scuppers.

Wes and the others just stood and stared, stunned by the swiftness of this tragedy. But Cameron launched himself, fully clothed, over the bulwark. Even as he jumped he saw the pearl plop into the water and start to sink. Cameron dived straight down. The salt stung his eyes but as his entry bubbles cleared he could still see it, gleaming in the clear water, dropping away fast.

He went down after it, taking two powerful strokes. He swallowed hard, but could not clear the air trapped in his eardrums. The pressure built quickly to a piercing agony but he forced himself down. He could not lose the pearl.

He reached out, knowing he would have just one chance. He felt it touch his palm and his fist closed triumphantly around it. Christ, his ears! He twisted in the water and struck out for the surface with his left hand, keeping the precious pearl clutched against his chest with his other hand.

He came up choking, and paddled to the boat. Wes's huge arm reached over the side, grabbing him by the shirt and dragging him out of the water.

'I lose you dat one pearl?' he groaned.

Cameron could not hear him. He put a hand up to his ear. Blood. He must have ruptured an eardrum. He laughed and held up his fist to show he had the pearl. And then he passed out.

Wes's first thought was to put the pearl safely in the pearl box but when he tried to lever open Cameron's fist, his fingers were locked so tight around the pearl that they would not open. Even unconscious, Cameron McKenzie was not about to release his ultimate prize.

43

They had christened her Elvira, but everyone called her
Elvie. She had a mop of fair hair and eyes as steely blue
as the sea at dusk. During the pearling season, when Cam
was away, she would go down to Buccaneer Rock every
morning before school and every afternoon on her way
home, and stare hopefully out to sea for the return of the
Roebuck. Even at five years old she had the uncanny ability
of knowing which one of the fleet was Cam's lugger when it
was still miles out at sea.

So when the *Roebuck* weighed anchor in the bay that
warm August morning, Elvie was already on the beach
waiting.

Cam could see her waving. He left Wes in charge of

unloading the shell, jumped in one of the lifeboats and rowed for the shore.

Elvie came splashing through the shallows. 'Pa!' she yelled and jumped into the boat, nearly capsizing it. 'Pa!'

'Elvie lass!' Cameron laughed and picked her up in his arms.

He had loved Elvie from the first day he had seen her, still wet and pink from the birth. It had never mattered to him that she had been fathered by another man. In those first moments she touched him as he had never been touched by anything in his life. Her eyes were open and as he stared into them it was like peering into a bottomless pool. In his mind she was his and she always would be.

She helped him drag the boat up onto the beach and then climbed up on his shoulders. Cameron bent to pick up the pearl box from the deck of the dinghy.

'Did you catch any pearls, Pa?' Elvie asked him, as she always did.

Cameron laughed. 'Aye, lassie, I caught myself a pearl. The biggest pearl you ever saw in your life! Let's go and tell your ma!' And he ran up the beach, Elvie bouncing and laughing on his shoulders.

✦   ✦   ✦

George Niland was in a bad mood. He was accustomed to having a freshly laundered shirt and suit laid out for him. This morning he had been forced to wear the same clothes he had worn the day before and the suit had telltale ochre stains on the trouser cuffs.

He blamed Kate for not organising things better. Liddy

had not been seen since yesterday morning. Lately she had succumbed to the wiles of the debil-debil and while Kate had partly welcomed her fall from grace, it had made the running of the house a little more difficult. She had found a week's laundry piled up in Liddy's shack at the bottom of the garden, when Kate had supposed it was all at Ah Song's laundry in Chinatown.

George tutted and fumed. He didn't blame Liddy – she was, after all, just a black. It was patently his wife's fault. If she had been a more competent manager she would have kept a careful check on Liddy's conduct.

'For God's sake, how was I to know she had it all stored up out there?'

'That's what you're here for. To know.'

'Guardian of the Shirts. Is that my role in life now, George?'

'I have no intention of discussing it further. You know my feelings about the matter.' George picked up his knife and fork and concentrated on his breakfast.

Jamie came out of his bedroom and sat down at the table. George frowned. 'Why are you so late? You're going to miss school.'

'Yes, Father,' Jamie said.

Kate studied her son. He had grown into a fine-looking boy. His eyebrows and eyelashes were thick and black and it added a striking intensity to his eyes. He was tall for his age and Kate guessed he would be as tall as his father – well, as tall as George anyway – before his fourteenth birthday. She was very proud of him.

'He might be better served coming to the office with you,' she said to her husband.

George looked at his wife, amazed. 'With me?'

'Why not?'

'He's been to the office many times. I've shown him around.'

'I mean properly. You want him to join you in the business one day, so he might as well start learning a few things. And not just the office either. You could show him the stores and the packing sheds and the luggers.'

'Please, Father, can I?' Jamie said eagerly.

'I have never heard such a nonsensical suggestion. The boy's only eleven years old.'

'He's bright and enthusiastic and he wants to learn.'

'Can I go on a lugger?' Jamie said. 'Will you take me on board one of the luggers?'

George put down his knife and fork and pushed his plate away. 'I am down to my last good suit, thanks to your mother. I most certainly will not take you on one of the luggers. The last time I couldn't get the stench out of my clothes. I had to throw away a perfectly good pair of trousers.'

Jamie looked at his mother for support. 'Why don't you have one of your minions show him around,' Kate said. He bridled at the word 'minions'; it was a word he had used once and she never let him forget it.

George wiped his mouth with a napkin and threw it petulantly on the table. 'For goodness sake!'

'Please,' Jamie repeated.

'Oh all right,' he sighed. 'It seems I am not to have a moment's peace otherwise. Hurry up and have your breakfast. I'll not have you make me late!'

He stormed out of the room. Jamie looked at his mother and grinned.

'Thanks,' he said.

44

Cameron had taken the lease on a rundown bungalow with a red iron roof and bare corrugated iron walls. Unlike the shaded, green Edens of the master pearlers, the garden boasted just two sad bauhinias overhanging the bullnose veranda, and the buffalo grass was struggling to put down roots in the baked red earth.

The house was situated on the edge of the town, where the white shell-grit streets merged into the scrub. Some nights the Aborigines gathered in the brush behind the shack for *corroboree*, their *karlis* clack-clacking long into the night in land-old rhythm.

Rose sat on the veranda, her hands folded across her swollen belly. It was a cruel irony that they had had to wait so long for another child when the conception of Elvie and Jamie – she had to include Jamie in her calculations – had been so unwelcome.

She felt the child kicking in her womb and gasped, shifting her position. A lively child, livelier than Elvie had ever been. The time was getting close now, and she was frightened. Elvie's birth had been difficult. The memory of the terrible pain was acute. She had lost a lot of blood and it had taken her weeks to recover from the labour. She hoped it would be easier this time. She did not know how they would quite afford another baby, but she supposed they would manage somehow; they always had.

She squinted against the glare and saw an enormously tall figure making its way up the wide, white road. She realised it was Cameron, with Elvie on his shoulders. 'Cameron!' she shouted, and struggled to her feet.

Rose had barely reached the bottom of the veranda steps when he was there, throwing his arms around her, with Elvie still clinging to his neck.

'Rosie!'

She was embarrassed about her pregnancy and after he had kissed her she pushed herself away from him. 'You've seen enough whales at sea,' she said.

'You look beautiful, lass.'

'He found a pearl,' Elvie said.

Rose feigned a look of pleasure and surprise. Cameron had found a lot of pearls, but only ever small ones. None of them were really worth anything. It was the shell that was important now.

'Was it a good voyage?' she asked him.

'Like Elvie said,' Cam told her, rattling the wooden

pearl box he held in his left hand, 'I found a pearl.'

'What sort of pearl?' she said, his enthusiasm infectious.

'We're rich, lass!'

Rose forced a smile. There had been so many disappointments. 'And what about the shell?'

Cameron took her by the shoulders. 'I mean it! Never mind the shell! It's the biggest pearl you ever saw in your whole life! It must be over two hundred grains!'

Rose stared at him, not really comprehending what he was saying.

'I'm going to take you down to the city and dress you in the finest dresses money can buy! We won't have to live in this shack any more! We'll get a bungalow in the town and I'll even buy myself a motor car! I told you I'd find my pearl, Rosie! We're rich!'

✦   ✦   ✦

The Niland and Company offices and stores had been built on the shore between the Streeter and Male jetty and Dampier Creek. Niland drove the red Buick to the front door, and as he stepped out the clerks and accountants were already lined up along the veranda to greet him.

'Come along, come along,' he snapped at Jamie, and stamped ahead up the steps. Jamie leaped out of the car and ran along behind to keep up.

A junior clerk got in behind the wheel of the Buick to park it in the shade of the poinciana tree at the back.

George put his briefcase in his office and barked at his chief accountant, a middle aged man with a green eyeshade, that he was going to the store. Jamie had barely reached his

office when George stormed out again and Jamie had to run
back through the row of desks to the veranda.

'Your mother doesn't seem to realise that I am a very
busy man,' George said as he hurried across the foreshore to
the stores.

'Where are we going?'

'If your mother wants you to see the packing sheds and
the stores, then you shall see them.'

There was always a crowd on the foreshore at the
Niland camp, a cosmopolitan mix of Japanese carpenters
and sail makers, Malay and Manilamen packers and
Koepangers. Order was maintained by George's bosun,
a big-boned Japanese called Matsuki. He was built like a
Sumo wrestler and he kept a cast-iron discipline in the
camp, with his fists if he had to. Even Japanese of higher
social rank deferred to him.

George found Matsuki on the beach, supervising the
unloading of shell from the *Mary Jane*. George called to him
from the wharf, unwilling to further deteriorate the state of
his trouser cuffs by trudging through the sand.

'Boss,' Matsuki said in greeting. Jamie disliked him
immediately. He was surly and Jamie thought the way he
looked at his father appeared disrespectful.

'I want you to show my son around the camp and the
sheds,' George said. 'Answer any questions he has.'

'Plenty work this morning,' Matsuki said.

'Do as I say.'

Matsuki looked at the young boy as if he would rather
break him in half with his hands. 'Boss,' he said finally.

'Aren't you coming with us?' Jamie said.

'I told you, I'm very busy this morning. Matsuki will

bring you back to the office when you've seen enough. I'll get someone to run you home.' He turned on his heel. 'I hope your mother will be satisfied.'

Jamie looked up at the big Japanese bosun. 'Hello,' he said.

Matsuki spat into the sand.

Jamie was not going to let himself be intimidated. 'Well,' he said brightly, 'shall we start with the packing sheds?'

45

Tom Ellies sat cross-legged, his pipe in his mouth, and turned the pearl in his fingers. If he was impressed by its size, he gave no hint of it. He never showed any emotion whatever when he was cleaning pearls. He considered it unwise.

'Well?' Cameron said eagerly.

'I have seen more tragedies than Shakespeare in this little room,' he said.

'That's no answer.'

'It has some dirt spots here and here,' Tom said, pointing to a nest of tiny black pinpricks on the pearl. 'It is impossible to tell if they go right to the heart of the stone. You may have a fortune, you may have nothing.'

'What do you think I should do, Tom?'

'It is not my stone, Mister McKenzie. The decision is yours. You could sell it to a buyer now for perhaps . . . four, five hundred pounds. Let him take the risk. If I clean it, it could be worth five thousand. Perhaps ten. Or perhaps it is worth nothing at all.'

He laid the pearl on the black velvet cloth. Cameron stared at it. It was huge, big as a sparrow's egg, and it seemed to glow and pulse like a tiny silver heart. Cameron swallowed hard.

'Clean it,' he said.

Tom Ellies put his pipe in the ashtray. It was always the same; they all took the risk. 'Come back in the morning, when the light is better. In the early morning sun I can see into a stone's heart, perhaps unlock its secret. In the afternoon, like now, the sun is too harsh.' He picked up the pearl and handed it to Cameron. He never kept pearls on the premises or worked on them when the customer was not there. That, too, was unwise. A pearler had once accused him of changing the shape of his pearl and he had never forgotten it.

Cameron put the pearl in his waistcoat pocket. He experienced the first doubt. 'I'll see you in the morning, then,' he said and got to his feet.

'Sleep well,' Tom said.

Cameron gave him a grim smile. 'I doubt it, Tom,' he murmured and went out.

＊　＊　＊

The dentist had his surgery at the back of the barber shop in Sheba Lane. He gave Wes a look of some apprehension as the big man lowered himself into the chair.

'Toothache?' he asked, turning from the primitive array of instruments on the little cabinet.

'Toof is hokkay,' Wes growled. He had never been to the dentist in his life, but he had seen plenty of men who had, cotton wool plugged in their jaws to stop the bleeding, groaning with pain.

The dentist's name was McKimmon. He was a good dentist when he was sober, but he wasn't sober often, which was the reason he had left Perth and set up practice here. Now he peered at Wes over the top of his wire-rimmed glasses. 'If your teeth are okay, what are you here for?'

'Want a gol' toof. Like dat Assan.'

'Assan's tooth was rotten.'

'I want a gol' toof. No, mebbe two gol' toof. More dan dat Assan. Yep.'

McKimmon frowned. 'It's expensive.'

Wes shrugged. He reckoned that with his commission from the big pearl he could afford a whole mouthful of gold teeth if he wanted.

'Well, open up,' McKimmon said. He picked up his instruments and bent to examine Wes's mouth. Just then he felt a massive fist close around his testicles.

'Now,' Wes whispered, 'you doan hurt me, I doan hurt you. Hokkay?'

✦　✦　✦

Ever since Jamie was a small boy, he had imagined his father as a modern day Viking, a cross between King George V and Douglas Fairbanks. Each morning, he watched him

281

climb into the red Buick and drive away to catch pearls. He had invented a vivid fantasy in which his father climbed aboard a lugger every day and sailed out of the bay, standing at the prow in his white tropical suit and sola topee, to return each night with the decks behind him laden with chests of huge, gleaming pearls.

There was no one day when he realised his father did not spend every day at sea; it came to him gradually, as part of the erosion of dreams and legends that accompany the passage from boyhood. Santa Claus did not drive along the palm-fringed streets each Christmas Eve, his sleigh loaded with toys, the tooth fairy did not leave threepence under his pillow for each molar he placed there, and his father did not go to sea to hunt pearls.

But even his sketchy knowledge of reality had not prepared him for his first adventure inside the mythologised offices of Niland and Company. He had expected grandeur, and found only a few desks, some ancient calculating machines, and dusty piles of ledgers. It had all the romance of a provisions store.

He dealt with the shattering moment of disillusion in the spirit of the redeemer. If his father was flawed with inaction, then he would himself restore the ideal by fulfilling those failings in his father's character. He himself would provide the daring, while his father took care of the books and figures. This was how they would grow to know and admire each other as men. In this way he was able to delay the crushing inevitability of disappointment that tied him to the man he knew as his father.

◆　◆　◆

He sat in a corner of George's office, his skin sticky damp with sweat under the shirt and tie his father had made him wear for that morning's expedition to the stores and packing sheds. George finally appeared and seemed surprised to see him sitting there. It occurred to Jamie that he had forgotten all about him.

'James,' he said, with something like disdain, and then: 'So, did you enjoy your little jaunt around the stores?'

'It was good,' Jamie said. It was true, he had enjoyed it – despite Matsuki's grim disposition.

'This is where the real work's done, of course. I can teach you all you need to know right here.'

'When?'

'When you're old enough.'

Jamie looked around the office and quickly decided he would rather be boiled in oil than spend a minute longer in here than he had to. 'Why don't you ever go out on the luggers?' he asked.

'What an extraordinary suggestion.'

'Some of the pearlers do.'

He laughed. 'Not many.'

'Mister McKenzie does.'

'Mister McKenzie has no other choice. He can't even afford to pay his divers. Besides, I have more important things to do here.'

'But mother says it's important for me to know how the business is run. Can't I go out on the *Mary Jane* next season?'

'Ridiculous.'

'But mother says –'

'Your mother says a great many things, not all of them

283

very sensible. While she may be an admirable organiser of the house . . .' he stared down at his trouser cuffs and frowned '. . . she doesn't understand business. You should not pay her too much attention. Weston, take Master James home please.'

One of his father's clerks jumped to his feet and came over to collect the car keys.

'And don't dawdle. It's not a pleasure jaunt. I expect you to be back here at your desk in half an hour.'

'Yes, sir.'

'And be careful with the car. I shall check for dents when you get back. The cost of any repairs will be deducted from your wages.'

Jamie followed the clerk out to the car. As he got in, Weston glared at him as if it was his fault he had been given this onerous and unwelcome responsibility.

Well, his mother was right. This morning had been educational. For the first time, he realised what a master pearler was, and he was disappointed and a little embarrassed. 'Not exactly Bluebeard,' he said to himself.

'What was that?' Weston said.

'Nothing,' Jamie said, and then, out of mischief, he added: 'Be careful you don't dent the car,' and relished Weston's white-lipped but impotent fury all the way home.

46

It was quiet in the little room except for the ticking of the clock on the mantle. Tom Ellies held the pearl between the index finger and thumb of his right hand while he worked on the skin with an ancient three-cornered file. The brown and stubby fingers did not look like the hands of an artist, but they had a magic in them. Tom Ellies could reveal the gem in even the most misshapen or flawed stone.

As he worked thin shavings fell onto the black velvet mat. Cameron fidgeted, trying not to calculate the cost to him of each translucent sliver. After half an hour Tom laid the pearl aside to massage the muscles of his hand. Cameron felt a tightness in his chest. He realised he had been holding his breath for minutes at a time while Tom worked.

'Well?' he snapped, unable to stand the tension any longer.

'It is just the first petal from the rose,' Tom answered. 'It is too early to say.'

After a few moments' rest, he began work again. He peeled away skin after skin, each layer of pearl blemished in some way.

Occasionally Cameron would look at the clock and then his eyes returned inevitably to the little pile of shavings. Two hundred and sixty grains! The greatest pearl anyone had ever found in Broome and it was shrinking in front of his eyes.

Tom continued with his painstaking work, his expression unfathomable.

After a while Cameron closed his eyes. The faint rasp of the file on the stone and the ticking of the clock dominated the room. Cameron felt his treasure slipping away. He was diving into the sea again, and the bright moon was sinking into the green, away from him. But this time it could not be retrieved, this time there was nothing he could do.

It was a long time before he dared open his eyes again and when he did Tom had stopped working and the little file with its cork handle lay on the table beside his elbow. In front of him was two hundred and sixty grains of pearl in tiny shavings.

Tom Ellies picked up his pipe and lit it. The two men stared in gloomy resignation at the worthless skins of nacre on the velvet mat. Finally Cameron got to his feet and went out the door.

There was nothing either of them could think of to say.

◆　◆　◆

It had been clear to Elvie for as long as she could remember that her father was the biggest, strongest, most handsome father in the world. She adored him, and when he was not at sea she would not let him out of her sight. Sometimes he would even take her into the Continental Hotel with him. He would lift her high onto the polished teak bar and buy her lemonade while he laughed and talked about pearls with the other men.

He had explained to her that he had to go away so much so that he could look for pearls. Elvie hated pearls. She asked him why he didn't just buy the pearls from Mister van Heusen and then he could stay home with her and Rosie. He had laughed and asked her where she thought Mister van Heusen got his pearls from in the first place.

Elvie didn't care where he got them from. She just wanted Cameron not to go away. She always remembered the weeks he was home as special, laughter-filled times. She had never seen him like this.

He sat on the veranda watching the sun sink down the sky, copper red now and tame after the fiery heat of the day. There was a bottle of square-face gin in his lap and the oyster shell ashtray between his feet. He had been sitting there like that all day, with just his tobacco tin and his drink for company.

Elvie knew that something must be very, very wrong and finally, she gathered the courage to approach him.

'Pa? What's wrong?'

'You wouldn't understand, lassie.'

Elvie frowned. 'I'm a big girl now.'

'Aye, I know that.'

'Ma said it was about a pearl.'

'Aye, it was a pearl. The biggest, bonniest thing you ever saw in your life.'

'Can I see?'

'It's gone.'

'Did you lose it?'

'Aye, I suppose I did.'

Elvie sucked a thumb and considered. She put out her hand, playing with the long, black curls of his hair, coiling them around her fingers. 'Why do we need pearls?'

'We need pearls to sell, lassie.'

'Why do you have to sell them?'

'A pearl is like a gate to another world, Elvie. Through the gate there are fine houses and fleets of luggers and even new cars. That's why I look for pearls, lassie. I'm looking for another world for me, for you and for your ma.'

'Are there new dolls in this world?'

'Aye, there's every kind of toy you can think of,' he said, and pulled her towards him. He kissed her gently on the forehead. 'Go inside, lassie. I want to be alone for a while.'

Elvie retreated, and Cameron continued his lonely vigil as the polar star rose in the western sky, a diamond in the gloaming.

Finally Rose came out onto the veranda, her hands on her hips. 'Are you going to sit there sulking all night?' she said.

'I can and I will,' he answered her, his voice even. 'Now leave me alone, lass, let me drown my misery in peace.'

'It was just a pearl.'

'It was not just a pearl! It was a fortune! It was a new house and food in Elvie's belly and maybe a couple more luggers. It was my self respect. That's what it was!'

Without warning Rose bent down and picked up the bottle of square-face between his legs and threw it into the garden where it smashed in the hard, red dirt.

Cameron looked disappointed rather than angry. 'Now why did you do that?'

'If you're looking for self respect, you'll not find it in a bottle.'

Cameron stood up, unsteady on his feet. He leaned against one of the veranda posts for support. 'Two hundred and sixty grains! How much would it have been worth if it had not been for a few tiny specks! That's the McKenzie luck!'

'Stop wallowing in self pity, Cam. It's not like you.'

'Aye, well, maybe it's about time.'

'It's never time. When they wanted to hang you for something you didn't do, you never cried about it. You've had disappointments before. You'll have them again.'

Cameron shook his head. 'I was going to be the greatest pearler on the coast. Look where it's got me.'

'Then give it up, Cam. Pearls are killing you a little bit every day. I've watched you getting out of bed in the morning. You've got the rheumatics, haven't you?'

'Nothing to worry about.'

'Nothing to worry about? You've seen what happens to some of these Japanese who won't give it up. They finish as cripples. Sure they strut and preen for a couple of years, but they end up as beggars. Is that what you want?'

'I'll find my pearl, Rosie. I'll not have you in rags for the rest of your life.'

Rose put her hand on his shoulder and said gently, 'Find something else to do, Cam. You're a fine sailor. There must be some other way.'

'I've come this far, Rosie. I'll not give up now.'

'For God's sake!'

'Rosie, it's out there somewhere.'

Rose took her hand away, as if she had been slapped. 'You're like a million other men, Cameron McKenzie, you only want what you don't have. What would you do with being a rich man, anyway? Be like George Niland and sit in an office every day poring over account books? Sit on your veranda like the dummy pearlers playing bridge and drinking gin?'

'I can't give it up, Rosie. Not now. It's taken too much of my life.'

Rose stared into his eyes. Pointless to argue with him. The search for that one fabulous pearl had become a direct contest of strength between him and the sea. It was beyond reason.

They heard footsteps on the grit road. Cameron saw Wes ambling along from the direction of the town. There was blood seeping from his mouth. He looked as if he had been in a fight. His handsome mahogany features were contorted in a grimace of pain.

'Dey say for true?' he said. 'Dat one pearl no good?'

'Aye, it's true,' Cameron told him. 'She was a bitch right to her heart.'

Wes spat out the cotton wool in his mouth. Where there had once been two perfect white teeth was a bloody gap. 'How Wes gonna pay for gol' toof now?' he wailed.

✦ ✦ ✦

Cam lay in the moonlit bedroom, watching the steady rise and fall of Rose's swollen breasts under the thin fabric of her nightdress. He reached out and gently touched the tight swelling of her belly. The infant felt his touch and gave a kick.

Rose gasped and put a hand to her belly.

'You think the bairn's a boy?'

'Just a feeling I have. Call it women's intuition.'

It was a full moon and Cameron could see her face clearly, the elfin nose, high cheekbones. Her long fair hair had fallen across her face and she brushed it away.

'Don't look at me,' she said.

'Why not?'

'I'm the size of a house.'

'You look bonnie to me, lass.'

'Do you love me, Cam?'

'Have you ever doubted it?' He moved closer to her in the bed. 'Rosie, I don't want to hurt the bairn, but . . .'

She laughed. 'I'm not a piece of china.' She sat up and finally managed to manoeuvre herself into a kneeling position. 'It doesn't hurt. It's just hard to get comfortable. Do you think I'd say no, Cam? I've been six weeks without you.' She lowered herself onto him, feeling the hardness of his erection between her thighs. She rubbed herself against him, and felt herself getting wet.

'Say it again, Cam.'

'Say what, lass?'

'Say you love me.'

She ran her fingers through the tight curls on his chest, feeling the hard bands of muscle beneath his skin, watching his face in the silver splash of moonlight, the sharp hawk's features, the hint of cruelty more pronounced in the darkness.

'I love you, Rosie.'

She guided him into her and as she moved on him she felt their child kick again. But then her own needs overtook her, and when the dam finally broke she came to her climax sobbing, needing him to love her, needing desperately to believe it, wondering if she ever would.

◆　　◆　　◆

George had not long left for the office with Jamie when Liddy came in to the drawing room to announce that they had a visitor.

'Who is it?' Kate asked her.

'Boss him b'long white hair,' Liddy said, and Kate recognised Conrad van Heusen from the description.

She felt a flutter of pleasure and panic. 'Show him in,' she said.

A few moments later Liddy ushered Conrad through the door.

Kate felt inexplicably nervous. 'Good afternoon, Mister van Heusen. I'm afraid my husband isn't here.'

'It's not your husband I've come to see.' He was staring at her openly with his intense, pale blue eyes. Only one other man had looked at her the way he did. The comparison had never occurred to her until now.

Kate felt her cheeks grow hot. She turned to Liddy. 'Will you bring us some iced tea?'

Liddy shuffled away.

'Won't you take a seat, Mister van Heusen?'

'Conrad, please.'

They sat down. He crossed his legs and lounged gracefully in the cane chair, studying her. Kate met his gaze. She was curious now. He seemed a little too diffident in his speech and manners to be the kind of man who might meddle with other men's wives.

'I know you'll think this presumptuous of me,' he said, 'but I've come to talk to you about Niland and Company.'

She stared at him, astonished. There was nothing she could think of to say to that opening gambit. But instead of going on, he folded his hands in his lap and smiled. She had the uncomfortable suspicion that he could read what she was thinking.

Finally she managed: 'You're correct, Mister van Heusen. That is presumptuous.'

'Shall I leave?'

'If you have any sympathy at all for my position, I think you should.'

'If I lacked sympathy for your position, I would not have come.'

Well, that took her breath away. She had no idea where this was leading. 'If you wish to discuss Niland and Company, you should talk to my husband.'

'I already have. But the company's affairs affect you too, don't they?' He did not wait for her to answer. He leaned forward, his elbows resting on his knees. 'If you report this conversation to your husband, I shall no doubt find myself unable to continue doing business here in Broome. There is considerable risk for me in doing what I am about to do. I assure you, it is not in my financial interest to do so.'

Liddy brought the tea on a sterling silver tray. While she arranged the glasses, Kate made her decision.

After Liddy had left the room, she said: 'Whatever you have to say will be kept in the strictest confidence.'

Conrad smiled. 'Thank you.' He leaned forward again. 'Do you know the real situation of the pearling industry here in Broome? Lays are down, the value of the pearl is decreasing every year. That, in itself, would be due cause for concern. But then there's the Japanese issue. Ever since the war their influence has been growing. For instance, very few of your husband's boats take to the sea under a white master now. Even those luggers with a white pearl-opener on board are effectively skippered by the number one diver, who is invariably Japanese. Everyone knows most of the pearls are finding their way into the pockets of the crews. They may even be cheating on the shell as well. The Japanese Club is effectively a trade union, and rates for divers are going through the roof. The writing's on the wall for any sensible businessman, Mrs Niland.' He paused. 'I wonder why your husband does not see it?'

Kate knew some of this, of course, but she had not realised the situation was as dire as he had painted it. 'You have spoken to him about this?' she asked.

'Of course. But he will countenance no other view but his own.'

Kate sipped her iced tea, giving herself time to think. 'Why are you telling me all this?'

'I supposed you had some influence with him,' he said, and smiled.

'I'm afraid you overestimate me. It's not for want of trying.'

He put down his glass. 'You know he bought me out?'

'What?'

'My fleet was for sale. His offer was a good one. I am a businessman, I was not about to refuse him.'

She shrugged, but the news alarmed her. 'He never talks to me about business.'

'He must reduce his exposure to risk. Someone has to make him see that.'

She had heard the talk for years about the Japanese, about the dummying, the constant harping and worrying over the price of shell. Listening to George, she had supposed the problem to be exaggerated, that everything would sort itself out in a year or two. 'There is nothing I can do about this,' she said.

Conrad nodded, and after a few moments he reached for his hat. He got to his feet. 'You're right. I have put you in a very difficult position. I am sorry.'

She stood up. 'Is that why you came here?' she asked him softly.

'I am by nature a cautious man. I think I have just made a terrible fool of myself. Thank you for your hospitality.'

He hesitated in the doorway. Kate stared at him, astonished at this bizarre conversation, this abrupt departure. 'Good day,' he said, and went out.

Kate slumped back into the cane chair. 'My God,' she murmured. 'What was all that about?'

47

Kate found Liddy peeling potatoes in the kitchen. This time she had succumbed to the devil only briefly.

'You're not to mention Mister van Heusen's visit to the master,' Kate told her.

Liddy sniffed. 'Liddy not lie. Liddy lie, she not go paradise b'long Jesus Christ.'

'I'm not asking you to lie. You just don't tell him.'

'You go longa debil-debil, you see.'

'Let me worry about my spiritual welfare. Do as you're told.'

Liddy's face was dark and disapproving. 'No good too mus, missus.'

Kate wagged her finger at her. 'Remember what else the

father says, Lidia. Jesus Christ wants you to be loyal.'

'Never mind that Jesus Christ,' Liddy said with a sudden and unexpected shift in her logic. 'What if master find out?' She went off, muttering to herself.

Kate made a face at her behind her back. So what if George did find out? She didn't care. Besides, nothing had happened. Nothing at all.

❖   ❖   ❖

George's Buick rolled to a stop outside Cameron's red-roofed shack. George climbed from behind the wheel. 'Get the hamper for me, will you?' he said to Jamie.

Rosie came out onto the veranda. 'Mister Niland,' she said, surprised. 'What can we do for you?'

George took off his sola topee and gave a slight bow. 'Good day, Mrs McKenzie. Is your husband at home?'

At that moment the screen door banged open and Cameron appeared. 'George,' he grunted. 'This is an unexpected pleasure.'

'I heard you had some bad luck.'

'Aye, well . . . It happens.'

'Things must be difficult.'

'No more than for anyone else.'

George nodded to Jamie, who was struggling to heft a large wicker basket from the back seat of the Buick. 'We thought you might need a little extra food to tide you over. I realise times are hard and I'm not averse to kindness for the less well off.'

Cameron's face flushed the colour of bronze. 'Put that back where you got it, young Jamie,' he said.

Jamie had just wrestled the hamper clear of the running board when Cameron came striding towards him. He had never seen anyone look so angry in his whole life and he dropped the basket on the ground; the tinned meat, tomatoes, bananas and bags of flour his father had just purchased tumbled into the red dirt.

He looked over at his father. 'I'm sorry,' he mumbled.

Cameron was standing in front of George, his fists clenched at his sides. 'Pick it up and take it out of my sight,' he growled.

'Now, look here, Cam –'

'Get it out of here, George! Now, or I'll break your bloody neck!'

George replaced his sola topee with a gesture of patient forbearance while Jamie scrambled in the dirt for the tins of meat. 'Leave it,' he said.

'You'll not leave it,' Cameron said. He picked up a handful of tomatoes and tossed them in the back of the Buick. One split open and the juice spattered over the upholstery. Cameron hurled the rest of the tins and flour bags in after them. 'Now get out of here!'

George climbed in behind the wheel. 'Come along, Jamie.'

Jamie was terrified, but as he climbed in the passenger seat he turned back to look at Cameron and thrust out his jaw. 'Imbecile,' he said, a word he had learned at school.

George started the car and drove off.

Cameron watched the fancy American motor car disappear up the road, a cloud of choking red dirt thrown up by the wheels. Rosie came to stand beside him.

'Cam . . .?'

'The bastard! The dirty, filthy bastard!'

'Come away.'

'That little scene was just for Jamie's benefit, you know that, don't you, lass?'

He turned. Elvie was framed in the doorway, and on her face was an expression he had never seen before. Jesus Christ. He kicked the gate off its hinges and stormed away, to be alone in the scrub and yell obscenities at the galahs and the boabs.

✦   ✦   ✦

George allowed himself a tight smile. 'So that's the man you said you admired so much,' he said. 'He's nothing but an oaf and a bully.'

Jamie was silent.

George shook his head. 'Extend the hand of friendship to that kind and you just lose your fingers!'

Jamie looked around. The tomato juice had already dried to a crust on the leather upholstery. He wondered what had made McKenzie so angry. They had only been trying to do him a good turn, after all. He decided his father must be right. McKenzie was an oaf and a bully.

48

The western veranda of the house had been enclosed with mesh and converted into a bedroom for Jamie. It was the most pleasant room in the whole house, open day and night to the cool breeze that came from the bay. Tonight it was heady with the scent of camphorwood and the strong incense Junzo had lit to keep away the mosquitoes.

Kate sat on the edge of Jamie's bed and brushed back the damp curls on his forehead. She felt him flinch. He did not like her touching him anymore. He was growing away from her. He would be a young man soon, and would not like her coming into his bedroom to kiss him goodnight.

She brushed her lips against his forehead. 'Goodnight, Jamie.'

'Goodnight, Mother.'

Just as she reached the doorway he asked her: 'Do you know a pearler called McKenzie?'

She felt as if her heart had stopped. 'Mister McKenzie? Yes, yes, I know him.' She hoped her voice had not betrayed her.

'He was rude to us today.'

'Rude to you? Why?'

'We went over there in the car, to take him and his family some food. Because they're poor.'

'We?'

'Me and Father. It was an enormous hamper. You would think people would be grateful when you do things for them.'

George had not mentioned the incident to her, of course. His vindictiveness amazed her sometimes, and she had lived with him for twelve years.

'What did Mister McKenzie say?'

'He got very angry. I don't know why.'

'I dare say Mister McKenzie's pride was offended.'

'There's tomato stains all over the car. Father should have him arrested.'

You sound just like George, she thought. 'Perhaps you'll understand when you get older. Go to sleep now.'

She went out, turning off the carbide lamp on the wall. Then she went to sit on the veranda to wait for George to come back from the office.

She looked up at the night sky. When you looked into space like this, she thought, it makes your own problems seem so insignificant. Yet if you believed what the astrologers said, the stars had a hand in every single person's fate,

like the workings of some enormous clock, each piece inter-
locking with another, each tiny cog and wheel an indispen-
sable part of the whole. Was that the way it was?

She wished she could decipher her own code among
all those blinking messages of celestial morse. Where was
she going with her life? It had all turned out so differently
from her childhood dreams. It had taken just a handful of
decisions to bring her to this ebb, all of them bad ones:
Cameron's baby, George's compromise. Yet she did not
regret Cameron, for he had given her Jamie. Her whole life
was lived for him now. Perhaps, when he was a man, she
could start thinking about herself again. If there was
anything to think about. She was, after all, a woman in a
man's world. Where else could she go?

Conrad.

His name slipped into her head like an intruder, a thief
silently slipping inside an unlocked door. Conrad had
reminded her that she was a woman after all, not just a wife
and a mother. But Conrad was an idle dream on a hot afternoon. She might as well chase the moon.

She heard the wheels of the Buick crunch on the
driveway. A few moments later she heard her husband's
footfall on the veranda. He seemed weary and defeated, as if
his briefcase was loaded with bricks instead of papers.

'You work too hard,' she said as he walked in.

'Oh,' he said. 'You're still up.'

'I was waiting for you.'

'Oh?'

'I want to talk to you.'

She heard him sigh. 'Can it wait until the morning?'

'You always say that, then in the morning you say it

has to wait until you come home. It's just your way of avoiding me.'

'You're a fine one to talk.' He stood in the shadows, thought about retreat to the study, then surrendered, throwing his briefcase on a table and slumping into one of the cane chairs. He rubbed his face with his hands. 'Well, what is it?'

'You bought Conrad van Heusen's fleet?'

Suddenly his voice had an edge to it. 'How did you know about that?'

'Gossip. Is it true?'

'I got a bargain. The man's a fool. If I were him, I should have held out for a much higher price.'

'Why didn't you tell me?'

'It's really none of your concern.'

'It is my concern, George. If the business fails, it's very much my concern. And Jamie's.'

'Are you going to tell me how to run my business now? Really, you presume too much!'

'Are there problems with Niland and Company?'

'Of course there aren't. What have you been hearing?'

'This talk about shell prices and the Japanese . . .'

'People talk a lot of rot about the Japanese. They're the future of the industry in Broome. If anyone –'

'But with shell prices the way they are, why did you buy van Heusen's fleet? If we go too deeply into debt –'

George jumped to his feet. 'How dare you! How dare you question my business judgment! Have you ever wanted for anything, you or the boy? Have you?'

'That's not the issue.'

'Don't you dare! Don't you dare just sit there like the

Queen of Egypt and tell me what the issues are. I'll tell you the issues! Five years you've denied me your love, your bed, even a fragment of human warmth and companionship, while I've done everything for you. Everything! I've worked my fingers to the bone to give you and the boy –'

Now Kate was on her feet too. 'Stop it! Stop it! I'm sick of men telling me what they've done for me when all this selflessness is just to disguise their own naked greed. I'm just another possession, your flagship for social occasions, so don't tell me it's all been to make me happy!'

'I've loved you more than you deserve!'

'Love? Don't make me sick!'

Kate stormed inside, slamming the screen door. She ran to her bedroom and sat down at her dresser, began furiously tearing a hairbrush through her curls. How could she have done this to herself? How could she have turned her life into such a ridiculous, painful farce?

She threw the tortoiseshell brush at the glass, cracking it.

The door flew open and George stood framed in the doorway.

'Get out,' she hissed at him.

His voice was strangely hoarse. 'Not tonight,' he said, and closed the door softly behind him.

Kate jumped up. 'I said, get out.'

George took off his jacket and threw it on the floor. His hands were shaking. 'I could have had any woman I wanted.'

'Don't you dare.'

He took two steps towards her and slapped her across the face. Kate gasped with shock. She slapped him back.

She was about to hit him again but he caught her wrist and threw her onto the bed, pinning her with his weight.

He held her arms above her head with one hand while the other fumbled at the hem of her skirt. 'For one night you'll damned well be my wife,' he whispered.

She smelled the sour taint of liquor on his breath. He must have a secret cache of gin at his office she thought. She was surprised by how strong he was. He hooked his fingers into the neck of her dress and pulled down savagely, ripping it open. 'I'd almost forgotten how beautiful you are,' he said.

Kate stopped struggling and closed her eyes. She lay quite still. She was neither frightened of him, nor much outraged; merely disgusted. She felt him pull her drawers down and try to push himself inside her.

It wasn't different from their usual lovemaking, she thought sourly. Let him have his way. She was his wife, after all.

'I love you,' he whispered as he entered her.

Her eyes snapped open. 'Just get it over with,' she said.

49

Elvie hated school. The other children taunted her sometimes, saying things about her mother she really didn't
understand. But she knew they were bad words and she
never let them go unavenged. Elvie was good with her fists;
she could beat any boy in her class in a fight. She knew her
father would be furious if he found out so she never told
him about the fights she had in the scrub behind the school.

Her feistiness won her the grudging admiration of her
classmates but it did not win her friends. The taunts became
less overt; they were replaced by pitying stares, whispered
remarks in the classroom, faces pulled behind her back.
Elvie hated it, hated being different in a way she did not
comprehend; the same way she hated having no shoes, and

having to wear the same frayed dress day after day. So whenever she could, she stayed away.

She knew the *Roebuck* would be in port for at least another day, taking on provisions, and that Cameron would not be on board this morning. She had overheard him telling her mother that he had an important meeting in town. So instead of heading up the road towards the school she ran through the scrub and made her way down to the foreshore camp to find Wes.

✦　✦　✦

Jamie passed an old Malay grandfather near the jetty. He was carrying four enormous white enamel billy cans, balanced on a bamboo pole he carried across his shoulders. The slopping seawater in the cans contained scores of small cockle oysters gathered from the rocks below Cable Beach. The old man would get a shilling a beerpot measure for them in town.

Jamie heard a high-pitched mewling, like the sound of a baby. He stopped and looked around, but could see nothing. As he walked out onto the jetty, the sound grew louder.

He peered over the edge. There was a hessian sack lying in the thick mud about ten yards out. Something was moving inside it. The sound was definitely coming from there. Jamie was reluctant to go out there, especially in his school clothes. His mother would kill him.

He found a split boom mast lying halfway up the beach and dragged it back to the tidal edge. He tried to hook the sack with the end of the pole and drag it towards him. Whatever was in the sack squealed even louder. Jamie tried again, overbalanced and took a step forward, sinking ankle deep into the mud. 'Hell!' he said.

He reached forward again with the pole. It was useless. Well, he had one shoe full of mud already, another wasn't going to make much difference. He waded in. It was like walking through sticky black treacle. He reached the sack and tried to lift it, but it was heavier than he imagined and sunk fast into the mud. He grabbed it with two hands and tried to drag it. His hands slipped on the wet hessian and he fell backwards into the mud.

'Bloody damned bloody rotten bloody bloody hell!' He stood and looked at his clothes. What a mess. He was done for.

The sack came alive again, something writhing and whimpering inside, trying to escape. Jamie took care to get a firmer grip this time and dragged the sack back through the mud to the beach.

It had been tied with rope and the seawater had soaked the knot, making it difficult to loosen. Instead he found a tear in the sack itself, hooked his fingers inside and ripped it open.

He reached in to rescue whatever was inside. It bit him.

'Hell!' He pulled his hand away. Blood!

Jamie leaped to his feet. 'You ungrateful little mongrel! I should have let you drown!' The pup snarled, bearing its small, needlesharp white teeth. 'To hell with you!' Jamie turned and stamped off down the road. But the puppy followed, dogging his heels, ignoring the rocks and curses hurled in his direction.

✦   ✦   ✦

'Well look hyar,' Wes said.

Jamie stood on top of the dune, his long grey socks and bare knees crusty with grey mud. A small black dog stood a few paces away.

'It's Jamie Niland,' Elvie whispered.

'I knows it,' Wes answered. He put his big ham fists in the pockets of his dungarees and shouted up: 'Mebbe you belong at school ri' now, boy.'

'So does she,' Jamie said, pointing at Elvie.

'Mebbe so.' He grinned. 'What can I do fer you, boy?'

'I'm just standing here.'

'Guess you is,' Wes said. He looked at Jamie's legs. 'Sweet Jay-sus, what you done to yo'self?'

Jamie did not answer. He turned to look for the black pup but it had wandered down the dune and was sniffing with interest at Elvie's leg. She bent to pat it, wrinkling her nose against the smell. It needed a good bath.

'Is this your dog?' she shouted.

'No. It bit me.'

'I know a feller got bit by a dawg,' Wes said. 'He up and die.'

Jamie blanched. 'I don't care. I'm not scared.'

Elvie picked up the little dog. It began to make soft, mewling noises. 'Can I have him?' she said.

Jamie couldn't believe it. Why didn't the dog bite *her*? 'I don't want him,' he lied. To cover his disappointment he shifted his attention to the rowboats scurrying to and from the *Roebuck*. 'What are you doing?' he said.

'Loading stores. We out to sea long time. Men get hungry. Mebbe you want to help.'

'Can I?' Jamie said, and immediately regretted how

eager he had sounded. 'I mean, I don't mind. If you think you need a hand.'

'Mebbe I do,' Wes told him. He put his arm on Jamie's shoulder. 'Come on, boy.'

Elvie watched them walk away down the beach, unsure what to make of this. She knew her da' did not like Jamie's father. She had seen him throw tomatoes at his car. Perhaps she was supposed to hate him too. But here was Wes putting his arm around Jamie Niland and talking to him like . . . well, like he talked to her. It was confusing.

And Jamie had given her his dog.

She carried it over to the water tank. 'You need a good bath, mister, you stink,' she scolded it. 'Then we'll have to think of a name for you, won't we?'

50

Next day Cameron was supervising the final loading of provisions on board the *Roebuck* when Wes touched Cameron's arm and pointed to the dunes above the foreshore. A small boy was picking his way through the jumble of iron and timber shacks and godowns of the McKenzie camp. Cameron felt a familiar clutch of sorrow and anger. It was him.

He waved. 'Hey, Jamie!'

Jamie waved back, hesitated when he saw Cameron. He stopped a dozen paces from where they were standing, his hands in the pockets of his shorts.

'Dis hyar the skip,' Wes said. 'Mebbe you go wid him today, hokkay?'

Jamie said nothing.

'Hello, Jamie,' Cameron said to him.

Jamie shuffled his feet. 'You want to know 'bout pearls?'
Wes coaxed him. 'De skip, he know everytin' dere is. He tell
you better even dan me.'

Silence.

'Why do you want to learn about pearling, boy?'
Cameron asked finally.

'I want to be like my father.'

Wes and Cameron exchanged a look. 'Like your father?'

'I want to be a big pearler.'

'Aye, well. That's a noble ambition. Come by me then.'

He walked off. And after a few moments, Jamie
followed.

✦ ✦ ✦

Cameron rowed him out to the *Roebuck* in the whaleboat.
He gave him a quick tour of the lugger, and then tossed him
an oyster shell.

'A pearl!' Jamie said in wonderment, fingering the small
round in the hollow of the shell.

'Your first lesson, boy,' Cameron said, taking the shell
from his hand and crushing the round under his thumb. An
ooze of mud spilled out of it. 'It's just a blister. A borer
worm gets into the shell and the water pressure does the
rest. It looks like a pearl but it's not real. Worthless.' He
tossed the shell back onto the deck. 'Here's a pearl!' He
reached into his pocket and took out a small leather pouch.
He dropped the contents into the palm of his hand; a small
pearl, slightly misshapen, thirty or forty grains. 'If it were

only a wee bit larger, a wee bit rounder. But it's a bonnie thing, do you not think?'

Jamie stared at it and nodded. 'Do all the shells have pearls?'

Cameron laughed. 'One in a hundred. And most of them are too small to be worth more than dropping in a barmaid's jar! Do you know how a pearl is made?'

Jamie shook his head.

'It's born by the tide. The tide is the pulse of the sea, it keeps the ocean and everything that's in it alive. The oyster feeds off the tide, its food is carried by the current. But sometimes a speck of sand finds its way inside the shell and the oyster can't get rid of it. It's like having a wee stone in your shoe, I suppose. So it puts a kind of saliva around the speck of sand, to protect itself, and there's nacre in it, and it gets hard and forms a pearl. Some pearls are misshapen, and that's what they call barrack. You can buy them from any of the pearlers by the carat; they keep them in jam tins. But a good round might be worth anything. It all depends on the size, the lustre of it, the colour, the smoothness. A man might wake up one morning poor, by sunset he can find a pearl and be rich as a czar!'

'How do you catch the oysters?'

'You don't catch them. They're just there, in the sea, like gold.' Cameron took him below deck and showed him the diving dresses and the heavy lead boots and the two sea-greened copper helmets. 'Try and lift one,' he said.

Jamie grunted and heaved but it was too heavy for him.

'Is it not a fierce weight to be carrying to the bottom of the ocean, Jamie? A man has to know what he's about, or it's his own coffin he climbs into.'

'You walk on the bottom of the sea with all that weight?'

'It does'nae feel so heavy down below. But you don't walk all the time. A canny diver sits in the loop of his lifeline and lets the lugger carry him over the bottom till he finds a likely place for shell. It's the diver who sails the boat, Jamie, he uses his lifeline to signal to his tender which way the boat sails and how fast or how slow, whether to drift or whether to turn into the wind.'

'Who's the tender?'

'The tender's job is to keep the air hose and the lifeline taut. He has to be a good man, for he has your life in his hands. To much line and you risk a snag, too little and you're pulled along the bottom like a dog chained to a cart. Your tender can save your life or lose it. I remember one diver on the *Alma* who fell through a crevice under the water. His tender could not hold the weight and the man sank. When they finally got him to the surface the water pressure had squeezed his whole body up inside his corselet and helmet. They had to bury him like that, for they couldn't get him out.'

Jamie felt suddenly ill. Cameron seemed so casual about such appalling risks. Jamie could not imagine dying that way. 'Do you still dive, Mister McKenzie?'

'Call me Cam. And no, I don't dive anymore. I've got the diver's sickness.'

'Why do you still go on the boats then?'

'To keep an eye on the crew. A man can't be a pearler in Broome and not go on the boats – his crew will steal every last pearl they find. Even if you have a shell opener on board they'll come out at night and try to find a pearl among the unopened shell. You have to keep respect and you can't do that in an office.'

Jamie bridled at such blatant criticism of his father. 'I think I should go back now,' he said.

'I didn't mean anything against your father.'

'He's the greatest pearler in Broome.'

'Who told you that?'

My father, Jamie thought, but he wasn't about to say it.

Cameron put his hand on the boy's shoulder. 'I'll take you back,' he said.

'Thanks.'

As he climbed into the whaleboat Cameron studied him and smiled. He was a fine boy. A man ought to be proud.

✦　✦　✦

The kerosene lamp hissed and spluttered on the bench, the night insects swarming around it. A tribe of Djuleun were dancing *corroboree* behind the tea-trees, the rhythm of their clapping sticks haunting the hot, still night. Cameron pushed away his dinner plate and lit a cigarette.

He looked around the barren kitchen at the stained canvas chairs and the bare iron walls and thought about his home in Glasgow, the grinding poverty of his life there that he had sworn to leave behind: *All I've done is exchange one kind of failure for another. Instead of grey, terraced houses and cold, misty rain there are mosquitoes and stultifying heat.*

Rose reached across the table and took his hand. 'Don't look so sad.'

'It was not meant to be this way, Rosie.'

'Let's leave here.'

Cameron shook his head. 'It's like admitting I'm beaten.'

'The pearls are gone, Cam. The days of quick fortunes are over.'

'I keep thinking that if I can just hold on for one more season . . . just one good pearl, Rosie. That's all it would take. One good pearl.'

'If you want to stay, I'll stay.'

He brushed a wisp of hair from her face. 'I was going to dress you in silk.'

'Can't milk the goat in silk, Cam.'

He kissed her. 'One day I'll find my pearl, Rosie. And you'll have everything a woman could want. You'll see!'

51

When George arrived home for lunch, Jamie was sitting on the veranda drinking a lemon squash. As soon as he saw his father's face, he knew he was in big trouble.

George did not even wait to reach the back steps before beginning the tirade. He pointed a finger at Jamie, his cheeks flushed. 'You've been lying to me!'

Jamie jumped to his feet. *How did he find out?*

George stamped onto the veranda. 'What were you doing at McKenzie's camp?'

'I wasn't doing anything wrong.'

'I asked you what you were doing there.'

'I wanted to learn about pearling.'

'I own the largest fleet in Broome and you go to a man who can barely keep one lugger in the water?'

Jamie said nothing.

'I've shown you the whole Niland and Company operation. What more do you need to know?'

'I wanted to go on one of the luggers. I wanted to see a diving dress.'

'Matsuki could have shown you all that.'

'Matsuki thinks I'm a nuisance.'

Kate heard the shouting and came out onto the veranda. 'What's going on?' she said to George.

'It seems your son has become a regular visitor to the McKenzie camp.'

'Jamie?'

'One of my divers saw him there and told Matsuki. You've been there all morning, haven't you?'

'I've only been three times,' Jamie said defiantly.

George turned to Kate. 'I thought you were supposed to be his mother. You're supposed to keep an eye on him.'

'He's eleven years old. I can't follow him everywhere!'

'This is absolutely outrageous!' George rounded on Jamie. 'It is to stop immediately! Do you understand?'

'Why?' Jamie said. 'What harm is it?'

A look passed between his mother and father. Then George said: 'You are never to speak to that man again. If I ever see you near him, ever . . .' The threat hung in the air. 'Do you understand?'

'. . . I suppose so.'

'I said, do you understand?'

'Yes!'

'Outrageous,' George shouted and went inside, slamming the screen door.

✦ ✦ ✦

The sun hung low over the pindan and the baobabs, silhouetted against a lavender sky. The angelus rang from the galvanised iron spire of the chapel.

The red Buick, parked in the dirt street outside the house, was a warning of trouble. George Niland. Cameron took off his panama and went inside. But it wasn't George, it was Kate. She and Rose were sitting in the kitchen, a pot of tea on the table between them. Elvie was watching from the veranda, her nose pressed against the tattered flywire of the screen door.

Kate got to her feet as he walked in. She was wearing a dress of pure white muslin and white cotton gloves. Her hair was tied behind her head. She looked like an aristocrat instead of the daughter of a bog Irish pearl thief, he thought sourly. He glanced at Rose, still in her work dress, long fair curls unkempt. Her face was a mask of anger and shame.

'Mrs Niland is here to see you,' she said.

'An unexpected pleasure.'

There was a heavy silence. 'Well, I have things to do,' Rose said, and went outside. Cameron heard her shout: 'Come away!' to Elvie as she went down the back steps.

Cameron and Kate stared at each other. 'How are you, Cam?'

'I'm fine.'

Kate sat and Cameron eased himself into Rose's chair.

'You shouldn't have come here,' he said softly.

319

'I have something important to discuss with you.'

'You should still not have come.'

She looked around the sparse kitchen. 'She seems like a nice person.'

'You're not here to discuss Rosie.'

Kate's cheeks flushed pink. 'Can we at least be friends, Cam?'

He didn't answer her.

Kate stared at the table. 'I need to talk to you about Jamie.'

'What about him?'

'He's been coming to see you at the camp.'

Cameron tried to cover his surprise. 'Aye. Does George know this?'

'He found out from Matsuki.'

'Aye well, it's true. But I never forced him to come. The boy wanted to learn about pearling.'

Kate's voice had an edge of steel. 'Then you have to discourage it.'

'I can't. I won't.'

Kate looked around the meagre kitchen again, then said: 'Has pearling made you your fortune, Cam? Has it brought you happiness? Or me?'

'Like I said, he's not my son.'

'But he is mine. And I don't want this sort of life for him. He deserves better.'

'That's for him to decide.'

'No, Cam, it isn't. George and I have forbidden him to go near the foreshore again. Next year he's going to Perth, to a boarding school. Hopefully he'll lose this fascination for pearling while he's away.'

'Your husband has not done so badly by it.'

'He's not a pearler, Cam, and you know it. He inherited the company from his father and all the money comes from the station and the agencies these days.'

Cameron shrugged. 'He's no pearler, that's a fact.'

'I'm sorry, Cam.'

'Don't be sorry. The boy's near grown now. What would he be wanting with a father like me anyway?'

She reached across the table and put her hand on his. 'I wish –'

Cameron jerked his hand away. 'There's no point in wishing. It won't change anything.'

When Kate stood up her tone was businesslike again. 'I hope you'll respect my wishes.'

'If the boy comes to the camp, I'll not turn him away. If you can stop him coming, well, that's up to you. But I think you're making a mistake, Kate. He has the sea in him.'

'Not if I can help it,' she said, and left.

At the back of the house there was a chicken run and a nanny goat chained to a post. Elvie had named her Brutus, not yet having mastered the complexities of gender. After Kate had gone, Cameron went outside and looked for Rose. She had just finished milking Brutus and was carrying a pail half full of warm milk. 'I'll start our supper,' she said.

'Do you not want to know what that was about?'

Rose put down the pail. 'No.'

He caught her by the shoulders and made her look at him. 'Then what's that face for?'

Rose twisted away from him. 'Look at me! Look at my hands! Working hands, Cam. And my clothes . . . I have two dresses . . . and she glides up the path in her lace and

321

her cotton gloves, smelling of French perfume and sits in my kitchen and wrinkles her nose and makes me feel like . . . like . . .'

'Rosie –'

'She still loves you! You can see it in her eyes! If she ever wanted to take you away from me, what could I do to stop her?'

Cameron reached for her but she backed away. 'And I know you still love her.'

'I don't love her, Rosie . . . not anymore.'

She shook her head. 'I don't blame you. It's just some-times I can't bear knowing that she's still here in the town. How does a whore compete with a lady?'

'You're not a whore!'

'You haven't been to the Tennis Club. Or the Residency. Or the Race Club. The ladies there all know what I am.'

'Rosie . . .'

She pushed past him and ran inside. Cam saw Elvie standing there, watching. 'Go on with you and feed the chickens,' he said to her.

She ignored him. Instead she stamped past him and went inside, slamming the screen door a second time.

Cam found Rosie sitting at her dresser, combing out her hair, her face wet with tears. Their eyes met in the mirror.

'I'm sorry,' he whispered. He put his arms around her shoulders. 'One day, Rosie, one day you'll have perfumes and dresses and –'

She put a hand on his lips to shush him. 'Stop. Just stop it. It doesn't matter.'

'It matters to me.'

'Just don't let her come here again.' She wiped her face with her sleeve and forced a smile. 'Next time she sniffs at my cabbage she wears it in her lap.'

52

Dalziel was escorted through the rows of clerks and accountants to George's office. When he was settled, George had an office boy bring two pots of lemon squash, the ice shavings melting on the surface, sweet and cool. George shouted out of the window for his *punkah wallah* to work harder at the fan.

The two men exchanged pleasantries, then George leaned back in his chair, his fingers interlocked on his paunch. 'Well, Charles, I've been considering your proposal.'

Dalziel smiled to cover his nervousness. Winning the Niland account away from the Bank of Western Australia would be a major coup if he could manage it. 'And?'

'I've decided that you're right. I believe we would be better served by a more progressive bank. So I have decided that we will transfer our accounts to the Commercial Union.'

Dalziel beamed. 'That's capital news, George!'

'I am confident that it will be a mutually profitable association.'

'I can assure you, George, that our bank will do everything –'

'Of course, this will have to be done gradually. It's a major step for us, and we have certain commitments to fulfil with your competitors.'

'Of course.'

'There is one other condition.'

Dalziel recovered his poise. He studied George's face for clues. An excellent bridge partner, Dalziel remembered. His expression never gave anything away. 'Condition?'

George gazed out of the window at the brooding mangroves and the lugger skeletons decaying in the mud. 'Well, not so much a condition. I'd like to think of it as a favour.'

'You just have to ask, George.'

'It's about Cameron McKenzie,' he said.

53

Cameron threw open the door of the bank so viciously that several of the customers stepped back in alarm. Cameron leaped the counter, a letter crumpled in his right fist. One of the ledger clerks jumped to his feet and tried to bar his way. He pushed him back into his seat and stormed into Dalziel's office, slamming the door behind him.

Dalziel was behind his desk, examining a ledger book, his accountant leaning over his right shoulder. Dalziel's face drained to the colour of chalk.

Cameron slapped the crumpled letter on the desk. 'What's this?'

'Mister McKenzie, you have no right –'

The accountant tried to slip past Cameron to the door.

Cameron rounded on him. 'You stay where you are!'

'If you wish to make an appointment to discuss this –'

'I've nae need to make an appointment, Dalziel. I'm here and we're discussing it. Now tell me what it means!'

'It's quite clear what it means. The bank is foreclosing on your loan.'

'Why?'

'It's bank policy –'

Cameron grabbed his tie and twisted the knot, choking him. 'Tell me one thing. Is this George Niland's doing?'

Dalziel made a squeaking sound, his eyes bulging in fright. He didn't answer.

'I guess that tells me all I need to know.' Cameron released him. 'You little bastard.'

He threw the letter in Dalziel's face and went out again, customers and staff gaping at him.

No one moved for a moment and then a junior clerk put his head around the door. 'Would you like your cup of tea now, sir?' he said to Dalziel.

✦ ✦ ✦

Elvie was in the yard, feeding the chickens. Something was wrong. Cameron had not spoken for days, and even Ma was in a bad mood. There were empty gin bottles piling up on the veranda. She wished someone would tell her what was happening.

She heard Black Jack – Cameron had called him that after he tried to stroke him and got bitten on the thumb for his pains – barking furiously in the front yard. She dropped the tin of chicken pellets and ran around the side of the house to see what the matter was. She hoped he hadn't baled up a snake.

There was a shiny black Sunbeam parked outside. A squat Japanese in a white suit and sola topee was trapped against the door, Black Jack chewing energetically on his right shin.

'Jack, come away!' Elvie grabbed the little dog by the scruff of the neck and pulled him off.

The Japanese examined his shredded trousers. His shin was bleeding. But instead of being angry, he smiled and bowed at the little girl. 'Most grateful,' he said.

At that moment Cameron stormed onto the veranda. 'What in God's name is going on out here?'

Elvie picked up Black Jack and ran for the tea-trees. Jack was really in trouble now. She heard Cameron's voice yelling: 'That bloody dog! Mister Tanaka – are you all right?'

◆   ◆   ◆

Tanaka sat with his leg propped on a stool while Rosie put a cold compress on his shin. Cameron came into the room holding a bottle of whiskey and two tumblers.

'My apologies, Mister Tanaka. The damned dog has ruined your suit.'

Tanaka grinned with embarrassment. 'Please, McKenzie-san, not to worry. Just accident.'

'No wonder that dog ended up in a sack.' Cameron sat down and poured two fingers of whiskey into each of the tumblers. 'Your health, Mister Tanaka.'

Tanaka raised his glass and drank the whiskey. He looked like a man who needed one.

'It's a fine motor car you've bought yourself.'

'Gods smile at me.'

Cameron smiled also. He knew that Tanaka's recent success had nothing at all to do with the gods. Tanaka was the single most prosperous Asian in Broome, with the possible exception of Tom Ellies. Tanaka was banker, merchant and financial adviser to almost all the Japanese divers in Broome and there were persistent rumours that he owned his own pearling fleet. This was supposedly illegal – no foreign national could own a pearling licence – but by now the practice was entrenched. White pearlers bought or leased luggers with Japanese money and then allowed Japanese crew to sail them. Sometimes they received a share of the profits, more often they received a basic yearly stipend and became 'veranda pearlers', seldom even venturing down to the foreshore on the pretence of checking on their 'fleet'. Because so many genuine pearlers used Japanese crews, the illegal practice – known as 'dummying' – was almost impossible to prove or to police.

'I hear you have bad luck,' Tanaka said.

'Not bad luck, bad blood.'

'Nilan'-san.'

'I can't prove it, but what else can a man think? Dalziel had no other reason to do what he did. Is that what you came here to see me about, Mister Tanaka?'

'I have business proposal for you.'

Cameron looked at Rosie, who was standing by the kitchen window, her arms folded, watching. 'Be careful,' she mouthed silently at him.

'Well, out with it, Mister Tanaka.'

'Perhaps you not lose your lugger. Perhaps other man can pay loan, buy boat. You sail as number one diver, get share of profit. Let someone else worry.'

'If this other man is Japanese, what you're suggesting is illegal, Mister Tanaka.' Cameron drained his glass. 'Thank you for your offer. I can't do it.'

'If you do not, bank take *Roebuck*.'

'I have my pride. I said I would not work for any other man, and I meant it.'

Tanaka was silent a moment. 'Many years gone, you save my life. You remember?'

'Aye, I remember.'

'I dead now but for you. Now perhaps I pay back my debt.'

'You paid your debt, when I came back to Broome after the war.'

'Life worth more than just one boat.' Tanaka ran his stubby index finger across the gritty surface of the table, tracing a faint outline of the coast. 'Look. Barred Creek just here. Here – Malay boat. No licence. What will custom boat do if he find?'

'He'd confiscate all his shell and throw it over the side.'

'Yes, that is what he will do. I suppose.'

'You mean –'

'Mean nothing. Only think perhaps knowledge useful for you. All knowledge is useful somehow.' Tanaka stood up, replaced his topee and bowed. 'Goodbye, McKenzie-san. Think about what I say.' He limped to the door.

After he had gone Cameron stood on the veranda watching the Sunbeam disappear in the direction of Dampier Terrace.

'What did he mean?' Rosie said, drawing him close. 'What was all that about the Malay poachers?'

'He meant that it was a chance to make myself some easy money and maybe get myself out of the hole,' he told her.

He went back inside the house, started sorting through the drawers in the dresser.

'Where's my old Navy uniform, Rosie?' he called to her. 'I hope to God the silverfish have 'nae eaten it all!'

54

It was eight years since Cameron had worn the uniform of a lieutenant in the Royal Navy. It reeked of mothballs and there were small holes at the back of the collar and on one sleeve where the insects had ravaged it. The gold braid on the cuffs was dirty and ragged.

Cameron slipped on the jacket and drew the lapels together. He buttoned it, and studied his reflection in the cracked dresser mirror.

He felt more than a little smug to discover that it still fitted him. In fact, he looked rather good in it, he thought. He grinned, then saw Rose's reflection. She was watching from the bedroom doorway. 'Not bad, eh, Rosie?'

'You're a shocking vain man. Now will you mind telling me what the goodness you're doing?'

✦　✦　✦

They came up on the big Malay *prahu* on Scott's Reef, just before sunset. The Malay skipper ignored the *Roebuck* until he realised, too late, that she was sailing straight for him. By the time he had hoisted sail Cameron was just a hundred yards off his stern. He abandoned his attempt to escape. There was only a light breeze and he knew that the *Roebuck*, with its auxiliary motor, could easily overtake them.

On the *Roebuck*, Wes rolled his eyes when he saw a *kris* flash in the sun on the deck of the *prahu*. 'Mebbe dis not such a good idea, skip,' he said.

'Easy, Mister Redonda,' Cameron murmured. He took out his heavy Navy revolver and clambered over the side into the whaleboat. Wes and two of the Malay crewmen, Assan and Ismael, took the oars.

A few minutes later they boarded the Malay poacher. There were a dozen crew manning the *prahu*. The captain was a sullen, yellow-eyed salt with brown tombstone teeth and a pearl-handled *kris* tucked into his sarong.

A huge pile of shell littered the deck. They must have been fishing here for a week, perhaps more. The shell was good size and quality.

Cameron turned to Assan. 'Tell the captain I am an officer in the Royal Australian Navy. Tell him he is fishing illegally in Australian waters.'

Assan relayed this information to the captain, who

shrugged his shoulders as if the matter could not be of less interest to him. He barked something back in Malay.

'What did he say?'

'He say he is sorry. He think he still in Malaya.'

Cameron pointed to the coastline a mile away to the east, at the long white beach and the scrubby flat bush beyond. 'Does that look like jungle to him?'

The captain smirked and shrugged his shoulders again.

Cameron turned back to Assan. 'Tell him we are confiscating his shell. Tell him he must throw it all over the side and leave Australian waters immediately.'

Assan repeated this in Malay and a ripple of angry whispers passed among the Malay crew. In response Cameron took the revolver from its holster and removed the safety.

'Mebbe you have to use dat pretty soon,' Wes whispered.

'I'd like to, Wes, but I don't have any ammunition for it.'

'Jay-sus!'

The captain started shouting and gesticulating wildly.

'What's he saying?'

'Boss, he say he not let you take all his shell. He say you cannot make him throw it away.'

'Is that what he believes?' Cameron turned Wes. 'Throw that shell in the water!'

Wes hesitated.

'Do it!'

Wes picked up an armful of shell, went to the port side and dumped it into the sea.

Immediately the captain raced towards him, drawing his *kris*. But Cameron was ready for him. He brought his revolver down on the man's wrist and there was a loud crack of snapping bone. The man screamed, high-pitched, and dropped the *kris* on the deck. Ismael immediately snatched it up, relieved to finally have a weapon.

The rest of the Malay crew hesitated. One of them put his hand on the handle of the knife at his waist but took it away again when Cameron pointed the revolver at his head. Please God, don't call my bluff, Cameron thought.

For a moment no one moved. A swell passed under the hull. The only sound was the squealing of the Malay captain as he writhed on the deck, clutching his wrist.

Wes broke the stalemate. He was a fearsome sight, Cameron supposed, especially now his two front teeth were gone. He grabbed two Malays standing between him and the shell, one under each arm, and threw them in the sea. The Malays backed off, astonished and awed by this display of strength and ferocity.

Cameron turned to Assan. 'Tell them to throw their weapons on the deck, in the name of His Majesty the King.'

Assan translated this and half a dozen *kris* clattered onto the deck. Cameron turned to Wes and Ismael. 'Carry on,' he said.

A quarter of an hour later all the shell had disappeared over the side of the boat into the ocean. As a precaution Cameron had Wes throw the *kris* knives over the side as well.

He allowed Ismael to make a splint for the captain's arm before climbing back into the whaleboat. 'Tell him if he wishes to make a complaint against me, he should write to King George the Fifth in London. For now, I shall let him off with a warning.'

As the sun set golden over the ocean, Cameron stood on

the bow of the *Roebuck* and watched the *prahu* disappear over the northern horizon. 'Put down a lead line and marker, Wes,' he said. 'I have a feeling that in the morning we'll find the best bed of shell in the history of the nor'west!'

55

The moment Cameron pushed open the door of the Commercial Union Bank on Dampier Terrace, the accountant jumped to his feet and took off out the back like a startled rabbit. Cameron ignored the tellers and secretaries and went straight in to Dalziel's office.

Dalziel grabbed the telephone but Cameron slammed the receiver down again, holding his wrist.

'I warn you,' Dalziel stammered, 'my staff have been instructed to inform Sergeant Clarke –'

'It'll not be necessary.' Cameron reached into his shirt pocket and slapped a cheque on the desk. 'That clears my loan, Mister Dalziel. It leaves me with nothing much else but my boat and the clothes I stand up in, but it gets your filthy hands from around my neck.' He leaned close to the other man's face. 'You'll regret this one day, Mister Dalziel. And so will George Niland. You can tell him that.'

And he walked out.

✦ ✦ ✦

Tanaka's bungalow nestled in the tea-tree scrub on the edge of town. All Tanaka's wealth could not buy him an address among the veranda pearlers in the white section of Broome. But it did buy him an army of native gardeners, and the veranda was wreathed in fragrant jasmine and honeysuckle. As Cameron climbed the front steps he heard the gentle tinkling of *furin*, little Japanese wind chimes, brought to life by a zephyr from the bay.

Fumiko, Tanaka's daughter, answered his knock. He heard the shuffle of her feet on the polished wooden floors.

'McKenzie-san,' she said in her soft singsong voice, and bowed.

'Fumiko-san.' Cameron had always thought her one of the most beautiful and delicate creatures he had ever seen. She was tall for a Japanese and moved with the grace of a dancer, as if she floated above the ground. She was reed-slim, with small, tapered hands and a perfect oval face. But it was her eyes and mouth that were her most striking features. Her soft, dark eyes shone like chips of jet, and her mouth was always curled at the corners in an impish smile, so that despite her taciturn demeanour, Cameron had the impression that she was quietly amused and entertained by everything she saw around her.

Cameron had thought her to be no more than twenty, though he had recently learned from Tanaka that she was twenty-seven – twenty-six by a western calendar. Her husband had been number one diver on one of her father's luggers and had died off the Lacepedes three years earlier. As far as Cameron knew she had no children, and now lived with Tanaka, taking care of his needs.

Cameron kicked off his boots on the veranda, after the Japanese custom, and Fumiko led him down the dark passageway to the enclosed veranda at the rear of the house. Tanaka was seated on a rush mat, cross-legged, dressed in a simple *yukata*. There was incense burning in the corners of the room.

Cameron bowed and held out the small gift he had brought with him, wrapped in a traditional, silk *furoshiki* handkerchief.

'McKenzie-san.'

'Mister Tanaka.'

He sat down, cross-legged, like his host. Tanaka nodded to Fumiko and she went to fetch tea.

'Very beautiful girl,' Tanaka said. '*Urizane-gao*. It means melon-seed face. Perfect shape, oval, like melon seed.'

'She's certainly a bonnie thing. Will she marry again, do you think?'

'If gods will it,' Tanaka answered. 'Am honoured you come to my poor house.'

'It's not as poor as mine,' Cameron said, and nodded at the huge clay animal that stood guard in one corner of the room. It was almost as tall as a man and stood on its hind legs, like a badger with a great flat tail and pointed ears. 'What kind of animal is that?'

'Is *tanuki*. We have many in Japan. Is very shy, also very cunning. Like fox, only come out at night. Japanese very fond of *tanuki*.'

'Oh aye?'

'*Tanuki* very clever. Cannot dig hole himself, so he live in hole other animal dig. Let other do work. *Tanuki* also very slow, but has big brain.'

'You admire that, do you, Mister Tanaka?'

'Of course.'

Fumiko came back into the room carrying an *uchiwa*, a flat fan that also served as a tray. On the *uchiwa* was a small kettle with a bamboo handle and two cups of Satsuma china. She knelt down and placed it on the rush mat between them. Then she poured tea into the two cups, bowed, and left the room.

Tanaka unwrapped the gift that Cameron had brought with him. Inside was a small pearl. 'Thank you, McKenzie-san.'

'It comes from the Malay poacher. It was a rich haul. Three wee seed pearls, some barrack, and a ton of good shell. Best day's pearling I've ever done. Thanks to you, Mister Tanaka.'

'Together, we make formidable team.'

'Aye, perhaps.'

Tanaka wrapped the pearl back in the folds of the *furoshiki*. 'You buy back *Roebuck*?'

'Aye, I did. I have not a thing to eat, I can't pay my crew or buy provisions for her, but I have Dalziel off my back.'

Tanaka returned his attention to the *tanuki* statue. 'They say *tanuki* has great magic. They say he make himself into human and play trick on mens. Sometime is important to change to something different, you know? Must wear disguise to win.'

'What do you have in mind?'

'How long you pearler now? Seven year?'

'This will be my ninth season.'

'You be pearler long time more and Nilan'-san still be boss. What if McKenzie-san want to be boss?'

'You know it's my ambition, Mister Tanaka. I've not made a secret of that.'

'Tanaka want to be boss also. Too bad. Tanaka Japanese man.'

'You've not done too bad by yourself.'

'Not too bad is not boss. Perhaps Tanaka need disguise.'

'You mean you want me to dummy for you?'

'You want to be boss, you need money. Tanaka has money. You need good crew, Tanaka President of Japanese Association. Know all Japanese, all Japanese know Tanaka.'

'Go on.'

'Tanaka want to be boss, need white face, white face get credit from bank, white face buy lugger, white face can be on Roads Board, have power with European mens. Tanaka need white face, McKenzie-san has white face. Tanaka need man with clean stomach, honest man. McKenzie has.'

'I'll not be honest if I dummy for you, Mister Tanaka. It's against the law.'

'What is honest? Honest for white man or honest for Japanese? More important you honest with Tanaka.'

'You don't need me for your dummying. You do that already, by all accounts.'

'Just little bit. One mans here, one mans there. No power that way. Tanaka want to be Broome boss, same like you want. Perhaps we do disguise, like *tanuki*. We change. You become Tanaka, Tanaka become you.'

Cameron thought about this. It was tempting. Tanaka was right; together they were far more powerful than they were alone. But he had his pride and his pride said no. 'I can't do it. I want to be master of this coast, sure enough, but I can't be master if I'm not master of myself.'

'That is very pity.'

'There's plenty of other men who'll front for you, if that's what you want. Broome's full of them.'

'Not understand. Not just front. Much, much more. Must be trust.'

'How do you know you can trust me?'

'I know I can trust you with life. What more trust is there?'

Cameron sighed. 'The answer's still the same. I can't do it. I must be my own master or I may as well be dead.'

Tanaka shook his head. 'You are brave mans, but you not have the clever. Without the clever, Nilan'-san always be boss.'

'Maybe.'

Tanaka sighed. 'So what you do now?'

'I'm not sure. I need to raise money from somewhere to pay my operating costs for the season.'

'Then Tanaka give you loan.' He held up his hand to still Cameron's protests. 'Just business. Ten per cent. You pay me back end of season.'

Cameron shrugged. 'It's more than the bank will do. I accept.'

Cameron got to his feet. Tanaka rose also. They bowed, formally.

'Thanks for your help, Mister Tanaka. You saved the *Roebuck*.'

'Am honoured my poor information was help to you.'

'You're a canny man, no mistake.'

'Think about *tanuki*,' Tanaka said. 'We make fine *tanuki* together. *Sayonara*.'

'Aye, *sayonara*, Mister Tanaka.'

56

It was dawn. A sliver of light crept into the bedroom through the cane window shades, leaving half the room in shadow. Rose, already awake, watched Cameron slip into his clothes, buttoning his flannel shirt and fastening the broad, brown leather belt with the money pouch, then tying the silk handkerchief at his throat.

'Rosie,' Cameron whispered. 'Are you awake, lass?'

'I'm awake.'

'I have to be going if we're to catch the morning tide.'

Rose reached up to him. He had not shaved and his chin was rough to the touch. She pulled his head to her breast, breathed in the warm, familiar scent of his hair and body. She was suddenly afraid.

'Doctor Halloran's close by. And Elvie's here. You'll be all right.'

'I know.'

'We've no money. I can't afford to lose another day of the neap tides.'

She watched him creep into Elvie's room across the passageway, heard the boards creak under his heavy canvas boots, heard him whisper some endearment, and Elvie's sleepy, murmured reply.

She had never got used to this. Sometimes he was away for up to three months at a time during the season. The leaving was the worst. Elvie was miserable for days afterwards. Rose always worried about him, but this time she was also afraid for herself, because he would be gone when the baby came.

Cameron crept back into the room. 'Rosie? Are you all right?'

'Hold me, Cam.'

He sat on the bed and she buried her face in his neck. Stupid to feel this way. But she remembered when Elvie was born, she had been in labour for twenty-four hours, a day and a night that seemed like a lifetime of pain and black despair. She had thought she would never be able to push the baby out and every few minutes spasms of unbelievable pain racked her body, leaving her utterly spent. She did not know if she could go through it again, not alone. She wished Cameron could stay until after the baby was born. But it was impossible. There were pearls to be harvested.

'Go now,' she whispered.

'I love you, Rosie.'

'Just go,' she said.

He picked up the canvas kit bag from the floor, kissed her once and was gone.

Elvie appeared in the doorway. She was crying. Rose held open her arms and the little girl crawled into bed beside her. Rose wrapped her arms around her, grateful for another warm body close to hers.

But inside she felt cold as the grave.

✦ ✦ ✦

The polished black Sunbeam was parked by the foreshore, the bonnet pointing towards the *Roebuck*, which was riding at anchor in the bay, its sails furled. Tanaka sat behind the wheel, resplendent in a white suit and topee.

Cameron approached the car, his kit bag slung casually over one shoulder, and leaned on the window. 'Come to pipe me aboard, Mister Tanaka?'

'One more favour for you, McKenzie-san.'

'Why?'

'You not want favour?'

'I want to know why I'm getting it.'

'Ah, you learn the clever now. See, we make fine *tanuki*.'

'You've not answered my question.'

'I want to show you how to become big boss in Broome. Show you the clever.'

'And how would you do that?'

'You sail to Hanlon Reef. Put diver down. Find good shell, very much.'

'How do you know that?'

'Diver belong Nilan'-san find this shell. But he not take.

When he come to Broome, he tell Tanaka. Usual times I send lugger to find. This time I tell you. Just favour.'

Cameron shook his head in admiration. 'You're using George Niland's divers to do your spotting for you, is that it? He pays the wages, you just have to pay commission.'

Tanaka grinned. But there was something else in those black eyes, an expression Cameron had not seen before. 'I show you the clever, then you–me become big boss in Broome. You think about it.'

'The answer's still the same. I'll beat George Niland my own way.'

Tanaka shrugged. 'Well, you still have favour and I protect my money. Not want to lose loan.'

'You'll have your money back, Mister Tanaka, I promise you.'

'I believe. Good luck. Good fishing.' He started up the Sunbeam and drove away.

57

Elvie was standing on a beer crate in the kitchen, washing the dishes, when she heard the scream.

She ran into the yard. Rose had crawled to the steps. The pail of chicken feed was on its side in the dirt, the chickens squabbling and fussing around it.

'Help me,' Rose said. There was a dark stain on her skirts, and her right hand was covered in blood.

Elvie grabbed her mother's arm, thinking to try and pull her to her feet, but Rose pushed her away. 'Go and get Doc Halloran!' she shouted. 'Quickly!'

Elvie took off. The shortest way to town was through the scrub at the back of the house. She ran from the sounds of her mother's screams and the bright gobs of blood in the dirt. She ran until her lungs burned and her legs ached and she tripped, pitching headlong into a thorn bush.

By the time she had disentangled herself, she was covered in cuts and her face was wet with sweat and tears. She looked around and realised she was just a few yards from the white picket fence of what the other children called the Japanese house. It belonged to the fat Japanese that Black Jack had bitten the afternoon he visited her da'. She could see him sitting on the veranda, in his shirtsleeves and braces, reading a newspaper. Elvie vaulted the fence, ripping the hem of her skirt on the palings.

Tanaka jumped up when he saw her, and at first he looked angry and shouted something at her in Japanese. But then he recognised her and the newspaper slipped out of his hand and his expression changed.

'Mister Tanaka!'

'What is wrong?'

She ran up the veranda steps and grabbed his hand. 'Please! My mother!'

Tanaka crouched down. 'She have baby now?'

'There's blood. There's blood everywhere. She was feeding the chickens. There's blood in the yard!'

'*Kuwabara!*' Tanaka swore. He pulled his hand free.

'Do something!' Elvie screamed. 'Hurry!'

Tanaka propelled her back down the steps. 'You go back to your mother! Quicktime! I fetch doctor, everything be all right. Hurry, hurry!'

Elvie did as he said. She hurdled the fence and ran back through the scrub towards her house, shouting her prayers into the hot wind that rushed past her face.

✦   ✦   ✦

Doctor Halloran's bungalow was less than half a mile away, but when Tanaka got there his ancient houseboy, Joseph, told him the doctor was not at home. He had gone to the Niland house.

Tanaka waddled back to the Sunbeam.

The thought did not come to him until he was running up the Nilands' white shell-grit path. It came to him with a fragment of conversation he had once had with Cameron.

Liddy answered the door.

'Must see Nilan'-san.'

Liddy gave him a long and searching look. 'What name you?'

'Tanaka-san. Is most urgent.'

A few moments later, George Niland came to the door. He looked down his long nose at Tanaka with the expression of a man contemplating a beggar. 'Yes?'

Tanaka bowed. 'Is doctor here?'

'Halloran's here. What do you want with him?'

'McKenzie-san's wife have baby now.'

George stroked his wispy moustache. 'I see. Is it urgent?'

Tanaka hesitated.

Opportunity.

Why has George Niland done this to me now?

Opportunity.

Cameron was a brave man, but he did not have the clever. Sometimes a man had to have the luck or the clever to win. If Cam would not help himself, perhaps he must have the clever for them both.

'No. No urgent.'

'I'll inform Doctor Halloran. Good day to you.'

And the door shut.

Doctor Halloran was playing contract bridge on the back veranda with Conrad van Heusen and the Governor. They were all in their shirtsleeves, the cards scattered on the table between them. Everyone, except Conrad, had tumblers of whiskey in front of them.

'Who was it, George?' the Governor asked.

'It was that Jap hawker, Tanaka.'

'What did he want?'

George sat down and picked up his cards. 'He wanted you, Pat,' he said to Halloran. 'McKenzie's wife's gone into labour.'

'Is it urgent?'

'No,' George said. He frowned as Halloran sighed and got to his feet. 'You're not leaving, are you?'

'Duty calls,' Halloran said, buttoning his shirtsleeves.

'Look, he said it wasn't urgent. Let's finish the game.'

Halloran hesitated. 'I suppose it will be all right,' he said, and sat down again. 'She was in labour over a day last time.'

'Have another drink,' George said, and yelled for Liddy to get the whiskey bottle. Then he picked up the cards and started to shuffle.

58

Halloran climbed into his Roadster and set off along the wide, dusty street for McKenzie's house on the outskirts of the town. It was a warm afternoon – August was heralding the end of the cool winter – and he loosened his tie. He had had one too many whiskies at George's.

As he drove he berated himself for his bad play. He had recklessly committed himself and his partner – the Governor – to an impossible contract and they had lost the game. It would be a while before he lived that down.

He was not in the least concerned about Rose McKenzie. She was a fit and healthy young woman. They invariably called on him too early.

The Roadster rolled to a stop outside McKenzie's iron

shack. He saw Tanaka's black Sunbeam parked outside and felt the first stab of apprehension. As he got out he heard the screams. They weren't the normal sounds of a woman in labour; not screams of pain, but of despair.

'Oh my God,' Halloran said.

He grabbed his black leather bag from the back seat of the Roadster and ran up the path. The door was wide open.

There were splashes of bright red blood on the wooden floorboards in the passage. He found Rose lying on the bedroom floor. Tanaka was crouched over her, and her little daughter stood in the doorway, her eyes wide as dinner plates, a hand clamped over her mouth.

Rose had pulled her skirts up to her waist and had used pieces of cloth torn from her skirt and her blouse to staunch the flow. Her hands and arms were slick with blood. Her skin was the colour of chalk, her eyes glassy, staring vacantly at the ceiling. As he watched, she started to convulse.

He realised he was already too late. There was absolutely nothing he could do.

Tanaka looked up at him in anger and bewilderment. 'I tell Nilan'-san is urgent!' he shouted. 'Why you take so long?'

59

The morning sunlight reflecting on Roebuck Bay was so bright it hurt the eyes. George Niland squinted against the glare as he drove along Dampier Terrace.

He passed a working party of Aboriginal prisoners by the side of the road. They were mostly naked, except for tattered and filthy trousers which they wore to spare the sensibilities of the ladies of the town. They were chained in pairs about the neck, and each man had a kerosene tin of stones on his head, which they were carrying from the gravel pit to the road repair site. A warden in a khaki uniform and white topee, his Winchester slung across one shoulder, marched beside them.

George examined them with proprietorial interest. As

Chairman of the Roads Board, the state of the town's thoroughfares was a constant source of vexation and criticism.

He did not see Cameron, partly because of the bright sun, partly because his attention was momentarily distracted by the chain gang. Suddenly he was there, beside the Buick. He leaped onto the running board on the passenger side and forced the door open. His face was ugly with rage.

George instinctively slammed his foot on the brake and the Buick lurched to a stop so violently that Cameron was thrown against the dashboard, cutting his cheek. George tried to escape but Cameron grabbed him, ripping his jacket pocket.

George threw himself out of the car and landed on his knees in the dirt.

'I'm going to kill you!' Cameron shouted.

George scrambled to his feet and ran.

The Aborigines had stopped in their tracks and were staring in bewilderment at this white man's business. The warden, unsure what was happening, unslung his rifle and ran towards the abandoned Buick.

George waved his arms at him. 'Shoot him, for God's sake! He's lost his mind!'

Something hit him hard in the back and he fell forward. Cameron's knee crunched onto his spine and then his fingers were around his throat, choking him.

'You killed Rosie! You filthy bastard!'

George wanted to tell him that it wasn't his fault, but he couldn't talk, couldn't even breathe. He started to black out.

Suddenly it stopped. He gasped and rolled onto his side and retched painfully into the dirt.

Cameron was lying face down on the road, his arms and

legs askew. There was blood in his hair and the warden was standing over him, the butt of his rifle raised.

'Are you all right, Mister Niland?'

The warden helped him to his feet but George's knees were shaking so violently they would not support him. He slumped back on his haunches. 'Get Sergeant Clarke,' he croaked.

60

The tapestry of a man's life is a delicate weave of gossamer thread. The final stitches see Nosiro Tanaka, sitting in his office in the Japanese Club, in white tailored suit, drinking heavily and taking inventory of his achievements in this white man's town. He had an appointment with Cameron McKenzie at eleven o'clock.

He downed another glass of Suntory. Lately the nights had been long and haunted by black dreams. He never thought to fret so much for one *gaijin* whore. His own *tanuki* was beset on all side by traps, clever but not so clever that he could get through the long days without the succour of whiskey.

There was a saying: to live with ambition is to sleep with

a rock beneath the pillow; to live with regret is never to sleep again. There had been many times since that afternoon that Tanaka had regretted what he had done. He was truly sorry about the woman and that McKenzie-san had taken it hard. These days he looked hollow, like his soul was torn out, gutted like a fish. Guilt made his grief twice as keen.

Perhaps McKenzie-san was right. If he had not left to go pearling, she would still be alive. Elvie would not have run to him, and he would not have been fated to be the one to fetch the doctor.

Fate. Opportunity.

Tanaka had heard the stories, how McKenzie-san had only married her because she had tried to help him, that he was still in love with the Niland woman. Tanaka had never thought he would take this so hard. But what was love anyway? One woman was just like any other.

He had done what he had done in the best interests of them both. Cameron would never get what he wanted without him. He could not see this for himself. It was a weakness common to many men.

As for himself, he was a yellow man who needed a white face, a white face he could trust. He knew McKenzie-san, understood him. They had the bond of life, forged under the sea thirteen years ago.

✦   ✦   ✦

The Japanese Club had been built from corrugated tin and asbestos. Outside the front door hung a Seibe and Gorman diving helmet, the emblem of the Japanese stock in trade. The building housed a function room crowded with tables

358

and chairs, and an office and sleeping room at the back for the Club Secretary. Grainy black and white photographs of committees past and present adorned the walls. There was also a shrine to Nakimiro-Fudo, the god of the sea, revered by the men of Wakayama prefecture, which was home to most of the Japanese in Broome.

The club served not only as a meeting place for the Japanese, but also as a trade union, and a symbol of their unity in a foreign land. It was precisely this unity that had enabled them to achieve their domination of the pearling industry. Unlike the Malays and the Koepangers and the Manilamen, they were a united force. They bargained collectively for wages, and had even formed their own credit societies. It was acknowledged that much of the credit for their burgeoning power lay with Tanaka-san, one of the founding members and now Club Secretary.

He received Cameron in his deceptively humble office. As he sat down on the tatami mat, he studied Cameron's bandaged head with weary resignation.

'So now you have to bail me out of gaol,' Cameron said.

'You have much stomach, McKenzie-san, but not the clever.'

'He killed her as sure as if he'd taken a gun to her head and shot her.'

'You cannot know for sure.'

'He told Halloran it was not urgent. There're witnesses. The bastard let her bleed to death! He as good as killed the bairn as well. A boy. Did you know?'

'So you kill him,' Tanaka said. 'Then they put you on rope. Not the clever.'

Cameron leaned across the little table, his face black

with rage. 'Do not lecture me, Mister Tanaka. I intend to get even with him!'

'Perhaps is another way.'

'I'm listening.'

'Tanaka want revenge also. I would make Nilan'-san bleed, all same.'

'How?'

'I tell you many time but you not listen. You tell me you wish to be own master. You own master now?'

Cameron accepted the rebuke. He was right, of course. 'You mean this *tanuki* business?'

Tanaka gave an almost imperceptible nod of the head.

'You kill him this one time, he bleed just once. You take his money, he bleed every day, as long as he live.'

The muscles in Cameron's jaw rippled. 'It will take too much time.'

'What else you have time for if not to use for what you want?'

He had a point, Cameron supposed. 'What do you have in mind?'

'We make partnership. Cannot do this without partner-ship.'

'A contract?' Cameron shook his head. 'Too dangerous. We can't put it to paper.'

'No, not contract. Something much more strong than paper. Fumiko-san.'

'Fumiko?'

'You marry.'

Cameron stared at him. Tanaka's smooth, bronzed cheeks and small black eyes were fathomless. 'Christ, man, Rosie's nae cold yet.'

'Not love, just marry. Not have to love. In Japan love not so important. Is business.'

Cameron jumped to his feet. 'I should not have left her alone!'

'So sorry for you. But perhaps nothing to do. Doctor say nothing can help, no matter what.'

'Aye well, the drunken auld bastard would say that.'

'Maybe for true. Is what gods wish.'

'I want George Niland's balls.'

'We will have them, sliced and raw, like sashimi. First you make marry with Fumiko-san. Yes?'

Cameron was silent for a long time. 'No. Enough with all that. I'll not do it any more. I'm sorry Tanaka-san. You have been a great friend to me, but I cannot do it.' He picked up his hat and left.

✦ ✦ ✦

Cameron held Elvie's hand and they walked slowly down the hill to the little plot where Rosie was buried with their baby son. Elvie took the posy of hibiscus from Cameron's hand and laid it on the tiny mound.

They sat for a while in silence, Elvie with her head resting on her knees.

'Elvie, when you grow up I want you to remember something.'

She looked up, her eyes wet and red-rimmed.

'Remember that love is the finest thing there is. Not just being loved, because I wager they'll be plenty of young men line up to fall in love with you one day. But being in love yourself. Now there's a thing.'

'How will I ever know?'

'Trust me, you'll know,' Cameron said and smiled.

She looked for all the world like a lost puppy, shivering and looking for a friend. He pulled her towards him and wrapped her in a bear hug.

'I can hear your heart beating,' she murmured.

'You know, Elvie, there was a time I would have done anything for revenge, or for ambition, for how I looked to the world. I want you to remember that none of that matters. What you hear right there, in your heart, that's all that matters. If you can find the one that makes it beat faster, then you have all the pearls in the world, and not a soul can take it away from you but you yourself.'

He held her tighter, watched the heavy copper sun dip below the ocean. He thought about his father, saw him wrapping the belt around his knuckles. When will you learn to be a man?

Learning to be a man had been a great deal more complicated than he had imagined. Perhaps the sun was setting on the best days of Cameron McKenzie, but he knew in his soul that he would break the chain. He would at least give Elvie the keys to heaven, let her know that vengeance and opportunity were not the finest things in life.

'I love you,' he whispered to his girl.

'Love you back, Pa,' she murmured and as the night gathered and the cool wind chased off the sea, she fell asleep in his arms.

61

Kate stood beside the Buick on Cable Beach, deciding whether to ask Junzo to take her to Cameron's house. He was alone now, she had heard, and distraught with grief. Should she go to him?

Is this what I want? She wondered. Why am I still drawn to him after so long? She had told herself she was weak, that it was a sickness in her to still love him so much. Perhaps she was wrong. Why did the thought of being alone with him again send this thrill through her still?

She had chided him for taking his vengeance so precisely. But wasn't that what she had done? He had hurt her once, as badly as any man alive. She had wanted him to pay. But what was it they said: when you set out for revenge, first dig two graves.

She imagined walking up the path to his house, saw him standing on the lamplit veranda, tried to divine what might be the expression on his face. Would the fire still burn in his eyes?

As it still burned in her.

'I miss you, Cam,' she murmured to the night wind.

She wondered what he might say, how he might look, whether tonight she might lie in his arms again and come home again, after so long holding life at arm's length. But if she went, what would life bring her? She was accustomed to her life of ease, and money, she knew at least this way what tomorrow would bring.

She turned to Junzo at the wheel of the Buick.

'Take me to the McKenzie house,' she said. His face was unreadable. She wondered if he would tell George about this. She didn't really care anymore.

Wavelets beat the shore. The breathless night closed in.

✦ ✦ ✦

A single yellow light shone from inside the house. She heard the screen door creak as he came out onto the veranda and stood there on the steps, watching her as she came up the path. His face was in shadow but his presence was overwhelming. She felt herself shiver even in the warm night wind.

'Hello Cam.'

He did not answer her.

'I'm sorry. About your wife.'

'Thank you.'

She stood there, waiting for him to say something else.

She felt a tear drop of perspiration start its long journey down her spine.

'I've missed you, Cam.'

He sagged against the veranda post. He sighed. 'Is that why you came?'

'You're not going to make this easy for me, are you?'

'It's too late, Kate.'

It was as if he had kicked her in the stomach. Of course, of course. What did you expect, Kate? Well, there had been a part of her that thought she would always be able to go back to him someday, that there would always be a time for them. And suddenly she realised that this was not true.

He shook his head. 'I did a terrible thing. No denying. But for years after I loved you, like no man has ever loved you. Perhaps there was a time, Kate. Just before your father got himself killed. But not now.'

'Cam . . .' She wanted to say something else.

'Go home, Kate.'

He turned and went back inside the house.

She heard the screen door slam.

She climbed back into the Buick. Without a word, Junzo started the engine and put the automobile into gear. Kate stared straight ahead but she did not see the dark and swelling sea beyond Cable Beach, the shadowed spinifex. She was seeing him come towards her on the veranda of that bungalow so long ago, a handsome and arrogant stranger in a white linen suit.

My turn for regrets now, she thought.

I never thought it would hurt so much.

'One day I'll get him back,' she promised the night. 'One

day I will make him love me again, see that look in his eyes one more time. One day. You see if I don't.'

The night closed around her like an oyster shell closing on the lustrous dream of a pearl.

ACKNOWLEDGEMENTS

My thanks once again to my agent and great friend Tim Curnow. Thanks also to Jude McGee, my fantastic publisher, for her unwavering support. My gratitude to Jo Jarrah, for another wonderful editing job, and for making sense of my scribblings. Thanks also to Peta Levett, my gorgeous publicist from the now notorious Sutherland shire, for her help and support. And to Katie Stackhouse, who took over at the end, for her endless patience with an absconding author, and taking *Pearls* over the line. Thank you all.

Also by Colin Falconer

MY BEAUTIFUL SPY

Nick Davis first saw Daniela Simonici in the American Bar of the Athenee Palace Hotel in Bucharest in June of 1940 . . . He couldn't take his eyes off her . . .

1940. Europe is at war and British spy Nick Davis is posing as a diplomat in Bucharest. A centre of fashion, art and culture, graced with beautiful boulevards, even an Arc de Triomphe, Bucharest is known as 'little Paris'. But the Nazis have recently arrived, and terror has overtaken the city.

When Nick rescues the beautiful but mysterious Daniela Simonici, mistress to a German businessman, his life is changed forever. Nick and Daniela fall for each other, hard, and soon Daniela is spying for Nick. But who is Daniela Simonici? Who does she really love? And who is she really spying for?

My Beautiful Spy is an unforgettable love story set against a dramatic backdrop by a master of historical fiction. Nick is a hero you'll fall in love with; Daniela a woman you'll never forget.

Also by Colin Falconer

ANASTASIA

Some men don't fall in love; they get lost. I was lost from the moment I saw Anastasia Romanov in the taxi club that first night . . .

When American journalist Michael Sheridan jumps into the Whangpoa River to save a woman he met in one of Shanghai's taxi clubs, his life is changed irrevocably. A Russian refugee, Anastasia Romanov bears an extraordinary resemblance to the princess said to have survived the brutal murder of her family at the hands of Bolshevik revolution-aries, but she is suffering from amnesia and remembers little of her life before Shanghai.

Unravelling the mystery of Anastasia's identity and past takes them both from Berlin to the pre-war London of the 1920s, from Bolshevik Russia to New York just before the Wall Street crash. Spanning the turbulent and romantic decade of the twenties, *Anastasia* is a tale of murder and betrayal, royal scandal and financial intrigue.

'Falconer weaves a pacy story of obsession, love, greed and corruption . . . [He] writes with skill and grace . . . really well done.'
Sydney Morning Herald

'A beauty . . . Falconer's grasp of his period and places is almost flawless . . . He's my kind of writer.'
The Australian

Also by Colin Falconer
(as Mark D'Arbanville)

THE NAKED HUSBAND

A raw, candid and heart-wrenching novel for any woman who ever wondered what men really feel.

By all accounts Mark D'Arbanville has the 'perfect life': a successful writer, he is happily married with a teenage son. But when he falls in love with another woman, the effect is catastrophic – his wife commits suicide.

In response to *The Bride Stripped Bare*, *The Naked Husband* takes a candid look at the way men think, act and feel inside a relationship. Shocking, disturbing but impossible to put down, it's a novel for every woman who ever found the reality of sex and marriage so different to the fairytale, and wondered why.

'The insights into the way men in relationships think and feel, or don't think and feel, are terrific.'
Sydney Morning Herald

Also by Colin Falconer
(as Mark D'Arbanville)

THE NAKED HEART

A powerful and surprising sequel to the bestselling novel The
Naked Husband.

What would it be like to wake in the middle of your life
with no memory of what had gone before? Would you run
straight back into the past – or would you take this chance
to start again – with a naked heart?

Anna wakes in a hospital bed, with no memory of anything
before the accident that almost took her life four months
before. Everyone tells her that her former life was perfect.
But as she starts to search for the pieces of the puzzle
herself, a completely different picture emerges . . .

The Naked Husband explored the world of a man who could
not face a future he had built for himself. *The Naked Heart*
explores a woman's history, and how it has ruled her.